1,000,000 Books

are available to read at

www.ForgottenBooks.com

Read online
Download PDF
Purchase in print

ISBN 978-1-4400-9727-0
PIBN 10057069

1 MONTH OF
FREE
READING

at

www.ForgottenBooks.com

By purchasing this book you are eligible for one month membership to ForgottenBooks.com, giving you unlimited access to our entire collection of over 1,000,000 titles via our web site and mobile apps.

To claim your free month visit:

www.forgottenbooks.com/free57069

English
Français
Deutsche
Italiano
Español
Português

www.forgottenbooks.com

Mythology Photography **Fiction**
Fishing Christianity **Art** Cooking
Essays Buddhism Freemasonry
Medicine **Biology** Music **Ancient
Egypt** Evolution Carpentry Physics
Dance Geology **Mathematics** Fitness
Shakespeare **Folklore** Yoga Marketing
Confidence Immortality Biographies
Poetry **Psychology** Witchcraft
Electronics Chemistry History **Law**
Accounting **Philosophy** Anthropology
Alchemy Drama Quantum Mechanics
Atheism Sexual Health **Ancient History**
Entrepreneurship Languages Sport
Paleontology Needlework Islam
Metaphysics Investment Archaeology
Parenting Statistics Criminology
Motivational

BY

A. E. W. MASON

AUTHOR OF "RUNNING WATER," "FOUR FEATHERS,
"THE COURTSHIP OF MORRICE BUCKLER," ETC.

Barzun & Taylor # 1561

TORONTO

THE MUSSON BOOK COMPANY LIMITED

LONDON: HODDER AND STOUGHTON

Printed by Hazell, Watson & Viney, Ld., London and Aylesbury, England.

CONTENTS

CONTENTS

CHAPTER XVII

CHAPTER XVIII

CHAPTER XIX

CHAPTER XX

CHAPTER XXI

CHAPTER I

SUMMER LIGHTNING

IT was Mr. Ricardo's habit as soon as the second week of August came round to travel to Aix-les-Bains, in Savoy, where for five or six weeks he lived pleasantly. He pretended to take the waters in the morning, he went for a ride in his motor-car in the afternoon, he dined at the Cercle in the evening, and spent an hour or two afterwards in the baccarat-rooms at the Villa des Fleurs. An enviable, smooth life without a doubt, and it is certain that his acquaintances envied him. At the same time, however, they laughed at him and, alas! with some justice; for he was an exaggerated person. He was to be construed in the comparative. Everything in his life was a trifle overdone, from the fastidious arrangement of his neckties to the feminine nicety of his little dinner-parties. In age Mr. Ricardo was approaching the fifties; in condition he was a widower—a state greatly to his liking, for he avoided at once the irksomeness of marriage and the reproaches justly levelled at the bachelor; finally, he was rich, having amassed a fortune in Mincing Lane, which he had invested in profitable securities.

Ten years of ease, however, had not altogether obliterated in him the business look. Though he lounged from January to December, he lounged with the air of a financier taking a holiday; and when he visited, as he frequently did, the studio of a painter, a stranger would have hesitated to decide whether he had been drawn thither by a love of art or by the possibility of an investment. His "acquaintances" have been mentioned, and the word is suitable. For while he mingled in many circles he stood aloof from all. He affected the company of artists, by whom he was regarded as one ambitious to become a connoisseur; and amongst the younger business men, who had never dealt with him, he earned the disrespect reserved for the dilettante. If he had a grief, it was that he had discovered no great man who in return for practical favours would engrave his memory in brass. He was a Mæcenas without a Horace, an Earl of Southampton without a Shakespeare. In a word, Aix-les-Bains in the season was the very place for him; and never for a moment did it occur to him that he was here to be dipped in agitations, and hurried from excitement to excitement. The beauty of the little town, the crowd of well-dressed and agreeable people, the rose-coloured life of the place, all made their appeal to him. But it was the Villa des Fleurs which brought him to Aix. Not that he played for anything more than an occasional louis; nor, on the other hand, was he merely a cold looker-on. He had a bank-note or

two in his pocket on most evenings at the service
of the victims of the tables.   But the pleasure to
his curious and dilettante mind lay in the spectacle
of the battle which was waged night after night
between raw nature and good manners. It was
extraordinary to him how constantly manners
prevailed. There were, however, exceptions.

For instance. On the first evening of this particular visit he found the rooms hot, and sauntered
out into the little semicircular garden at the back.
He sat there for half an hour under a flawless
sky of stars watching the people come and go in
the light of the electric lamps, and appreciating
the gowns and jewels of the women with the eye
of a connoisseur ; and then into this starlit quiet
there came suddenly a flash of vivid life. A girl
in a soft, clinging frock of white satin darted swiftly
from the rooms and flung herself nervously upon
a bench. She could not, to Ricardo's thinking, be
more than twenty years of age. She was certainly
quite young. The supple slenderness of her figure
proved it, and he had moreover caught a glimpse,
as she rushed out, of a fresh and very pretty face ;
but he had lost sight of it now. For the girl wore
a big black satin hat with a broad brim, from which
a couple of white ostrich feathers curved over at
the back, and in the shadow of that hat her face
was masked. All that he could see was a pair
of long diamond eardrops, which sparkled and
trembled as she moved her head—and that she did
constantly. Now she stared moodily at the ground ;

now she flung herself back; then she twisted nervously to the right, and then a moment afterwards to the left; and then again she stared in front of her, swinging a satin slipper backwards and forwards against the pavement with the petulance of a child. All her movements were spasmodic; she was on the verge of hysteria. Ricardo was expecting her to burst into tears, when she sprang up and as swiftly as she had come she hurried back into the rooms. "Summer lightning," thought Mr. Ricardo.

Near to him a woman sneered, and a man said, pityingly: "She was pretty, that little one. It is regrettable that she has lost."

A few minutes afterwards Ricardo finished his cigar and strolled back into the rooms, making his way to the big table just on the right hand of the entrance, where the play as a rule runs high. It was clearly running high to-night. For so deep a crowd thronged about the table that Ricardo could only by standing on tiptoe see the faces of the players. Of the banker he could not catch a glimpse. But though the crowd remained, its units were constantly changing, and it was not long before Ricardo found himself standing in the front rank of the spectators, just behind the players seated in the chairs. The oval green table was spread out beneath him littered with bank-notes. Ricardo turned his eyes to the left, and saw seated at the middle of the table the man who was holding the bank. Ricardo recognised him with a start of surprise. He was a young Englishman, Harry

Wethermill, who, after a brilliant career at Oxford and at Munich, had so turned his scientific genius to account that he had made a fortune for himself at the age of twenty-eight.

He sat at the table with the indifferent look of the habitual player upon his cleanly chiselled face. But it was plain that his good fortune stayed at his elbow to-night, for opposite to him the croupier was arranging with extraordinary deftness piles of bank-notes in the order of their value. The bank was winning heavily. Even as Ricardo looked Wethermill turned up "a natural," and the croupier swept in the stakes from either side.

"Faites vos jeux, messieurs. Le jeu est fait?" the croupier cried, all in a breath, and repeated the words. Wethermill waited with his hand upon the wooden frame in which the cards were stacked. He glanced round the table while the stakes were being laid upon the cloth, and suddenly his face flashed from languor into interest. Almost opposite to him a small, white-gloved hand holding a five-louis note was thrust forward between the shoulders of two men seated at the table. Wethermill leaned forward and shook his head with a smile. With a gesture he refused the stake. But he was too late. The fingers of the hand had opened, the note fluttered down on to the cloth, the money was staked.

At once he leaned back in his chair

"Il y a une suite," he said quietly. He relinquished the bank rather than play against that five-louis note. The stakes were taken up by their owners.

The croupier began to count Wethermill's winnings, and Ricardo, curious to know whose small, delicately gloved hand it was which had brought the game to so abrupt a termination, leaned forward. He recognised the young girl in the white satin dress and the big black hat whose nerves had got the better of her a few minutes since in the garden. He saw her now clearly, and thought her of an entrancing loveliness. She was moderately tall, fair of skin, with a fresh colouring upon her cheeks which she owed to nothing but her youth. Her hair was of a light brown with a sheen upon it, her forehead broad, her eyes dark and wonderfully clear. But there was something more than her beauty to attract him. He had a strong belief that somewhere, some while ago, he had already seen her. And this belief grew and haunted him. He was still vaguely puzzling his brains to fix the place when the croupier finished his reckoning.

" There are two thousand louis in the bank," he cried. "Who will take on the bank for two thousand louis ?"

No one, however, was willing. A fresh bank was put up for sale, and Wethermill, still sitting in the dealer's chair, bought it. He spoke at once to an attendant, and the man slipped round the table, and, forcing his way through the crowd, carried a message to the girl in the black hat. She looked towards Wethermill and smiled : and the smile made her face a miracle of tenderness. Then she disappeared, and in a few moments Ricardo saw a way open in the throng behind the banker, and she appeared again only a yard or two away, just behind Wethermill. He turned, and taking her hand into his shook it chidingly.

"I couldn't let you play against me, Celia," he said, in English; "my luck's too good to-night. So you shall be my partner instead. I'll put in the capital and we'll share the winnings."

The girl's face flushed rosily. Her hand still lay clasped in his. She made no effort to withdraw it.

"I couldn't do that," she exclaimed.

"Why not?" said he. " See l" and loosening her fingers he took from them the five-louis note and tossed it over to the croupier to be added to his bank. " Now you can't help yourself. We're partners."

The girl laughed, and the company at the table smiled, half in sympathy, half with amusement. A chair was brought for her, and she sat down behind Wethermill, her lips parted, her face joyous with excitement. But all at once Wethermill's luck deserted him. He renewed his bank three times, and had lost the greater part of his winnings when he had dealt the cards through. He took a fourth bank, and rose from that, too, a loser.

"That's enough, Celia," he said. " Let us go out into the garden; it will be cooler there."

"I have taken your good luck away," said the girl remorsefully. Wethermill put his arm through hers.

" You'll have to take yourself away before you
can do that," he answered, and the couple walked
together out of Ricardo's hearing.

Ricardo was left to wonder about Celia. She was
just one of those problems which made Aix-les-Bains
so unfailingly attractive to him. She dwelt in some
street of Bohemia; so much was clear. The
frankness of her pleasure, of her excitement, and
even of her distress proved it. She passed from
one to the other while you could deal a pack of
cards. She was at no pains to wear a mask. Moreover, she was a young girl of nineteen or twenty,
running about those rooms alone, as unembarrassed
as if she had been at home. There was the free use,
too, of Christian names. Certainly she dwelt in
Bohemia. But it seemed to Ricardo that she could
pass in any company and yet not be overpassed.
She would look a little more picturesque than most
girls of her age, and she was certainly a good deal
more *soignée* than many, and she had the French-
woman's knack of putting on her clothes. But
those would be all the differences, leaving out the
frankness. Ricardo wondered in what street of
Bohemia she dwelt. He wondered still more when
he saw her again half an hour afterwards at the
entrance to the Villa des Fleurs. She came down
the long hall with Harry Wethermill at her side.
The couple were walking slowly, and talking as they
walked with so complete an absorption in each
other that they were unaware of their surroundings.
At the bottom of the steps a stout woman of fifty-

five, over-jewelled and over-dressed and raddled
with paint, watched their approach with a smile of
good-humoured amusement. When they came near
enough to hear she said in French :

" Well, Célie, are you ready to go home ? "

The girl looked up with a start.

" Of course, madame," she said, with a certain
submissiveness which surprised Ricardo. " I hope
I have not kept you waiting."

She ran to the cloak-room, and came back again
with her cloak.

" Good-bye, Harry," she said, dwelling upon his
name and looking out upon him with soft and
smiling eyes.

" I shall see you to-morrow evening," he said,
holding her hand. Again she let it stay within his
keeping, but she frowned, and a sudden gravity
settled like a cloud upon her face. She turned to
the elder woman with a sort of appeal.

" No, I do not think we shall be here to-morrow,
shall we, madame ? " she said reluctantly.

" Of course not," said madame briskly. " You
have not forgotten what we have planned ? No, we
shall not be here to-morrow ; but the night after—
yes."

Celia turned back again to Wethermill.

" Yes, we have plans for to-morrow," she said,
with a very wistful note of regret in her voice ; and,
seeing that madame was already at the door, she
bent forward and said timidly, " But the night after
I shall want you."

"I shall thank you for wanting me," Wethermill rejoined; and the girl tore her hand away and ran up the steps.

Harry Wethermill returned to the rooms. Mr. Ricardo did not follow him. He was too busy with the little problem which had been presented to him that night. What could that girl, he asked himself, have in common with the raddled woman she addressed so respectfully? Indeed, there had been a note of more than respect in her voice. There had been something of affection. Again Mr. Ricardo found himself wondering in what street in Bohemia Celia dwelt—and as he walked up to the hotel there came yet other questions to amuse him.

"Why," he asked, "could neither Celia nor madame come to the Villa des Fleurs to-morrow night? What are the plans they have made? And what was it in those plans which brought the sudden gravity and reluctance into Celia's face?"

Ricardo had reason to remember those questions during the next few days, though he only idled with them now.

CHAPTER II

A CRY FOR HELP

It was on a Monday evening that Ricardo saw Harry Wethermill and the girl Celia together. On the Tuesday he saw Wethermill in the rooms alone and had some talk with him.

Wethermill was not playing that night, and about ten o'clock the two men left the Villa des Fleurs together.

"Which way do you go?" asked Wethermill.

"Up the hill to the Hôtel Majestic," said Ricardo.

"We go together, then. I, too, am staying there," said the young man, and they climbed the steep streets together. Ricardo was dying to put some questions about Wethermill's young friend of the night before, but discretion kept him reluctantly silent. They chatted for a few seconds in the hall upon indifferent topics, and separated for the night. Mr. Ricardo, however, was to learn something more of Celia the next morning; for while he was fixing his tie before the mirror Wethermill burst into his dressing-room. Mr. Ricardo forgot his curiosity in the surge of his indignation. Such an invasion was an unprecedented outrage upon

the gentle tenor of his life.   The business of the
morning toilette was sacred.   To interrupt it carried
a subtle suggestion of anarchy.   Where was his
valet?   Where was Charles, who should have
guarded the door like the custodian of a chapel?

"I cannot speak to you for at least another half-
hour," said Mr. Ricardo sternly.

But Harry Wethermill was out of breath and
shaking with agitation.

"I can't wait," he cried, with a passionate appeal.
"I have got to see you.   You must help me, Mr
Ricardo—you must, indeed!"

Ricardo spun round upon his heel.   At first he
had thought that the help wanted was the help
usually wanted at Aix-les-Bains.   A glance at
Wethermill's face, however, and the ringing note
of anguish in his voice, told him that the thought
was wrong.   Mr. Ricardo slipped out of his affec-
tations as out of a loose coat.   "What has happened?" he asked quietly.

"Something terrible."   With shaking fingers
Wethermill held out a newspaper.   "Read it,"
he said.

It was a special edition of a local newspaper,
Le Journal de Savoie, and it bore the date of that
morning.

"They are crying it in the streets," said Wethermill.   "Read!"

A short paragraph was printed in large black
letters on the first page, and leaped to the eyes.

"Late last night," it ran, "an appalling murder

was committed at the Villa Rose, on the road to Lac Bourget. Mme. Camille Dauvray, an elderly rich woman, who was well known at Aix, and had occupied the villa every summer for the last few years, was discovered on the floor of her salon, fully dressed and brutally strangled, while upstairs, her maid, Héléne Vauquier, was found in bed, chloroformed, with her hands tied securely behind her back. At the time of going to press she had not recovered consciousness, but the doctor, Emile Peytin, is in attendance upon her, and it is hoped that she will be able shortly to throw some light on this dastardly affair. The police are properly reticent as to the details of the crime, but the following statement may be accepted without hesitation.

" The murder was discovered at twelve o'clock at night by the *sergent-de-ville* Perrichet, to whose intelligence more than a word of praise is due, and it is obvious from the absence of all marks upon the door and windows that the murderer was admitted from within the villa. Meanwhile Mme. Dauvray's motor-car has disappeared, and with it a young Englishwoman who came to Aix with her as her companion. The motive of the crime leaps to the eyes. Mme. Dauvray was famous in Aix for her jewels, which she wore with too little prudence. The condition of the house shows that a careful search was made for them, and they have disappeared. It is anticipated that a description of the young Englishwoman, with a reward for her apprehension, will be issued immediately.

And it is not too much to hope that the citizens of Aix, and indeed of France, will be cleared of all participation in so cruel and sinister a crime."

Ricardo read through the paragraph with a growing consternation, and laid the paper upon his dressing-table.

"It is infamous," cried Wethermill passionately.

"The young Englishwoman is, I suppose, your friend Miss Celia?" said Ricardo slowly.

Wethermill started forward.

"You know her, then?" he cried in amazement.

"No; but I saw her with you in the rooms. I heard you call her by that name."

"You saw us together?" exclaimed Wethermill. "Then you can understand how infamous the suggestion is."

But Ricardo had seen the girl alone half an hour before he had seen her with Harry Wethermill. He could not but vividly remember the picture of her as she flung herself on to the bench in the garden in a moment of hysteria, and petulantly kicked a satin slipper backwards and forwards against the stones. She was young, she was pretty, she had a charm of freshness, but—but—strive against it as he would, this picture in the recollection began more and more to wear a sinister aspect. He remembered some words spoken by a stranger. "She is pretty, that little one. It is regrettable that she has lost."

Mr. Ricardo arranged his tie with even a greater deliberation than he usually employed.

"And Mme. Dauvray?" he asked. "She was the stout woman with whom your young friend went away?"

"Yes," said Wethermill.

Ricardo turned round from the mirror.

"What do you want me to do?"

"Hanaud is at Aix. He is the cleverest of the French detectives. You know him. He dined with you once."

It was Mr. Ricardo's practice to collect celebrities round his dinner-table, and at one such gathering Hanaud and Wethermill had been present together.

"You wish me to approach him?"

"At once."

"It is a delicate position," said Ricardo. "Here is a man in charge of a case of murder, and we are quietly to go to him——"

To his relief Wethermill interrupted him.

"No, no," he cried; "he is not in charge of the case. He is on his holiday. I read of his arrival two days ago in the newspaper. It was stated that he came for rest. What I want is that he should take charge of the case."

The superb confidence of Wethermill shook Mr. Ricardo for a moment, but his recollections were too clear.

"You are going out of your way to launch the acutest of French detectives in search of this girl. Are you wise, Wethermill?"

Wethermill sprang up from his chair in desperation.

"You, too, think her guilty! You who have seen her. You think her guilty—like this detestable newspaper, like the police."

"Like the police?" asked Ricardo sharply.

"Yes," said Harry Wethermill sullenly. "As soon as I saw that rag I ran down to the villa. The police are in possession. They would not let me into the garden. But I talked with one of them. They, too, think that she let in the murderers."

Ricardo took a turn across the room. Then he came to a stop in front of Wethermill.

"Listen to me," he said solemnly. "I saw this girl half an hour before I saw you. She rushed out into the garden. She flung herself on to a bench. She could not sit still. She was hysterical. You know what that means. She had been losing. That's point number one.

Mr. Ricardo ticked it off upon his finger.

"She ran back into the rooms. You asked her to share the winnings of your bank. She consented eagerly. And you lost. That's point number two. A little later, as she was going away, you asked her whether she would be in the rooms the next night—yesterday night—the night when the murder was committed. Her face clouded over. She hesitated. She became more than grave. There was a distinct impression as though she shrank from the contemplation of what it was proposed she should do on the next night. And then she answered you, 'No, we have other plans.' That's number three." And Mr. Ricardo ticked off his third point.

"Now," he asked, "do you still ask me to launch Hanaud upon the case?"

"Yes, and at once," cried Wethermill.

Ricardo called for his hat and his stick.

"You know where Hanaud is staying?" he asked.

"Yes," replied Wethermill, and he led Ricardo to an unpretentious little hotel in the centre of the town. Ricardo sent in his name, and the two visitors were immediately shown into a small sitting-room, where M. Hanaud was enjoying his morning chocolate. He was stout and broad-shouldered, with a full and almost heavy face. In his morning suit at his breakfast-table he looked like a prosperous comedian.

He came forward with a smile of welcome, extending both his hands to Mr. Ricardo.

"Ah, my good friend," he said, "it is pleasant to see you. And Mr. Wethermill," he exclaimed, holding a hand out to the young inventor.

"You remember me, then?" said Wethermill gladly.

"It is my profession to remember people," said Hanaud, with a laugh "You were at that amusing dinner-party of Mr. Ricardo's in Grosvenor Square."

"Monsieur," said Wethermill, "I have come to ask your help."

The note of appeal in his voice was loud.

M. Hanaud drew up a chair by the window and motioned to Wethermill to take it. He pointed to another, with a bow of invitation to Mr. Ricardo.

"Let me hear," he said gravely.

"It is the murder of Mme. Dauvray," said Wethermill.

Hanaud started.

"And in what way, monsieur," he asked, "are you interested in the murder of Mme. Dauvray?"

"Her companion," said Wethermill, "the young English girl—she is a great friend of mine."

Hanaud's face grew stern. Then came a sparkle of anger in his eyes.

"And what do you wish me to do, monsieur?" he asked coldly.

"You are upon your holiday, M. Hanaud. I wish you—no, I implore you," Wethermill cried, his voice ringing with passion, "to take up this case, to discover the truth, to find out what has become of Celia."

Hanaud leaned back in his chair with his hands upon the arms. He did not take his eyes from Harry Wethermill, but the anger died out of them.

"Monsieur," he said, "I do not know what your procedure is in England. But in France a detective does not take up a case or leave it alone according to his pleasure. We are only servants. This affair is in the hands of M. Fleuriot, the Juge d'Instruction of Aix."

"But if you offered him your help it would be welcomed," cried Wethermill. "And to me that would mean so much. There would be no bungling. There would be no waste of time. Of that one would be sure."

Hanaud shook his head gently. His eyes were softened now by a look of pity. Suddenly he stretched out a forefinger.

"You have, perhaps, a photograph of the young lady in that card-case in your breast-pocket."

Wethermill flushed red, and, drawing out the card-case, handed the portrait to Hanaud. Hanaud looked at it carefully for a few moments.

"It was taken lately, here?" he asked.

"Yes; for me," replied Wethermill quietly.

"And it is a good likeness?"

"Very."

"How long have you known this Mlle. Célie?" he asked.

Wethermill looked at Hanaud with a certain defiance.

"For a fortnight."

Hanaud raised his eyebrows.

"You met her here?"

"Yes."

"In the rooms, I suppose? Not at the house of one of your friends?"

"That is so," said Wethermill quietly. "A friend of mine who had met her in Paris introduced me to her at my request."

Hanaud handed back the portrait and drew forward his chair nearer to Wethermill. His face had grown friendly. He spoke with a tone of respect.

" Monsieur, I know something of you.   Our
friend, Mr. Ricardo, told me your history; I asked
him for it when I saw you at his dinner.   You are
of those about whom one does ask questions, and I
know that you are not a romantic boy, but who
shall say that he is safe from the appeal of beauty?
I have seen women, monsieur, for whose purity of
soul I would myself have stood security, condemned for complicity in brutal crimes on evidence
that could not be gainsaid; and I have known them
turn foul-mouthed, and hideous to look upon, the
moment after their just sentences have been pro-
nounced."

"No doubt, monsieur," said Wethermill, with
perfect quietude.   "But Celia Harland is not one
of those women."

"I do not now say that she is," said Hanaud.
"But the Juge d'Instruction here has already sent
to me to ask for my assistance, and I refused.   I
replied that I was just a good bourgeois enjoying
his holiday.   Still it is difficult quite to forget one's
profession.   It was the Commissaire of Police who
came to me, and naturally I talked with him for a
little while.   The case is dark, monsieur, I warn
you."

" How dark?" asked Harry Wethermill.

" I will tell you," said Hanaud, drawing his chair
still closer to the young man.   " Understand this
in the first place.   There was an accomplice within
the villa.   Some one let the murderers in.   There
is no sign of an entrance being forced; no lock

was picked, there is no mark of a thumb on any panel, no sign of a bolt being forced. There was an accomplice within the house. We start from that."

Wethermill nodded his head sullenly. Ricardo drew his chair up towards the others. But Hanaud was not at that moment interested in Ricardo.

" Well, then, let us see who there are in Mme. Dauvray's household. The list is not a long one. It was Mme. Dauvray's habit to take her luncheon and her dinner at the restaurants, and her maid was all that she required to get ready her 'petit déjeuner' in the morning and her 'sirop' at night. Let us take the members of the household one by one. There is first the chauffeur, Henri Servettaz. He was not at the villa last night. He came back to it early this morning.

" Ah ! " said Ricardo, in a significant exclamation. Wethermill did not stir. He sat still as a stone, with a face deadly white and eyes burning upon Hanaud's face.

" But wait," said Hanaud, holding up a warning hand to Ricardo. " Servettaz was in Chambéry, where his parents live. He travelled to Chambéry by the two-o'clock train yesterday. He was with them in the afternoon. He went with them to a café in the evening. Moreover, early this morning the maid, Hélène Vauquier, was able to speak a few words in answer to a question. She said Servettaz was in Chambéry. She gave his address.

A telephone message was sent to the police in that town, and Servettaz was found in bed. I do not say that it is impossible that Servettaz was concerned in the crime. That we shall see. But it is quite clear, I think, that it was not he who opened the house to the murderers, for he was at Chambéry in the evening, and the murder was already discovered here by midnight. Moreover—it is a small point—he lives, not in the house, but over the garage in a corner of the garden. Then besides the chauffeur there was a charwoman, a woman of Aix, who came each morning at seven and left in the evening at seven or eight. Sometimes she would stay later if the maid was alone in the house, for the maid is nervous. But she left last night before nine—there is evidence of that—and the murder did not take place until afterwards. That is also a fact, not a conjecture. We can leave the charwoman, who for the rest has the best of characters, out of our calculations. There remain then the maid, Héléne Vauquier, and "—he shrugged his shoulders—" Mlle. Célie."

Hanaud reached out for the matches and lit a cigarette.

" Let us take first the maid, Héléne Vauquier. Forty years old, a Normandy peasant woman—they are not bad people, the Normandy peasants, monsieur—avaricious, no doubt, but on the whole honest and most respectable. We know something of Héléne Vauquier, monsieur. See ! " and he took up a sheet of paper from the table. The paper was folded lengthwise, written upon only on the inside. " I have some details here. Our police system is, I think, a little more complete than yours in England. Héléne Vauquier has served Mme. Dauvray for seven years. She has been the confidential friend rather than the maid. And mark this, M. Wethermill ! During those seven years how many opportunities has she had of conniving at last night's crime ? She was found chloroformed and bound. There is no doubt that she was chloroformed. Upon that point Dr. Peytin is quite, quite certain. He saw her before she recovered consciousness. She was violently sick on awakening. She sank again into unconsciousness. She is only now in a natural sleep. Besides those people, there is Mlle. Célie. Of her, monsieur, nothing is known. You yourself know nothing of her. She comes suddenly to Aix as the companion of Mme. Dauvray—a young and pretty English girl. How did she become the companion of Mme. Dauvray ? "

Wethermill stirred uneasily in his seat. His face flushed. To Mr. Ricardo that had been from the beginning the most interesting problem of the case. Was he to have the answer now ?

" I do not know," answered Wethermill, with some hesitation, and then it seemed that he was at once ashamed of his hesitation. His accent gathered strength, and in a low but ringing voice he added : " But I say this. You have told me, M. Hanaud, of women who looked innocent and were guilty. But you know also of women and girls who can live untainted and unspoilt amidst surroundings which are suspicious."

Hanaud listened, but he neither agreed nor denied. He took up a second slip of paper.

" I shall tell you something now of Mme. Dauvray," he said. " We will not rake up her early history. It might not be edifying, and, poor woman, she is dead. Let us not go back beyond her marriage seventeen years ago to a wealthy manufacturer of Nancy, whom she had met in Paris. Seven years ago M. Dauvray died, leaving his widow a very rich woman. She had a passion for jewellery, which she was now able to gratify. She collected jewels. A famous necklace, a well-known stone— she was not, as you say, happy till she got it. She had a fortune in precious stones—oh, but a large fortune! By the ostentation of her jewels she paraded her wealth here, at Monte Carlo, in Paris. Besides that, she was kind-hearted and most impressionable. Finally, she was, like so many of her class, superstitious to the degree of folly."

Suddenly Mr. Ricardo started in his chair. Superstitious! The word was a sudden light upon his darkness. Now he knew what had perplexed him during the last two days. Clearly—too clearly—he remembered where he had seen Celia Harland, and when. A picture rose before his eyes, and it seemed to strengthen like a film in a developing-dish as Hanaud continued :

" Very well! take Mme. Dauvray as we find her— rich, ostentatious, easily taken by a new face, generous, and foolishly superstitious—and you have in her a living provocation to every rogue. By a hundred instances she proclaimed herself a dupe. She threw down a challenge to every criminal to come and rob her. For seven years Héléne Vauquier stands at her elbow and protects her from serious trouble. Suddenly there is added to her— your young friend, and she is robbed and murdered. And, follow this, M. Wethermill, our thieves are, I think, more brutal to their victims than is the case with you."

Wethermill shut his eyes in a spasm of pain and the pallor of his face increased.

"Suppose that Celia were one of the victims?" he cried in a stifled voice.

Hanaud glanced at him with a look of commiseration.

"That perhaps we shall see," he said. "But what I meant was this. A stranger like Mlle. Célie might be the accomplice in such a crime as the crime of the Villa Rose, meaning only robbery. A stranger might only have discovered too late that murder would be added to the theft."

Meanwhile, in strong, clear colours, Ricardo's picture stood out before his eyes. He was startled by hearing Wethermill say, in a firm voice:

"My friend Ricardo has something to add to what you have said."

"I!" exclaimed Ricardo. How in the world could Wethermill know of that clear picture in his mind?

"Yes. You saw Celia Harland on the evening before the murder."

Ricardo stared at his friend. It seemed to him that Harry Wethermill had gone out of his mind. Here he was corroborating the suspicions of the police by facts—damning and incontrovertible facts.

"On the night before the murder," continued Wethermill quietly, "Celia Harland lost money at the baccarat-table. Ricardo saw her in the garden behind the rooms, and she was hysterical. Later on that same night he saw her again with me, and he heard what she said. I asked her to come to the rooms on the next evening—yesterday, the night of the crime—and her face changed, and she said, 'No, we have other plans for to-morrow But the night after I shall want you.'"

Hanaud sprang up from his chair.

"And *you* tell me these two things!" he cried.

"Yes," said Wethermill. "You were kind enough to say to me I was not a romantic boy. I am not. I can face facts."

Hanaud stared at his companion for a few moments. Then, with a remarkable air of consideration, he bowed.

"You have won, monsieur," he said. "I will take up this case. But," and his face grew stern and he brought his fist down upon the table with a bang, "I shall follow it to the end now, be the consequences bitter as death to you."

"That is what I wish, monsieur," said Wethermill.

Hanaud locked up the slips of paper in his

letter-case. Then he went out of the room and returned in a few minutes.

"We will begin at the beginning," he said briskly. "I have telephoned to the Depôt. Perrichet, the *sergent-de-ville* who discovered the crime, will be here at once. We will walk down to the villa with him, and on the way he shall tell us exactly what he discovered and how he discovered it. At the villa we shall find Monsieur Fleuriot, the Juge d'Instruction, who has already begun his examination, and the Commissaire of Police. In company with them we will inspect the villa. Except for the removal of Mme. Dauvray's body from the salon to her bedroom and the opening of the windows, the house remains exactly as it was."

"We may come with you?" cried Harry Wethermill eagerly.

"Yes, on one condition—that you ask no questions, and answer none unless I put them to you. Listen, watch, examine—but no interruptions!"

Hanaud's manner had altogether changed. It was now authoritative and alert. He turned to Ricardo.

"You will swear to what you saw in the garden and to the words you heard?" he asked. "They are important."

"Yes," said Ricardo.

But he kept silence about that clear picture in his mind which to him seemed no less important, no less suggestive.

The Assembly Hall at Leamington, a crowded audience chiefly of ladies, a platform at one end on which a black cabinet stood. A man, erect and with something of the soldier in his bearing, led forward a girl, pretty and fair-haired, who wore a black velvet dress with a long, sweeping train. She moved like one in a dream. Some half-dozen people from the audience climbed on to the platform, tied the girl's hands with tape behind her back, and sealed the tape. She was led to the cabinet, and in full view of the audience fastened to a bench. Then the door of the cabinet was closed, the people upon the platform descended into the body of the hall, and the lights were turned very low. The audience sat in suspense, and then abruptly in the silence and the darkness there came the rattle of a tambourine from the empty platform. Rappings and knockings seemed to flicker round the panels of the hall, and in the place where the door of the cabinet should be there appeared a splash of misty whiteness. The whiteness shaped itself dimly into the figure of a woman, a face dark and Eastern became visible, and a deep voice spoke in a chant of the Nile and Antony. Then the vision faded, the tambourines and cymbals rattled again. The lights were turned up, the door of the cabinet thrown open, and the girl in the black velvet dress was seen fastened upon the bench within.

It was a spiritualistic performance at which Julius Ricardo had been present two years ago. The young, fair-haired girl in black velvet, the medium, was Celia Harland.

That was the picture which was in Ricardo's mind, and Hanaud's description of Mme. Dauvray made a terrible commentary upon it. " Easily taken by a new face, generous, and foolishly superstitious, a living provocation to every rogue." Those were the words, and here was a beautiful girl of twenty versed in those very tricks of imposture which would make Mme. Dauvray her natural prey!

Ricardo looked at Wethermill, doubtful whether he should tell what he knew of Celia Harland or not. But before he had decided a knock came upon the door.

" Here is Perrichet," said Hanaud, taking up his hat. " We will go down to the Villa Rose."

CHAPTER III

PERRICHET'S STORY

PERRICHET was a young, thick-set man, with a red, fair face, and a moustache and hair so pale in colour that they were almost silver. He came into the room with an air of importance.

"Aha!" said Hanaud, with a malicious smile. "You went to bed late last night, my friend. Yet you were up early enough to read the newspaper. Well, I am to have the honour of being associated with you in this case."

Perrichet twirled his cap awkwardly and blushed.

"Monsieur is pleased to laugh at me," he said. "But it was not I who called myself intelligent. Though indeed I would like to be so, for the good God knows I do not look it."

Hanaud clapped him on the shoulder.

"Then congratulate yourself! It is a great advantage to be intelligent and not to look it. We shall get on famously. Come!"

The four men descended the stairs, and as they walked towards the villa Perrichet related, concisely and clearly, his experience of the night.

"I passed the gate of the villa about half-past

nine," he said. "The gate was closed. Above the
wall and bushes of the garden I saw a bright light
in the room upon the first floor which faces the road
at the south-western corner of the villa. The lower
windows I could not see. More than an hour afterwards I came back, and as I passed the villa again I
noticed that there was now no light in the room
upon the first floor, but that the gate was open. I
thereupon went into the garden, and, pulling the
gate, let it swing to and latch. But it occurred to
me as I did so that there might be visitors at the
villa who had not yet left, and for whom the gate
had been set open. I accordingly followed the
drive which winds round to the front door. The
front door is not on the side of the villa which faces
the road, but at the back. When I came to the
open space where the carriages turn, I saw that the
house was in complete darkness. There were
wooden latticed doors to the long windows on the
ground floor, and these were closed. I tried one to
make certain, and found the fastenings secure. The
other windows upon that floor were shuttered. No
light gleamed anywhere. I then left the garden,
closing the gate behind me. I heard a clock strike
the hour a few minutes afterwards, so that I can be
sure of the time. It was now eleven o'clock. I
came round a third time an hour after, and to my
astonishment I found the gate once more open. I
had left it closed and the house shut up and dark.
Now it stood open ! I looked up to the windows,
and I saw that in a room on the second floor, close

beneath the roof, a light was burning brightly. That room had been dark an hour before. I stood and watched the light for a few minutes, thinking that I should see it suddenly go out. But it did not: it burned quite steadily. This light and the gate opened and reopened aroused my suspicions. I went again into the garden, but this time with greater caution. It was a clear night, and, although there was no moon, I could see without the aid of my lantern. I stole quietly along the drive. When I came round to the front door, I noticed immediately that the shutters of one of the ground-floor windows were swung back, and that the inside glass window which descended to the ground stood open. The sight gave me a shock. Within the hour those shutters had been opened. I felt the blood turn to ice in my veins, and a chill crept along my spine. I thought of that solitary light burning steadily under the roof. I was convinced that something terrible had happened."

"Yes, yes. Quite so," said Hanaud. "Go on, my friend."

"The interior of the room gaped black," Perrichet resumed. "I crept up to the window at the side of the wall and flashed my lantern into the room. The window, however, was in a recess which opened into the room through an arch, and at each side of the arch curtains were draped. The curtains were not closed, but between them I could see nothing but a strip of the room. I stepped carefully in taking heed not to walk on the patch

of grass before the window. The light of my
lantern showed me a chair overturned upon the
floor, and to my right, below the middle one of
the three windows in the right-hand side wall, a
woman lying huddled upon the floor. It was
Mme. Dauvray. She was dressed. There was a
little mud upon her shoes, as though she had
walked after the rain had ceased. Monsieur will
remember that two heavy showers fell last evening
between six and eight."

"Yes," said Hanaud, nodding his approval.

"She was quite dead. Her face was terribly
swollen and black, and a piece of thin strong cord
was knotted so tightly about her neck and had
sunk so deeply into her flesh that at first I did
not see it, for Mme. Dauvray was stout."

"Then what did you do?" asked Hanaud.

"I went to the telephone which was in the hall
and rang up the police. Then I crept upstairs
very cautiously, trying the doors. I came upon
no one until I reached the room under the roof
where the light was burning; there I found Héléne
Vauquier, the maid, snoring in bed in a terrible
fashion."

The four men turned a bend in the road. A few
paces away a knot of people stood before a gate
which a *sergent-de-ville* guarded.

"But here we are at the villa," said Hanaud.

They all looked up, and from a window at the
corner upon the first floor a man looked out and
drew in his head.

"That is M. Besnard, the Commissaire of our police in Aix," said Perrichet.

"And the window from which he looked," said Hanaud, "must be the window of that room in which you saw the bright light at half-past nine on your first round?"

"Yes, m'sieur," said Perrichet; "that is the window."

They stopped at the gate. Perrichet spoke to the *sergent-de-ville*, who at once held the gate open. The party passed into the garden of the villa.

CHAPTER IV

AT THE VILLA

THE drive curved between trees and high bushes towards the back of the house, and as the party advanced along it a small, trim, soldier-like man, with a pointed beard, came to meet them. It was the man who had looked out from the window, Louis Besnard, the Commissaire of Police.

"You are coming, then, to help us, M. Hanaud!" he cried, extending his hands. "You will find no jealousy here; no spirit amongst us of anything but good will; no desire except one to carry out your suggestions. All we wish is that the murderers should be discovered. Mon Dieu, what a crime! And so young a girl to be involved in it! But what will you?"

"So you have already made your mind up on that point!" said Hanaud sharply.

The Commissaire shrugged his shoulders.

"Examine the villa and then judge for yourself whether any other explanation is conceivable," he said; and turning, he waved his hand towards the house. Then he cried, "Ah!" and drew himself into an attitude of attention. A tall, thin man of

35

about forty-five years, dressed in a frock coat and a high silk hat, had just come round an angle of the drive and was moving slowly towards them. He wore the soft, curling brown beard of one who has never used a razor on his chin, and had a narrow face with eyes of a very light grey, and a round bulging forehead.

"This is the Juge d'Instruction?" asked Hanaud.

"Yes; M. Fleuriot," replied Louis Besnard in a whisper.

M. Fleuriot was occupied with his own thoughts, and it was not until Besnard stepped forward noisily on the gravel that he became aware of the group in the garden.

"This is M. Hanaud, of the Sûreté in Paris," said Louis Besnard.

M. Fleuriot bowed with cordiality.

"You are very welcome, M. Hanaud. You will find that nothing at the villa has been disturbed. The moment the message arrived over the telephone that you were willing to assist us I gave instructions that all should be left as we found it. I trust that you, with your experience, will see a way where our eyes find none."

Hanaud bowed in reply.

"I shall do my best, M. Fleuriot. I can say no more," he said.

"But who are these gentlemen?" asked Fleuriot, waking, it seemed, now for the first time to the presence of Harry Wethermill and Mr. Ricardo.

"They are both friends of mine," replied Hanaud.

"If you do not object, I think that their assistance may be useful. Mr. Wethermill, for instance, was acquainted with Celia Harland."

"Ah!" cried the judge; and his face took on suddenly a keen and eager look. "You can tell me about her perhaps?"

"All that I know I will tell readily," said Harry Wethermill.

Into the light eyes of M. Fleuriot there came a cold, bright gleam. He took a step forward. His face seemed to narrow to a greater sharpness. In a moment, to Mr. Ricardo's thought, he ceased to be the judge; he dropped from his high office; he dwindled into a fanatic.

"She is a Jewess, this Celia Harland?" he cried.

"No, M. Fleuriot, she is not," replied Wethermill. "I do not speak in disparagement of that race, for I count many friends amongst its members. But Celia Harland is not one of them."

"Ah!" said Fleuriot; and there was something of disappointment, something, too, of incredulity, in his voice. "Well, you will come and report to me when you have made your investigation." And he passed on without another question or remark.

The group of men watched him go, and it was not until he was out of earshot that Besnard turned with a deprecating gesture to Hanaud.

"Yes, yes, he is a good judge, M. Hanaud— quick, discriminating, sympathetic; but he has that bee in his bonnet, like so many others. Everywhere he must see l'affaire Dreyfus. He cannot get it out of his head. No matter how insignificant a woman is murdered, she must have letters in her possession which would convict Dreyfus. But you know! There are thousands like that—good, kindly, just people in the ordinary ways of life, but behind every crime they see the Jew."

Hanaud nodded his head.

"I know; and in a Juge d'Instruction it is very embarrassing. Let us walk on."

Half-way between the gate and the villa a second carriage-road struck off to the left, and at the entrance to it stood a young, stout man in black leggings."

"The chauffeur?" asked Hanaud. "I will speak to him."

The Commissaire called the chauffeur forward.

"Servettaz," he said, "you will answer any questions which monsieur may put to you."

"Certainly, M. le Commissaire," said the chauffeur. His manner was serious, but he answered readily. There was no sign of fear upon his face.

"How long have you been with Mme. Dauvray?" Hanaud asked.

"Four months, monsieur. I drove her to Aix from Paris."

"And since your parents live at Chambéry you wished to seize the opportunity of spending a day with them while you were so near?"

"Yes, monsieur."

"When did you ask for permission?"

"On Saturday, monsieur."

"Did you ask particularly that you should have yesterday, the Tuesday?"

"No, monsieur; I asked only for a day whenever it should be convenient to madame."

"Quite so," said Hanaud. "Now, when did Mme. Dauvray tell you that you might have Tuesday?"

Servettaz hesitated. His face became troubled. When he spoke, he spoke reluctantly.

"It was not Mme. Dauvray, monsieur, who told me that I might go on Tuesday," he said.

"Not Mme. Dauvray! Who was it, then?" Hanaud asked sharply.

Servettaz glanced from one to another of the grave faces which confronted him.

"It was Mlle. Célie," he said, "who told me."

"Oh!" said Hanaud slowly. "It was Mlle. Célie. When did she tell you?"

"On Monday morning, monsieur. I was cleaning the car. She came to the garage with some flowers in her hand which she had been cutting in the garden, and she said: 'I was right, Alphonse. Madame has a kind heart. You can go to-morrow by the train which leaves Aix at 1.52 and arrives at Chambéry at nine minutes after two.'"

Hanaud started.

"'I was right, Alphonse.' Were those her words? And 'Madame has a kind heart'? Come, come, what is all this?" He lifted a warning finger and said gravely, "Be very careful, Servettaz."

" Those were her words, monsieur."

" ' I was right, Alphonse. Madame has a kind heart ' ? "

" Yes, monsieur."

"Then Mlle. Célie had spoken to you before about this visit of yours to Chambéry," said Hanaud, with his eyes fixed steadily upon the chauffeur's face. The distress upon Servettaz's face increased. Suddenly Hanaud's voice rang sharply. "You hesitate. Begin at the beginning. Speak the truth, Servettaz!"

" Monsieur, I am speaking the truth," said the chauffeur. " It is true I hesitate ... I have heard this morning what people are saying ... I do not know what to think. Mlle. Célie was always kind and thoughtful for me. . . . But it is true "—and with a kind of desperation he went on—" yes, it is true that it was Mlle. Célie who first suggested to me that I should ask for a day to go to Chambéry."

" When did she suggest it ? "

" On the Saturday."

To Mr. Ricardo the words were startling. He glanced with pity towards Wethermill. Wethermill, however, had made up his mind for good and all. He stood with a dogged look upon his face, his chin thrust forward, his eyes upon the chauffeur. Besnard, the Commissaire, had made up his mind too. He merely shrugged his shoulders. Hanaud stepped forward and laid his hand gently on the chauffeur's arm.

"Come, my friend," he said, "let us hear exactly how this happened!"

"Mlle. Célie," said Servettaz, with genuine compunction in his voice, "came to the garage on Saturday morning and ordered the car for the afternoon. She stayed and talked to me for a little while, as she often did. She said that she had been told that my parents lived at Chambéry, and since I was so near I ought to ask for a holiday. For it would not be kind if I did not go and see them."

"That was all?"

"Yes, monsieur."

"Very well." And the detective resumed at once his brisk voice and alert manner. He seemed to dismiss Servettaz's admission from his mind. Ricardo had the impression of a man tying up an important document which he has done with, and putting it away ticketed in some pigeon-hole in his desk. "Let us see the garage!"

They followed the road between the bushes until a turn showed them the garage with its doors open.

"The doors were found unlocked?"

"Just as you see them."

Hanaud nodded. He spoke again to Servettaz. "What did you do with the key on Tuesday?"

"I gave it to Héléne Vauquier, monsieur, after I had locked up the garage. And she hung it on a nail in the kitchen."

"I see," said Hanaud. "So any one could easily have found it last night?"

"Yes, monsieur—if one knew where to look for it."

At the back of the garage a row of petrol-tins stood against the brick wall.

"Was any petrol taken?" asked Hanaud.

"Yes, monsieur; there was very little petrol in the car when I went away. More was taken, but it was taken from the middle tins—these." And he touched the tins.

"I see," said Hanaud, and he raised his eyebrows thoughtfully. The Commissaire moved with impatience.

"From the middle or from the end—what does it matter?" he exclaimed. "The petrol was taken."

Hanaud, however, did not dismiss the point so lightly.

"But it is very possible, that it does matter," he said gently. "For example, if Servettaz had had no reason to examine his tins it might have been some while before he found out that the petrol had been taken."

"Indeed, yes," said Servettaz. "I might even have forgotten that I had not used it myself."

"Quite so," said Hanaud, and he turned to Besnard. "I think that may be important. I do not know," he said.

"But since the car is gone," cried Besnard, "how could the chauffeur not look immediately at his tins?"

The question had occurred to Ricardo, and he wondered in what way Hanaud meant to answer it. Hanaud, however, did not mean to answer it. He took little notice of it at all. He put it aside with a superb indifference to the opinion which his companions might form of him.

"Ah, yes," he said carelessly. "Since the car is gone, as you say, that is so." And he turned again to Servettaz.

"It was a powerful car?" he asked.

"Sixty horse-power," said Servettaz.

Hanaud turned to the Commissaire.

"You have the number and description, I suppose? It will be as well to advertise for it. It may have been seen; it must be somewhere."

The Commissaire replied that the description had already been printed, and Hanaud, with a nod of approval, examined the ground. In front of the garage there was a small stone courtyard, but on its surface there was no trace of a footstep.

"Yet the gravel was wet," he said, shaking his head. "The man who fetched that car fetched it carefully."

He turned and walked back with his eyes upon the ground. Then he ran to the grass border between the gravel and the bushes.

"Look!" he said to Wethermill; "a foot has pressed the blades of grass down here, but very lightly—yes, and there again. Some one ran along the border here on his toes. Yes, he was very careful."

They turned again into the main drive, and, following it for a few yards, came suddenly upon a space in front of the villa. It was a small toy pleasure-house, looking on to a green lawn gay with flower-beds. It was built of yellow stone, and was almost square in shape. A couple of ornate pillars flanked the door, and a gable roof, topped by a gilt vane, surmounted it. To Ricardo it seemed impossible that so sordid and sinister a tragedy had taken place within its walls during the last twelve hours. It glistened so gaudily in the blaze of sunlight. Here and there the green outer shutters were closed; here and there the windows stood open to let in the air and light. Upon each side of the door there was a window lighting the hall, which was large; beyond those windows again, on each side, there were glass doors opening to the ground and protected by the ordinary green latticed shutters of wood, which now stood hooked back against the wall. These glass doors opened into rooms oblong in shape, which ran through towards the back of the house, and were lighted in addition by side windows. The room upon the extreme left, as the party faced the villa, was the dining-room, with the kitchen at the back; the room on the right was the salon in which the murder had been committed. In front of the glass door to this room a strip of what had once been grass stretched to the gravel drive. But the grass had been worn away by constant use, and the black mould showed through. This strip was about three yards wide, and as they approached they saw, even at a distance, that since the rain of last night it had been trampled down.

" We will go round the house first," said Hanaud,

and he turned along the side of the villa and walked in the direction of the road. There were four windows just above his head, of which three lighted the salon, and the fourth a small writing-room behind it. Under these windows there was no disturbance of the ground, and a careful investigation showed conclusively that the only entrance used had been the glass doors of the salon facing the drive. To that spot, then, they returned. There were three sets of footmarks upon the soil. One set ran in a distinct curve from the drive to the side of the door, and did not cross the others.

"Those," said Hanaud, "are the footsteps of my intelligent friend, Perrichet, who was careful not to disturb the ground."

Perrichet beamed all over his rosy face, and Besnard nodded at him with condescending approval.

"But I wish, M. le Commissaire"—and Hanaud pointed to a blur of marks—"that your other officers had been as intelligent. Look! These run from the glass door to the drive, and, for all the use they are to us, a harrow might have been dragged across them."

Besnard drew himself up.

"Not one of my officers has entered the room by way of this door. The strictest orders were given and obeyed. The ground, as you see it, is the ground as it was at twelve o'clock last night."

Hanaud's face grew thoughtful.

"Is that so?" he said, and he stooped to examine

the second set of marks. They were at the right-
hand side of the door. "A woman and a man," he
said. "But they are mere hints rather than prints.
One might almost think——" He rose up without finishing his sentence, and he turned to the
third set and a look of satisfaction gleamed upon
his face. "Ah! here is something more interesting,"
he said.

There were just three impressions; and, whereas
the blurred marks were at the side, these three
pointed straight from the middle of the glass doors
to the drive. They were quite clearly defined, and
all three were the impressions made by a woman's
small, arched, high-heeled shoe. The position of
the marks was at first sight a little peculiar. There
was one a good yard from the window, the impression of the right foot, and the pressure of the sole
of the shoe was more marked than that of the heel.
The second, the impression of the left foot, was not
quite so far from the first as the first was from the
window, and here again the heel was the more
lightly defined. But there was this difference—
the mark of the toe, which was pointed in the first
instance, was, in this, broader and a trifle blurred.
Close beside it the right foot was again visible;
only now the narrow heel was more clearly defined
than the ball of the foot. It had, indeed, sunk
half an inch into the soft ground. There were no
further imprints. Indeed, these two were not merely
close together, they were close to the gravel of the
drive and on the very border of the grass.

Hanaud looked at the marks thoughtfully. Then he turned to the Commissaire.

"Are there any shoes in the house which fit those marks?"

"Yes. We have tried the shoes of all the women —Célie Harland, the maid, and even Mme. Dauvray. The only ones which fit at all are those taken from Célie Harland's bedroom."

He called to an officer standing in the drive, and a pair of grey suéde shoes were brought to him from the hall.

"See, M. Hanaud, it is a pretty little foot which made those clear impressions," he said, with a smile; "a foot arched and slender. Mme. Dauvray's foot is short and square, the maid's broad and flat. Neither Mme. Dauvray nor Héléne Vauquier could have worn these shoes. They were lying, one here, one there, upon the floor of Célie Harland's room, as though she had kicked them off in a hurry. They are almost new, you see. They have been worn once perhaps, no more, and they fit with absolute precision into those footmarks, except just at the toe of that second one."

Hanaud took the shoes and, kneeling down, placed them one after the other over the impressions. To Ricardo it was extraordinary how exactly they covered up the marks and filled the indentations.

"I should say," said the Commissaire, "that Célie Harland went away wearing a new pair of shoes made on the very same last as those."

As those she had left carelessly lying on the floor
of her room for the first person to notice, thought
Ricardo! It seemed as if the girl had gone out
of her way to make the weight of evidence against
her as heavy as possible.   Yet, after all, it was
just through inattention to the small details, so
insignificant at the red moment of crime, so terribly
instructive the next day, that guilt was generally
brought home.

Hanaud rose to his feet and handed the shoes
back to the officer.

"Yes," he said, "so it seems. The shoemaker
can help us here. I see the shoes were made in
Aix."

Besnard looked at the name stamped in gold
letters upon the lining of the shoes.

"I will have inquiries made," he said.

Hanaud nodded, took a measure from his pocket
and measured the ground between the window and
the first footstep, and between the first footstep
and the other two.

"How tall is Mlle. Célie?" he asked, and he
addressed the question to Wethermill. It struck
Ricardo as one of the strangest details in all this
strange affair that the detective should ask with
confidence for information which might help to
bring Célia Harland to the guillotine from the man
who had staked his happiness upon her innocence.

"About five feet seven," he answered.

Hanaud replaced his measure in his pocket. He
turned with a grave face to Wethermill.

" I warned you fairly, didn't I ? " he said.

Wethermill's white face twitched.

" Yes," he said. " I am not afraid." But there was more of anxiety in his voice than there had been before.

Hanaud pointed solemnly to the ground.

" Read the story those footprints write in the mould there. A young and active girl of about Mlle. Célie's height, and wearing a new pair of Mlle. Célie's shoes, springs from that room where the murder was committed, where the body of the murdered woman lies. She is running. She is wearing a long gown. At the second step the hem of the gown catches beneath the point of her shoe. She stumbles. To save herself from falling she brings up the other foot sharply and stamps the heel down into the ground. She recovers her balance. She steps on to the drive. It is true the gravel here is hard and takes no mark, but you will see that some of the mould which has clung to her shoes has dropped off. She mounts into the motor-car with the man and the other woman and drives off—some time between eleven and twelve."

" Between eleven and twelve ? Is that sure ? " asked Besnard.

" Certainly," replied Hanaud. " The gate is open at eleven, and Perrichet closes it. It is open again at twelve. Therefore the murderers had not gone before eleven. No ; the gate was open for them to go, but they had not gone. Else why should the gate again be open at midnight ? "

Besnard nodded in assent, and suddenly Perrichet
started forward, with his eyes full of horror.

"Then, when I first closed the gate," he cried,
"and came into the garden and up to the house
they were here—in that room? Oh, my God!"
He stared at the window, with his mouth open.

"I am afraid, my friend, that is so," said Hanaud
gravely.

"But I knocked upon the wooden door, I tried
the bolts; and they were within—in the darkness
within, holding their breath not three yards from
me."

He stood transfixed.

"That we shall see," said Hanaud.

He stepped in Perrichet's footsteps to the sill of
the room. He examined the green wooden doors
which opened outwards, and the glass doors which
opened inwards, taking a magnifying-glass trom his
pocket. He called Besnard to his side.

"See!" he said, pointing to the woodwork.

"Finger-marks?" asked Besnard eagerly.

"Yes; of hands in gloves," returned Hanaud.
"We shall learn nothing from these marks except
that the assassins knew their trade."

Then he stooped down to the sill, where some
traces of steps were visible. He rose with a gesture
of resignation.

"Rubber shoes," he said, and so stepped into the
room, followed by Wethermill and the others.
They found themselves in a small recess which was
panelled with wood painted white, and here and

there delicately carved into festoons of flowers. The recess ended in an arch, supported by two slender pillars, and on the inner side of the arch thick curtains of pink silk were hung. These were drawn back carelessly, and through the opening between them the party looked down the length of the room beyond. They passed within.

CHAPTER V

IN THE SALON

JULIUS RICARDO pushed aside the curtains with a thrill of excitement. He found himself standing within a small oblong room which was prettily, even daintily, furnished. On his left, close by the recess, was a small fireplace with the ashes of a burnt-out fire in the grate. Beyond the grate a long settee covered in pink damask, with a crumpled cushion at each end, stood a foot or two away from the wall, and beyond the settee the door of the room opened into the hall. At the end a long mirror was let into the panelling, and a writing-table stood by the mirror. On the right were the three windows, and between the two nearest to Mr. Ricardo was the switch of the electric light. A chandelier hung from the ceiling, an electric lamp stood upon the writing-table, a couple of electric candles on the mantelshelf. A round satin-wood table stood under the windows, with three chairs about it, of which one was overturned, one was placed with its back to the electric switch, and the third on the opposite side facing it.

Ricardo could hardly believe that he stood

actually upon the spot where, within twelve hours, a cruel and sinister tragedy had taken place. There was so little disorder. The three windows on his right showed him the blue sunlit sky and a glimpse of flowers and trees; behind him the glass doors stood open to the lawn, where birds piped cheerfully and the trees murmured of summer. But he saw Hanaud stepping quickly from place to place, with an extraordinary lightness of step for so big a man, obviously engrossed, obviously reading here and there some detail, some custom of the inhabitants of that room.

Ricardo leaned with careful artistry against the wall.

"Now, what has this room to say to me?" he asked importantly. Nobody paid the slightest attention to his question, and it was just as well. For the room had very little information to give him. He ran his eye over the white Louis Seize furniture, the white panels of the wall, the polished floor, the pink curtains. Even the delicate tracery of the ceiling did not escape his scrutiny. Yet he saw nothing likely to help him but an overturned chair and a couple of crushed cushions on a settee. It was very annoying, all the more annoying because M. Hanaud was so uncommonly busy. Hanaud looked carefully at the long settee and the crumpled cushions, and he took out his measure and measured the distance between the cushion at one end and the cushion at the other. He examined the table, he measured the distance between the chairs. He came to the fireplace and raked in the ashes of the burnt-out fire. But Ricardo noticed a singular thing. In the midst of his search Hanaud's eyes were always straying back to the settee, and always with a look of extreme perplexity, as if he read there something, definitely something, but something which he could not explain. Finally he went back to it; he drew it farther away from the wall, and suddenly with a little cry he stooped and went down on his knees. When he rose he was holding some torn fragments of paper in his hand. He went over to the writing-table and opened the blotting-book. Where it fell open there were some sheets of note-paper, and one particular sheet of which half had been torn off. He compared the pieces which he held with that torn sheet, and seemed satisfied.

There was a rack for note-paper upon the table, and from it he took a stiff card.

" Get me some gum or paste, and quickly," he said. His voice had become brusque, the politeness had gone from his address. He carried the card and the fragments of paper to the round table. There he sat down and, with infinite patience, gummed the fragments on to the card, fitting them together like the pieces of a Chinese puzzle.

The others over his shoulders could see spaced words, written in pencil, taking shape as a sentence upon the card. Hanaud turned abruptly in his seat toward Wethermill.

"You have, no doubt, a letter written by Mlle. Célie?"

Wethermill took his letter-case from his pocket and a letter out of the case. He hesitated for a moment as he glanced over what was written. The four sheets were covered. He folded back the letter, so that only the two inner sheets were visible, and handed it to Hanaud. Hanaud compared it with the handwriting upon the card.

"Look!" he said at length, and the three men gathered behind him. On the card the gummed fragments of paper revealed a sentence:

"Je ne sais pas."

"'I do not know,'" said Ricardo; "now this is very important."

Beside the card Celia's letter to Wethermill was laid.

"What do you think?" asked Hanaud.

Besnard, the Commissaire of Police, bent over Hanaud's shoulder.

"There are strong resemblances," he said guardedly.

Ricardo was on the look-out for deep mysteries. Resemblances were not enough for him; they were inadequate to the artistic needs of the situation.

"Both were written by the same hand," he said definitely; "only in the sentence written upon the card the handwriting is carefully disguised."

"Ah!" said the Commissaire, bending forward again. "Here is an idea! Yes, yes, there are strong differences."

Ricardo looked triumphant.

"Yes, there are differences," said Hanaud. "Look how long the up stroke of the 'P' is, how it wavers! See how suddenly this 's' straggles off, as though some emotion made the hand shake. Yet this," and touching Wethermill's letter he smiled ruefully, "this is where the emotion should have affected the pen." He looked up at Wethermill's face and then said quietly :

"You have given us no opinion, monsieur. Yet your opinion should be the most valuable of all. Were these two papers written by the same hand?"

"I do not know," answered Wethermill.

"And I, too," cried Hanaud, in a sudden ex-asperation, "je ne sais pas. I do not know. It may be her hand carelessly counterfeited. It may be her hand disguised. It may be simply that she wrote in a hurry with her gloves on."

"It may have been written some time ago," said Mr. Ricardo, encouraged by his success to another suggestion.

"No; that is the one thing it could not have been," said Hanaud. "Look round the room. Was there ever a room better tended? Find me a little pile of dust in any one corner if you can! It is all as clean as a plate. Every morning, except this one morning, this room has been swept and polished. The paper was written and torn up yesterday."

He enclosed the card in an envelope as he spoke, and placed it in his pocket. Then he rose and crossed again to the settee. He stood at the side of

it, with his hands clutching the lapels of his coat
and his face gravely troubled. After a few moments
of silence for himself, of suspense for all the others
who watched him, he stooped suddenly. Slowly,
and with extraordinary care, he pushed his hands
under the head-cushion and lifted it up gently, so
that the indentations of its surface might not be dis-
arranged. He carried it over to the light of the
open window. The cushion was covered with silk,
and as he held it to the sunlight all could see a small
brown stain.

Hanaud took his magnifying-glass from his pocket
and bent his head over the cushion. But at that
moment, careful though he had been, the down
swelled up within the cushion, the folds and indentations disappeared, the silk covering was
stretched smooth.

"Oh!" cried Besnard tragically. "What have
you done?"

Hanaud's face flushed. He had been guilty of a
clumsiness—even he.

Mr. Ricardo took up the tale.

"Yes," he exclaimed, "what have you done?"

Hanaud looked at Ricardo in amazement at his
audacity.

"Well, what have I done?" he asked. "Come!
tell me!"

"You have destroyed a clue," replied Ricardo
impressively.

The deepest dejection at once overspread Hanaud's
burly face.

"Don't say that, M. Ricardo, I beseech you!" he implored. "A clue! and I have destroyed it! But what kind of a clue? And how have I destroyed it? And to what mystery would it be a clue if I hadn't destroyed it? And what will become of me when I go back to Paris, and say in the Rue de Jerusalem, 'Let me sweep the cellars, my good friends, for M. Ricardo knows that I destroyed a clue. Faithfully he promised me that he would not open his mouth, but I destroyed a clue, and his perspicacity forced him into speech.'"

It was the turn of Mr. Ricardo to grow red.

Hanaud turned with a smile to Besnard.

"It does not really matter whether the creases in this cushion remain," he said, "we have all seen them." And he replaced the glass in his pocket.

He carried that cushion back and replaced it. Then he took the other, which lay at the foot of the settee, and carried it in its turn to the window. This was indented too, and ridged up, and just at the marks the nap of the silk was worn, and there was a slit where it had been cut. The perplexity upon Hanaud's face greatly increased. He stood with the cushion in his hands, no longer looking at it, but looking out through the doors at the footsteps so clearly defined —the footsteps of a girl who had run from this room and sprung into a motor-car and driven away. He shook his head, and, carrying back the cushion, laid it carefully down. Then he stood erect, gazed about the room as though even yet he might force its secrets out from its silence, and cried, with a sudden violence :

" There is something here, gentlemen, which I do not understand."

Mr. Ricardo heard some one beside him draw a deep breath, and turned. Wethermill stood at his elbow. A faint colour had come back to his cheeks, his eyes were fixed intently upon Hanaud's face.

"What do you think ? " he asked; and Hanaud replied brusquely :

" It's not my business to hold opinions, monsieur ; my business is to make sure."

There was one point, and only one, of which he had made every one in that room sure. He had started confident. Here was a sordid crime, easily understood. But in that room he had read something which had troubled him, which had raised the sordid crime on to some higher and perplexing level.

" Then M. Fleuriot after all might be right ? " asked the Commissaire timidly.

Hanaud stared at him for a second, then smiled.

" L'affaire Dreyfus ? " he cried. " Oh la, la, la ! No, but there is something else."

What was that something ? Ricardo asked himself. He looked once more about the room. He did not find his answer, but he caught sight of an ornament upon the wall which drove the question from his mind. The ornament, if so it could be called, was a painted tambourine with a bunch of bright ribbons tied to the rim ; and it was hung upon the wall between the settee and the fireplace

at about the height of a man's head. Of course it
might be no more than it seemed to be—a rather
gaudy and vulgar toy, such as a woman like Mme.
Dauvray would be very likely to choose in order to
dress her walls. But it swept Ricardo's thoughts
back of a sudden to the concert-hall at Leamington
and the apparatus of a spiritualistic show. After all,
he reflected triumphantly, Hanaud had not noticed
everything, and as he made the reflection Hanaud's
voice broke in to corroborate him.

"We have seen everything here; let us go up-
stairs," he said. "We will first visit the room of
Mlle. Célie. Then we will question the maid, Héléne
Vauquier."

The four men, followed by Perrichet, passed out
by the door into the hall and mounted the stairs.
Celia's room was in the south-west angle of the villa,
a bright and airy room, of which one window overlooked the road, and two others, between which
stood the dressing-table, the garden. Behind the
room a door led into a little white-tiled bathroom.
Some towels were tumbled upon the floor beside
the bath. In the bedroom a dark-grey frock of
tussore and a petticoat were flung carelessly on the
bed; a big grey hat of Ottoman silk was lying upon
a chest of drawers in the recess of a window; and
upon a chair a little pile of fine linen and a pair of
grey silk stockings, which matched in shade the
grey suéde shoes, were tossed in a heap.

"It was here that you saw the light at half-past
nine?" Hanaud said, turning to Perrichet.

"Yes, monsieur," replied Perrichet.

"We may assume, then, that Mlle. Célie was changing her dress at that time."

Besnard was looking about him, opening a drawer here, a wardrobe there.

"Mlle. Célie," he said, with a laugh, "was a particular young lady, and fond of her fine clothes, if one may judge from the room and the order of the cupboards. She must have changed her dress last night in an unusual hurry."

There was about the whole room a certain daintiness, almost, it seemed to Mr. Ricardo, a fragrance, as though the girl had impressed something of her own delicate self upon it. Wethermill stood upon the threshold watching with a sullen face the violation of this chamber by the officers of the police.

No such feelings, however, troubled Hanaud. He went over to the dressing-room and opened a few small leather cases which held Celia's ornaments. In one or two of them a trinket was visible; others were empty. One of these latter Hanaud held open in his hand, and for so long that Besnard moved impatiently.

"You see it is empty, monsieur," he said, and suddenly Wethermill moved forward into the room.

"Yes, I see that," said Hanaud dryly.

It was a case made to hold a couple of long ear-drops—those diamond ear-drops, doubtless, which Mr. Ricardo had seen twinkling in the garden.

"Will monsieur let me see?" asked Wethermill, and he took the case in his hands. "Yes," he said. "Mlle. Célie's ear-drops," and he handed the case back with a thoughtful air.

It was the first time he had taken a definite part in the investigation. To Ricardo the reason was clear. Harry Wethermill had himself given those ear-drops to Celia. Hanaud replaced the case and turned round.

"There is nothing more for us to see here," he said. "I suppose that no one has been allowed to enter the room?" And he opened the door.

"No one except Héléne Vauquier," replied the Commissaire.

Ricardo felt indignant at so obvious a piece of carelessness. Even Wethermill looked surprised. Hanaud merely shut the door again.

"Oho, the maid!" he said. "Then she has recovered!"

"She is still weak," said the Commissaire. "But I thought it was necessary that we should obtain at once a description of what Célie Harland wore when she left the house. I spoke to M. Fleuriot about it, and he gave me permission to bring Héléne Vauquier here, who alone could tell us. I brought her here myself just before you came. She looked through the girl's wardrobe to see what was missing."

"Was she alone in the room?"

"Not for a moment," said M. Besnard haughtily. "Really, monsieur, we are not so ignorant of how an affair of this kind should be conducted. I was in the room myself the whole time, with my eye upon her."

"That was just before I came," said Hanaud. He crossed carelessly to the open window which overlooked the road and, leaning out of it, looked up the road to the corner round which he and his friends had come, precisely as the Commissaire had done. Then he turned back into the room.

"Which was the last cupboard or drawer that Héléne Vauquier touched?" he asked.

"This one."

Besnard stooped and pulled open the bottom drawer of a chest which stood in the embrasure of the window. A light-coloured dress was lying at the bottom.

"I told her to be quick," said Besnard, "since I had seen that you were coming. She lifted this dress out and said that nothing was missing there. So I took her back to her room and left her with the nurse."

Hanaud lifted the light dress from the drawer, shook it out in front of the window, twirled it round, snatched up a corner of it and held it to his eyes, and then, folding it quickly, replaced it in the drawer.

"Now show me the first drawer she touched." And this time he lifted out a petticoat, and, taking it to the window, examined it with a greater care. When he had finished with it he handed it to Ricardo to put away, and stood for a moment or two thoughtful and absorbed. Ricardo in his turn examined the petticoat. But he could see nothing unusual. It was an attractive petticoat, dainty with frills and lace, but it was hardly a thing to grow thoughtful over. He looked up in perplexity and saw that Hanaud was watching his investigations with a smile of amusement.

"When M. Ricardo has put that away," he said, "we will hear what Hélène Vauquier has to tell us."

He passed out of the door last, and, locking it, placed the key in his pocket.

"Hélène Vauquier's room is, I think, upstairs," he said. And he moved towards the staircase.

But as he did so a man in plain clothes, who had been waiting upon the landing, stepped forward. He carried in his hand a piece of thin, strong whipcord.

"Ah, Durette!" cried Besnard. "Monsieur Hanaud, I sent Durette this morning round the shops of Aix with the cord which was found knotted round Mme. Dauvray's neck."

Hanaud advanced quickly to the man.

"Well! Did you discover anything?"

"Yes, monsieur," said Durette. "At the shop of M. Corval, in the Rue du Casino, a young lady in a dark-grey frock and hat bought some cord of this kind at a few minutes after nine last night. It was just as the shop was being closed. I showed Corval the photograph of Célie Harland which M. le Commissaire gave me out of Mme.

Dauvray's room, and he identified it as the portrait of the girl who had bought the cord."

Complete silence followed upon Durette's words. The whole party stood like men stupefied. No one looked towards Wethermill; even Hanaud averted his eyes.

"Yes, that is very important," he said awkwardly. He turned away and, followed by the others, went up the stairs to the bedroom of Héléne Vauquier.

CHAPTER VI

HÉLÈNE VAUQUIER'S EVIDENCE

A NURSE opened the door. Within the room Héléne Vauquier was leaning back in a chair. She looked ill, and her face was very white. On the appearance of Hanaud, the Commissaire, and the others, however, she rose to her feet. Ricardo recognised the justice of Hanaud's description. She stood before them a hard-featured, tall woman of thirty-five or forty, in a neat black stuff dress, strong with the strength of a peasant, respectable, reliable. She looked what she had been, the confidential maid of an elderly woman. On her face there was now an aspect of eager appeal.

"Oh, monsieur!" she began, "let me go from here—anywhere—into prison if you like. But to stay here—where in years past we were so happy—and with madame lying in the room below. No, it is insupportable."

She sank into her chair, and Hanaud came over to her side.

"Yes, yes," he said, in a soothing voice. "I can understand your feelings, my poor woman.

We will not keep you here. You have, perhaps, friends in Aix with whom you could stay?"

"Oh yes, monsieur!" Héléne cried gratefully. "Oh, but I thank you! That I should have to sleep here to-night! Oh, how the fear of that has frightened me!"

"You need have had no such fear. After all, we are not the visitors of last night," said Hanaud, drawing a chair close to her and patting her hand sympathetically. "Now, I want you to tell these gentlemen and myself all that you know of this dreadful business. Take your time, mademoiselle! We are human."

"But, monsieur, I know nothing," she cried. "I was told that I might go to bed as soon as I had dressed Mlle. Célie for the séance."

"Séance!" cried Ricardo, startled into speech. The picture of the Assembly Hall at Leamington was again before his mind. But Hanaud turned towards him, and, though Hanaud's face retained its benevolent expression, there was a glitter in his eyes which sent the blood into Ricardo's face.

"Did you speak again, M. Ricardo?" the detective asked. "No? I thought it was not possible. He turned back to Héléne Vauquier. "So Mlle. Célie practised séances. That is very strange. We will hear about them. Who knows what thread may lead us to the truth?"

Héléne Vauquier shook her head.

"Monsieur, it is not right that you should seek the truth from me. For, consider this! I cannot speak with justice of Mlle. Célie. No, I cannot! I did not like her. I was jealous—yes, jealous. Monsieur, you want the truth—I hated her!" And the woman's face flushed and she clenched her hand upon the arm of her chair. "Yes, I hated her. How could I help it?" she asked.

"Why?" asked Hanaud gently. "Why could you not help it?"

Héléne Vauquier leaned back again, her strength exhausted, and smiled languidly.

"I will tell you. But remember it is a woman speaking to you, and things which you will count silly and trivial mean very much to her. There was one night last June—only last June! To think of it! So little while ago there was no Mlle. Célie—— " and, as Hanaud raised his hand, she said hurriedly, "Yes, yes; I will control myself. But to think of Mme. Dauvray now!"

And thereupon she blurted out her story and explained to Mr. Ricardo the question which had so perplexed him. how a girl of so much distinction as Celia Harland came to be living with a woman of so common a type as Mme. Dauvray.

"Well, one night in June," said Héléne Vauquier, "madame went with a party to supper at the Abbaye Restaurant in Montmartre. And she brought home for the first time Mlle. Célie. But you should have seen her! She had on a little plaid skirt and a coat which was falling to pieces, and she was starving—yes, starving. Madame told me the story that night as I undressed her. Mlle.

Célie was there dancing amidst the tables for a supper with any one who would be kind enough to dance with her."

The scorn of her voice rang through the room. She was the rigid, respectable peasant woman, speaking out her contempt. And Wethermill must needs listen to it. Ricardo dared not glance at him.

"But hardly any one would dance with her in her rags, and no one would give her supper except madame. Madame did. Madame listened to her story of hunger and distress. Madame believed it, and brought her home. Madame was so kind, so careless in her kindness. And now she lies murdered for a reward!" An hysterical sob checked the woman's utterances, her face began to work, her hands to twitch.

"Come, come!" said Hanaud gently, "calm yourself, mademoiselle."

Hélène Vauquier paused for a moment or two to recover her composure. "I beg your pardon, monsieur, but I have been so long with madame— oh, the poor woman! Yes, yes, I will calm myself. Well, madame brought her home, and in a week there was nothing too good for Mlle. Célie. Madame was like a child. Always she was being deceived and imposed upon. Never she learnt prudence. But no one so quickly made her way to madame's heart as Mlle. Célie. Mademoiselle must live with her. Mademoiselle must be dressed by the first modistes. Mademoiselle must have lace petticoats and the softest linen, long white gloves, and pretty ribbons for her hair, and hats from Caroline Réboux at twelve hundred francs. And madame's maid must attend upon her and deck her out in all these dainty things. Bah!"

Vauquier was sitting erect in her chair, violent, almost rancorous with anger. She looked round upon the company and shrugged her shoulders.

"I told you not to come to me!" she said. "I cannot speak impartially, or even gently of mademoiselle. Consider! For years I had been more than madame's maid—her friend; yes, so she was kind enough to call me. She talked to me about everything, consulted me about everything, took me with her everywhere. Then she brings home, at two o'clock in the morning, a young girl with a fresh, pretty face, from a Montmartre restaurant, and in a week I am nothing at all—oh, but nothing—and mademoiselle is queen."

"Yes, it is quite natural," said Hanaud sympathetically. "You would not have been human, mademoiselle, if you had not felt some anger. But tell us frankly about these séances. How did they begin?"

"Oh, monsieur," Vauquier answered, "it was not difficult to begin them. Mme. Dauvray had a passion for fortune-tellers and rogues of that kind. Any one with a pack of cards and some nonsense about a dangerous woman with black hair or a man with a limp — Monsieur knows the stories they string together in dimly lighted rooms to deceive the credulous—any one could make a harvest out of madame's superstitions. But monsieur knows the type."

" Indeed I do," said Hanaud, with a laugh.

" Well, after mademoiselle had been with us three weeks, she said to me one morning when I was dressing her hair that it was a pity madame was always running round the fortune-tellers, that she herself could do something much more striking and impressive, and that if only I would help her we could rescue madame from their clutches. Sir, I did not think what power I was putting into Mlle. Célie's hands, or assuredly I would have refused. And I did not wish to quarrel with Mlle. Célie ; so for once I consented, and, having once consented, I could never afterwards refuse, for, if I had, mademoiselle would have made some fine excuse about the psychic influence not being *en rapport*, and meanwhile would have had me sent away. While if I had confessed the truth to madame, she would have been so angry that I had been a party to tricking her that again I would have lost my place. And so the séances went on."

"Yes," said Hanaud. " I understand that your position was very difficult. We shall not, I think," and he turned to the Commissaire confidently for corroboration of his words, " be disposed to blame you."

"Certainly not," said the Commissaire. " After all, life is not so easy."

"Thus, then, the séances began," said Hanaud,

leaning forward with a keen interest. "This is a
strange and curious story you are telling me, Mlle.
Vauquier. Now, how were they conducted? How
did you assist? What did Mlle. Célie do? Rap
on the tables in the dark and rattle tambourines
like that one with the knot of ribbons which hangs
upon the wall of the salon?"

There was a gentle and inviting irony in Hanaud's
tone. Mr. Ricardo was disappointed. Hanaud had
after all not overlooked the tambourine. Without
Ricardo's reason to notice it, he had none the less
observed it and borne it in his memory.

"Well?" he asked.

"Oh, monsieur, the tambourines and the rapping
on the table!" cried Héléne. "That was nothing
—oh, but nothing at all. Mademoiselle Célie would
make spirits appear and speak!"

"Really! And she was never caught out! But
Mlle. Célie must have been a remarkably clever
girl."

"Oh, she was of an address which was surprising.
Sometimes madame and I were alone. Sometimes
there were others, whom madame in her pride had
invited. For she was very proud, monsieur, that
her companion could introduce her to the spirits of
dead people. But never was Mlle. Célie caught out.
She told me that for many years, even when quite
a child, she had travelled through England giving
these exhibitions."

"Oho!" said Hanaud, and he turned to Wethermill. "Did you know that?" he asked in English.

"I did not," he said. "I do not now."

Hanaud shook his head.

"To me this story does not seem invented," he replied. And then he spoke again in French to Héléne Vauquier. "Well, continue, mademoiselle! Assume that the company is assembled for our séance."

"Then Mlle. Célie, dressed in a long gown of black velvet, which set off her white arms and shoulders well—oh, mademoiselle did not forget those little trifles," Héléne Vauquicr interrupted her story, with a return of her bitterness, to interpolate—"mademoiselle would sail into the room with her velvet train flowing behind her, and perhaps for a little while she would say there was a force working against her, and she would sit silent in a chair while madame gaped at her with open eyes. At last mademoiselle would say that the powers were favourable and the spirits would manifest themselves to-night. Then she would be placed in a cabinet, perhaps with a string tied across the door outside—you will understand it was my business to see after the string—and the lights would be turned down, or perhaps out altogether. Or at other times we would sit holding hands round a table, Mlle. Célie between Mme. Dauvray and myself. But in that case the lights would be turned out first, and it would be really my hand which held Mme. Dauvray's. And whether it was the cabinet or the chairs, in a moment mademoiselle would be creeping silently about the room in a little pair

of soft-soled slippers without heels, which she wore
so that she might not be heard, and tambourines
would rattle as you say, and fingers touch the
forehead and the neck, and strange voices would
sound from corners of the room, and dim ap-
paritions would appear—the spirits of great ladies
of the past, who would talk with Mme. Dauvray
Such ladies as Mme. de Castiglione, Marie Antoin-
ette, Mme. de Medici—I do not remember all the
names, and very likely I do not pronounce them
properly. Then the voices would cease and the
lights be turned up, and Mlle. Célie would be found
in a trance just in the same place and attitude as
she had been when the lights were turned out.
Imagine, messieurs, the effect of such séances upon
a woman like Mme. Dauvray. She was made for
them. She believed in them implicitly. The words
of the great ladies from the past—she would remember and repeat them, and be very proud that
such great ladies had come back to the world merely
to tell her—Mme. Dauvray—about their lives. She
would have had séances all day, but Mlle. Célie
pleaded that she was left exhausted at the end of
them. But Mlle. Célie was of an address! For
instance—it will seem very absurd and ridiculous to
you, gentlemen, but you must remember what Mme.
Dauvray was—for instance, madame was particularly anxious to speak with the spirit of Mme.
de Montespan. Yes, yes! She had read all the
memoirs about that lady. Very likely Mlle. Célie
had put the notion into Mme. Dauvray's head, for

madame was not a scholar. But she was dying to hear that famous woman's voice and to catch a dim glimpse of her face. Well, she was never gratified. Always she hoped. Always Mlle. Célie tantalised her with the hope. But she would not gratify it. She would not spoil her fine affairs by making these treats too common. And she acquired —how should she not?—a power over Mme. Dauvray which was unassailable. The fortune-tellers had no more to say to Mme. Dauvray. She did nothing but felicitate herself upon the happy chance which had sent her Mlle. Célie. And now she lies in her room murdered!"

Once more Héléne's voice broke upon the words. But Hanaud poured her out a glass of water and held it to her lips. Héléne drank it eagerly.

"There, that is better, is it not?" he said.

"Yes, monsieur," said Héléne Vauquier, recovering herself. "Sometimes, too," she resumed, "messages from the spirits would flutter down in writing on the table."

"In writing?" exclaimed Hanaud quickly.

"Yes; answers to questions. Mlle. Célie had them ready. Oh, but she was of an address altogether surprising."

"I see," said Hanaud slowly; and he added, "But sometimes, I suppose, the questions were questions which Mlle. Célie could not answer?"

"Sometimes," Héléne Vauquier admitted, "when visitors were present. When Mme. Dauvray was alone—well, she was an ignorant woman, and any answer would serve. But it was not so when there were visitors whom Mlle. Célie did not know, or only knew slightly. These visitors might be putting questions to test her, of which they knew the answers, while Mlle. Célie did not."

"Exactly," said Hanaud. "What happened then?" All who were listening understood to what point he was leading Héléne Vauquier. All waited intently for her answer.

She smiled.

"It was all one to Mlle. Célie."

"She was prepared with an escape from the difficulty?"

"Perfectly prepared."

Hanaud looked puzzled.

"I can think of no way out of it except the one," and he looked round to the Commissaire and to Ricardo as though he would inquire of them how many ways they had discovered. "I can think of no escape except that a message in writing should flutter down from the spirit appealed to saying frankly," and Hanaud shrugged his shoulders, "'I do not know.'"

"Oh no no, monsieur," replied Héléne Vauquier in pity for Hanaud's misconception. "I see that you are not in the habit of attending séances. It would never do for a spirit to admit that it did not know. At once its authority would be gone, and with it Mlle. Célie's as well. But on the other hand, for inscrutable reasons the spirit might not be allowed to answer."

"I understand," said Hanaud, meekly accepting the correction. "The spirit might reply that it was forbidden to answer, but never that it did not know."

"No, never that," said Hélène. So it seemed that Hanaud must look elsewhere for the explanation of that sentence, "I do not know." Hélène continued : "Oh, Mlle. Célie—it was not easy to baffle her, I can tell you. She carried a lace scarf which she could drape about her head, and in a moment she would be, in the dim light, an old, old woman, with a voice so altered that no one could know it. Indeed, you said rightly, monsieur—she was clever."

To all who listened Hélène Vauquier's story carried its conviction. Mme. Dauvray rose vividly before their minds as a living woman. Celia's trickeries were so glibly described that they could hardly have been invented, and certainly not by this poor peasant-woman whose lips so bravely struggled with Medici, and Montespan, and the names of the other great ladies. How, indeed, should she know of them at all? She could never have had the inspiration to concoct the most convincing item of her story—the queer craze of Mme. Dauvray for an interview with Mme. de Montespan. These details were assuredly the truth.

Ricardo, indeed, knew them to be true. Had he not himself seen the girl in her black velvet dress shut up in a cabinet, and a great lady of the past dimly appear in the darkness? Moreover, Hélène Vauquier's jealousy was so natural and inevitable a thing. Her confession of it corroborated all her story.

"Well, then," said Hanaud, "we come to last night. There was a séance held in the salon last night."

"No, monsieur," said Vauquier, shaking her head; "there was no séance last night."

"But already you have said——" interrupted the Commissaire; and Hanaud held up his hand.

"Let her speak, my friend."

"Yes, monsieur shall hear," said Vauquier.

It appeared that at five o'clock in the afternoon Mme. Dauvray and Mlle. Célie prepared to leave the house on foot. It was their custom to walk down at this hour to the Villa des Fleurs, pass an hour or so there, dine in a restaurant, and return to the Rooms to spend the evening. On this occasion, however, Mme. Dauvray informed Hélène that they should be back early and bring with them a friend who was interested in, but entirely sceptical of, spiritualistic manifestations. "But we shall convince her to-night, Célie," she said confidently; and the two women then went out. Shortly before eight Hélène closed the shutters both of the upstair and the downstair windows and of the glass doors into the garden, and returned to the kitchen, which was at the back of the house—that is, on the side facing the road. There had been a fall of rain at seven which had lasted for the greater part of the hour, and soon after she had shut the windows the rain fell again in a heavy shower, and Hélène, knowing that madame felt the chill, lighted a small fire in the salon. The shower lasted until nearly nine, when it ceased altogether and the night cleared up.

It was close upon half-past nine when the bell rang from the salon. Vauquier was sure of the hour, for the charwoman called her attention to the clock.

" I found Mme. Dauvray, Mlle. Célie, and another woman in the salon," continued Héléne Vauquier. " Madame had let them in with her latchkey."

" Ah, the other woman!" cried Besnard. " Had you seen her before?"

" No, monsieur."

" What was she like?"

" She was sallow, with black hair and bright eyes like beads. She was short and about forty-five years old, though it is difficult to judge of these things. I noticed her hands, for she was taking her gloves off, and they seemed to me to be unusually muscular for a woman."

" Ah!" cried Louis Besnard. " That is important."

" Mme. Dauvray was, as she always was before a séance, in a feverish flutter. 'You will help Mlle. Célie to dress, Hélène, and be very quick,' she said; and with an extraordinary longing she added, 'Perhaps we shall see *her* to-night.' Her, you understand, was Mme. de Montespan. And she turned to the stranger and said, 'You will believe, Adéle, after to-night.'"

"Adéle!" said the Commissaire wisely. "Then Adéle was the strange woman's name?"

"Perhaps," said Hanaud dryly.

Héléne Vauquier reflected.

"I think Adéle was the name," she said in a more doubtful tone. "It sounded like Adéle."

The irrepressible Mr Ricardo was impelled to intervene.

"What Monsieur Hanaud means," he explained, with the pleasant air of a man happy to illuminate the dark intelligence of a child, "is that Adéle was probably a pseudonym."

Hanaud turned to him with a savage grin.

"Now that is sure to help her!" he cried. "A pseudonym! Héléne Vauquier is sure to understand that simple and elementary word. How bright this M. Ricardo is! Where shall we find a new pin more bright? I ask you," and he spread out his hands in a despairing admiration.

Mr. Ricardo flushed red, but he answered never a word. He must endure gibes and humiliations like a schoolboy in a class. His one constant fear was lest he should be turned out of the room. The Commissaire diverted wrath from him however.

"What he means by pseudonym," he said to Héléne Vauquier, explaining Mr. Ricardo to her as Mr. Ricardo had presumed to explain Hanaud, "is a false name. Adéle may have been, nay, probably was, a false name adopted by this strange woman."

"Adéle, I think, was the name used," replied Héléne, the doubt in her voice diminishing as she searched her memory. "I am almost sure."

"Well, we will call her Adéle," said Hanaud impatiently. "What does it matter? Go on, Mademoiselle Vauquier."

"The lady sat upright and squarely upon the edge of a chair, with a sort of defiance, as though she was determined nothing should convince her, and she laughed incredulously."

Here, again, all who heard were able vividly to conjure up the scene—the defiant sceptic sitting squarely on the edge of her chair, removing her gloves from her muscular hands; the excited Mme. Dauvray, so absorbed in the determination to convince; and Mlle. Célie running from the room to put on the black gown which would not be visible in the dim light.

"Whilst I took off mademoiselle's dress," Vauquier continued, "she said: 'When I have gone down to the salon you can go to bed, Héléne. Mme. Adéle'—yes, it was Adéle—'will be fetched by a friend in a motor-car, and I can let her out and fasten the door again. So if you hear the car you will know that it has come for her.'"

"Oh, she said that!" said Hanaud quickly.

"Yes, monsieur."

Hanaud looked gloomily towards Wethermill. Then he exchanged a sharp glance with the Commissaire, and moved his shoulders in an almost imperceptible shrug. But Mr. Ricardo saw it, and

6

construed it into one word. He imagined a jury uttering the word "Guilty."

Héléne Vauquier saw the movement too.

"Do not condemn her too quickly, monsieur," she said, with an impulse of remorse. "And not upon my words. For, as I say, I—hated her."

Hanaud nodded reassuringly, and she resumed:

"I was surprised, and I asked mademoiselle what she would do without her confederate. But she laughed, and said there would be no difficulty. That is partly why I think there was no séance held last night. Monsieur, there was a note in her voice that evening which I did not as yet understand. Mademoiselle then took her bath while I laid out her black dress and the slippers with the soft, noiseless soles. And now I tell you why I am sure there was no séance last night—why Mlle. Célie never meant there should be one."

"Yes, let us hear that," said Hanaud curiously, and leaning forward with his hands upon his knees.

"You have here, monsieur, a description of how mademoiselle was dressed when she went away." Héléne Vauquier picked up a sheet of paper from the table at her side. "I wrote it out at the request of M. le Commissaire." She handed the paper to Hanaud, who glanced through it as she continued. "Well, except for the white lace coat, monsieur, I dressed Mlle. Célie just in that way. She would have none of her plain black robe. No, Mlle. Célie must wear her fine new evening frock of pale reseda-green chiffon over soft clinging satin, which set off her fair beauty so prettily. It left her white arms and shoulders bare, and it had a long train, and it rustled as she moved. And with that she must put on her pale green silk stockings, her new little satin slippers to match, with the large paste buckles—and a sash of green satin looped through another glittering buckle at the side of the waist, with long ends loosely knotted together at the knee. I must tie her fair hair with a silver ribbon, and pin upon her curls a large hat of reseda green with a golden-brown ostrich feather drooping behind. I warned mademoiselle that there was a tiny fire burning in the salon. Even with the fire-screen in front of it there would still be a little light upon the floor, and the glittering buckles on her feet would betray her, even if the rustle of her dress did not. But she said she would kick her slippers off. Ah, gentlemen, it is, after all, not so that one dresses for a séance," she cried, shaking her head. "But it is just so—is it not?—that one dresses to go to meet a lover."

The suggestion startled every one who heard it. It fairly took Mr. Ricardo's breath away. Wether-mill stepped forward with a cry of revolt. The Commissaire exclaimed, admiringly, " But here is an idea!" Even Hanaud sat back in his chair, though his expression lost nothing of its impassivity, and his eyes never moved from Héléne Vauquier's face.

"Listen!" she continued, "I will tell you what I think. It was my habit to put out some sirop

and lemonade and some little cakes in the dining-
room, which, as you know, is at the other side of
the house across the hall.   I think it possible,
messieurs, that while Mlle. Célie was changing her
dress Mme. Dauvray and the stranger, Adéle, went
into the dining-room.   I know that Mlle. Célie, as
soon as she was dressed, ran downstairs to the
salon.   Well, then, suppose Mlle. Célie had a lover
waiting with whom she meant to run away.   She
hurries though the empty salon, opens the glass
doors, and is gone, leaving the doors open.   And
the thief, an accomplice of Adéle, finds the doors
open and hides himself in the salon until Mme.
Dauvray returns from the dining-room.   You see,
that leaves Mlle. Célie innocent."

Vauquier leaned forward eagerly, her white face
flushing.   There was a moment's silence, and then
Hanaud said:

"That is all very well, Mlle. Vauquier.   But it
does not account for the lace coat in which the
girl went away.   She must have returned to her
room to fetch that after you had gone to bed."

Héléne Vauquier leaned back with an air of
disappointment.

"That is true.   I had forgotten the coat.   I did
not like Mlle. Célie, but I am not wicked——"

"Nor for the fact that the sirop and the lemonade
had not been touched in the dining-room," said the
Commissaire, interrupting her.

Again the disappointment overspread Vauquier's
face.

" Is that so ?" she asked.   " I did not know—I have been kept a prisoner here."

The Commissaire cut her short with a cry of satisfaction.

" Listen ! listen !" he exclaimed excitedly.   " Here is a theory which accounts for all, which combines Vauquier's idea with ours, and Vauquier's idea is, I think, very just, up to a point.   Suppose, M. Hanaud, that the girl was going to meet her lover, but the lover is the murderer.   Then all becomes clear.   She does not run away to him ; she opens the door for him and lets him in."

Both Hanaud and Ricardo stole a glance at Wethermill.   How did he take the theory ? Wethermill was leaning against the wall, his eyes closed, his face white and contorted with a spasm of pain.   But he had the air of a man silently enduring an outrage rather than struck down by the conviction that the woman he loved was worthless.

" It is not for me to say, monsieur," Héléne Vauquier continued.   " I only tell you what I know. I am a woman, and it would be very difficult for a girl who was eagerly expecting her lover so to act that another woman would not know it.   However uncultivated and ignorant the other woman was, that at all events she would know.   The knowledge would spread to her of itself, without a word.   Consider, gentlemen !"   And suddenly Héléne Vauquier smiled.   " A young girl tingling with excitement from head to foot, eager that her beauty just at this moment should be more fresh, more sweet than ever it was, careful that her dress should set it exquisitely off. Imagine it! Her lips ready for the kiss! Oh, how should another woman not know? I saw Mlle. Célie, her cheeks rosy, her eyes bright. Never had she looked so lovely. The pale-green hat upon her fair head heavy with its curls! From head to foot she looked herself over, and then she sighed—she sighed with pleasure because she looked so pretty. That was Mlle. Célie last night, monsieur. She gathered up her train, took her long white gloves in the other hand, and ran down the stairs, her heels clicking on the wood, her buckles glittering. At the bottom she turned and said to me:

"'Remember, Hélène, you can go to bed.' That was it, monsieur."

And now violently the rancour of Héléne Vauquier's feelings burst out once more.

"For her the fine clothes, the pleasure, and the happiness. For me—I could go to bed!"

Hanaud looked again at the description which Héléne Vauquier had written out, and read it through carefully. Then he asked a question, of which Ricardo did not quite see the drift.

"So," he said, "when this morning you suggested to Monsieur the Commissaire that it would be advisable for you to go through Mlle. Célie's wardrobe, you found that nothing more had been taken away except the white lace coat?"

"That is so."

"Very well. Now, after Mlle. Célie had gone down the stairs——"

"I put the lights out in her room and, as she had ordered me to do, I went to bed. The next thing that I remember—but no! It terrifies me too much to think of it."

Héléne shuddered and covered her face spasmodically with her hands. Hanaud drew her hands gently down.

"Courage! You are safe now, mademoiselle. Calm yourself!"

She lay back with her eyes closed.

"Yes, yes; it is true. I am safe now. But oh! I feel I shall never dare to sleep again!" And the tears swam in her eyes. "I woke up with a feeling of being suffocated. Mon Dieu! There was the light burning in the room, and a woman, the strange woman with the strong hands, was holding me down by the shoulders, while a man with his cap drawn over his eyes and a little black moustache pressed over my lips a pad from which a horribly sweet and sickly taste filled my mouth. Oh, I was terrified! I could not scream. I struggled. The woman told me roughly to keep quiet. But I could not. I must struggle. And then with a brutality unheard of she dragged me up on to my knees while the man kept the pad right over my mouth. The man, with the arm which was free, held me close to him, and she bound my hands with a cord behind me. Look!"

She held out her wrists. They were terribly

bruised. Red and angry lines showed where the cord had cut deeply into her flesh.

"Then they flung me down again upon my back, and the next thing I remember is the doctor standing over me and this kind nurse supporting me."

She sank back exhausted in her chair and wiped her forehead with her handkerchief. The sweat stood upon it in beads.

"Thank you, mademoiselle," said Hanaud gravely "This has been a trying ideal for you. I understand that. But we are coming to the end. I want you to read this description of Mlle. Célie through again to make sure that nothing is omitted." He gave the paper into the maid's hands. "It will be advertised, so it is important that it should be complete. See that you have left out nothing."

Héléne Vauquier bent her head over the paper

"No," said Héléne at last. "I do not think I have omitted anything." And she handed the paper back.

"I asked you," Hanaud continued suavely, "because I understand that Mlle. Célie usually wore a pair of diamond ear-drops, and they are not mentioned here."

A faint colour came into the maid's face.

"That is true, monsieur. I had forgotten. It is quite true."

"Any one might forget," said Hanaud, with a reassuring smile. "But you will remember now. Think! think! Did Mlle. Célie wear them last night ? " He leaned forward, waiting for her reply. Wethermill, too, made a movement. Both men evidently thought the point of great importance. The maid looked at Hanaud for a few moments without speaking.

" It is not from me, mademoiselle, that you will get the answer," said Hanaud quietly.

" No, monsieur. I was thinking," said the maid, her face flushing at the rebuke.

" Did she wear them when she went down the stairs last night ? " he insisted.

" I think she wore them," she said doubtfully. "Ye-es—yes," and the words came now firm and clear. " I remember well. Mlle. Célie had taken them off before her bath, and they lay on the dressing-table. She put them into her ears while I dressed her hair and arranged the bow of ribbon in it."

" Then we will add the earrings to your description," said Hanaud, as he rose from his chair with the paper in his hand, "and for the moment we need not trouble you any more about Mademoiselle Célie." He folded the paper up, slipped it into his letter-case, and put it away in his pocket. "Let us consider that poor Madame Dauvray! Did she keep much money in the house ? "

" No, monsieur; very little. She was well known in Aix and her cheques were everywhere accepted without question. It was a high pleasure to serve madame, her credit was so good," said Hélène

Vauquier, raising her head as though she herself had a share in the pride of that good credit.

"No doubt," Hanaud agreed. "There are many fine households where the banking account is overdrawn, and it cannot be pleasant for the servants."

"They are put to so many shifts to hide it from the servants of their neighbours," said Héléne. "Besides," and she made a little grimace of contempt, "a fine household and an overdrawn banking account—it is like a ragged petticoat under a satin dress. That was never the case with Madame Dauvray."

"So that she was under no necessity to have ready money always in her pocket," said Hanaud. "I understand that. But at times perhaps she won at the Villa des Fleurs?"

Héléne Vauquier shook her head.

"She loved the Villa des Fleurs, but she never played for high sums and often never played at all. If she won a few louis, she was as delighted with her gains and as afraid to lose them again at the tables as if she were of the poorest, and she stopped at once. No, monsieur; twenty or thirty louis—there was never more than that in the house."

"Then it was certainly for her famous collection of jewellery that Madame Dauvray was murdered?"

"Certainly, monsieur."

"Now, where did she keep her jewellery?"

"In a safe in her bedroom, monsieur. Every night

she took off what she had been wearing and locked it up with the rest. She was never too tired for that."

"And what did she do with the keys?"

"That I cannot tell you. Certainly she locked her rings and necklaces away whilst I undressed her. And she laid the keys upon the dressing-table or the mantelshelf—anywhere. But in the morning the keys were no longer where she had left them. She had put them secretly away."

Hanaud turned to another point.

"I suppose that Mademoiselle Célie knew of the safe and that the jewels were kept there?"

"Oh yes! Mademoiselle indeed was often in Madame Dauvray's room when she was dressing or undressing. She must often have seen madame take them out and lock them up again. But then, monsieur, so did I."

Hanaud nodded to her with a friendly smile.

"Thank you once more, mademoiselle," he said. "The torture is over. But of course Monsieur Fleuriot will require your presence."

Héléne Vauquier looked anxiously towards him.

"But meanwhile I can go from this villa, monsieur?" she pleaded, with a trembling voice.

"Certainly; you shall go to your friends at once."

"Oh, monsieur, thank you!" she cried, and suddenly she gave way. The tears began to flow from her eyes. She buried her face in her hands and sobbed. "It is foolish of me, but what would you?" She jerked out the words between her sobs. "It has been too terrible."

"Yes, yes," said Hanaud soothingly. "The nurse will put a few things together for you in a bag. You will not leave Aix, of course, and I will send some one with you to your friends."

The maid started violently.

"Oh, not a *sergent-de-ville*, monsieur, I beg of you. I should be disgraced."

"No. It shall be a man in plain clothes, to see that you are not hindered by reporters on the way."

Hanaud turned towards the door. On the dressing-table a cord was lying. He took it up and spoke to the nurse.

"Was this the cord with which Héléne Vauquier's hands were tied?"

"Yes, monsieur," she replied.

Hanaud handed it to the Commissaire.

"It will be necessary to keep that," he said.

It was a thin piece of strong whipcord. It was the same kind of cord as that which had been found tied round Mme. Dauvray's throat. Hanaud opened the door and turned back to the nurse.

"We will send for a cab for Mlle. Vauquier. You will drive with her to her door. I think after that she will need no further help. Pack up a few things and bring them down. Mlle. Vauquier can follow, no doubt, now without assistance." And, with a friendly nod, he left the room.

Ricardo had been wondering, through the examination, in what light Hanaud considered Héléne Vauquier. He was sympathetic, but the sympathy might merely have been assumed to deceive. His questions betrayed in no particular the colour of his mind. Now, however, he made himself clear. He informed the nurse, in the plainest possible way, that she was no longer to act as jailer. She was to bring Vauquier's things down ; but Vauquier could follow by herself. Evidently Héléne Vauquier was cleared.

CHAPTER VII

A STARTLING DISCOVERY

HARRY WETHERMILL, however, was not so easily satisfied.

"Surely, monsieur, it would be well to know whither she is going," he said, "and to make sure that when she has gone there she will stay there—until we want her again?"

Hanaud looked at the young man pityingly.

"I can understand, monsieur, that you hold strong views about Hélène Vauquier. You are human, like the rest of us. And what she has said to us just now would not make you more friendly. But—but——" and he preferred to shrug his shoulders rather than to finish in words his sentence. "However," he said, "we shall take care to know where Hélène Vauquier is staying. Indeed, if she is at all implicated in this affair we shall learn more if we leave her free than if we keep her under lock and key. You see that? If we leave her quite free, but watch her very, very carefully, so as to awaken no suspicion, she may be emboldened to do something rash—or the others may."

Mr. Ricardo approved of Hanaud's reasoning.

"That is quite true," he said. "She might write a letter."

"Yes, or receive one," added Hanaud, "which would be still more satisfactory for us—supposing, of course, that she has anything to do with this affair"; and again he shrugged his shoulders. He turned towards the Commissaire.

"You have a discreet officer whom you can trust?" he asked.

"Certainly. A dozen."

"I want only one."

"And here he is," said the Commissaire.

They were descending the stairs. On the landing of the first floor Durette, the man who had discovered where the cord was bought, was still waiting. Hanaud took Durette by the sleeve in the familiar way which he so commonly used and led him to the top of the stairs, where the two men stood for a few moments apart. It was plain that Hanaud was giving, Durette receiving, definite instructions. Durette descended the stairs; Hanaud came back to the others.

"I have told him to fetch a cab," he said, "and convey Hélène Vauquier to her friends." Then he looked at Ricardo, and from Ricardo to the Commissaire, while he rubbed his hand backwards and forwards across his shaven chin.

"I tell you," he said, "I find this sinister little drama very interesting to me. The sordid, miserable struggle for mastery in this household of Mme.

Dauvray—eh? Yes, very interesting. Just as much patience, just as much effort, just as much planning for this small end as a general uses to defeat an army—and, at the last, nothing gained. What else is politics? Yes, very interesting."

His eyes rested upon Wethermill's face for a moment, but they gave the young man no hope. He took a key from his pocket.

"We need not keep this room locked," he said. "We know all that there is to be known." And he inserted the key into the lock of Celia's room and turned it.

"But is that wise, monsieur?" said Besnard.

Hanaud shrugged his shoulders.

"Why not?" he asked.

"The case is in your hands," said the Commissaire. To Ricardo the proceedings seemed singularly irregular. But if the Commissaire was content, it was not for him to object.

"And where is my excellent friend Perrichet?" asked Hanaud; and leaning over the balustrade he called him up from the hall.

"We will now," said Hanaud, "have a glance into this poor murdered woman's room."

The room was opposite to Celia's. Besnard produced the key and unlocked the door. Hanaud took off his hat upon the threshold and then passed into the room with his companions. Upon the bed, outlined under a sheet, lay the rigid form of Mme. Dauvray. Hanaud stepped gently to the bedside and reverently uncovered the face.

For a moment all could see it—livid, swollen, unhuman.

"A brutal business," he said in a low voice, and when he turned again to his companions his face was white and sickly. He replaced the sheet and gazed about the room.

It was decorated and furnished in the same style as the salon downstairs, yet the contrast between the two rooms was remarkable.

Downstairs, in the salon, only a chair had been overturned. Here there was every sign of violence and disorder. An empty safe stood open in one corner; the rugs upon the polished floor had been tossed aside; every drawer had been torn open, every wardrobe burst; the very bed had been moved from its position.

"It was in this safe that Madame Dauvray hid her jewels each night," said the Commissaire as Hanaud gazed about the room.

"Oh, was it so?" Hanaud asked slowly. It seemed to Ricardo that he read something in the aspect of this room too which troubled his mind and increased his perplexity.

"Yes," said Besnard confidently. "Every night Mme. Dauvray locked her jewels away in this safe. Vauquier told us so this morning. Every night she was never too tired for that. Besides, here"— and putting his hand into the safe he drew out a paper—"here is the list of Mme. Dauvray's jewellery."

Plainly, however, Hanaud was not satisfied. He

took the list and glanced through the items. But his thoughts were not concerned with it.

" If that is so," he said slowly, "if Mme. Dauvray kept her jewels in this safe, why has every drawer been ransacked, why was the bed moved? Perrichet, lock the door—quietly—from the inside. That is right. Now lean your back against it."

Hanaud waited until he saw Perrichet's broad back against the door. Then he went down upon his knees, and, tossing the rugs here and there, examined with the minutest care the inlaid floor. By the side of the bed a Persian mat of blue silk was spread. This in its turn he moved quickly aside. He bent his eyes to the ground, lay prone, moved this way and that to catch the light upon the floor, and then with a spring he rose upon his knees. He lifted his finger to his lips. In a dead silence he drew a pen-knife quickly from his pocket and opened it. He bent down again and inserted the blade between the cracks of the blocks. The three men in the room watched him with an intense excitement. A block of wood rose from the floor, he pulled it out, laid it noiselessly down, and inserted his hand into the opening.

Wethermill at Ricardo's elbow uttered a stifled cry. " Hush!" whispered Hanaud angrily. He drew out his hand again. It was holding a green leather jewel-case. He opened it, and a diamond necklace flashed its thousand colours in their faces. He thrust in his hand again and again and again, and each time that he withdrew it, it held a jewel-case. Before the astonished eyes of his companions he opened them. Ropes of pearls, collars of diamonds, necklaces of emeralds, rings of pigeon-blood rubies, bracelets of gold studded with opals— Mme. Dauvray's various jewellery was disclosed.

"But that is astounding," said Besnard, in an awestruck voice.

"Then she was never robbed after all?" cried Ricardo.

Hanaud rose to his feet.

"What a piece of irony!" he whispered. "The poor woman is murdered for her jewels, the room's turned upside down, and nothing is found. For all the while they lay safe in this *cache*. Nothing is taken except what she wore. Let us see what she wore."

"Only a few rings, Héléne Vauquier thought," said Besnard. "But she was not sure."

"Ah!" said Hanaud. "Well, let us make sure!" and, taking the list from the safe, he compared it with the jewellery in the cases on the floor, ticking off the items one by one. When he had finished he knelt down again, and, thrusting his hand into the hole, felt carefully about.

"There is a pearl necklace missing," he said—"a valuable necklace, from the description in the list— and some rings. She must have been wearing them"; and he sat back upon his heels. "We will send the intelligent Perrichet for a bag," he said, "and we will counsel the intelligent Perrichet not

to breathe a word to any living soul of what he
has seen in this room. Then we will seal up in
the bag the jewels, and we will hand it over to
M. le Commissaire, who will convey it with the
greatest secrecy out of this villa. For the list—I
will keep it," and he placed it carefully in his
pocket-book.

He unlocked the door and went out himself on
to the landing. He looked down the stairs and
up the stairs ; then he beckoned Perrichet to him.

"Go!" he whispered. "Be quick, and when
you come back hide the bag carefully under your
coat."

Perrichet went down the stairs with pride written
upon his face. Was he not assisting the great
M. Hanaud from the Sûreté in Paris? Hanaud
returned into Mme. Dauvray's room and closed the
door. He looked into the eyes of his companions.

"Can't you see the scene?" he asked, with a
queer smile of excitement. He had forgotten
Wethermill; he had forgotten even the dead
woman shrouded beneath the sheet. He was
absorbed. His eyes were bright, his whole face
vivid with life. Ricardo saw the real man at this
moment—and feared for the happiness of Harry
Wethermill. For nothing would Hanaud now turn
aside until he had reached the truth and set his
hands upon the quarry. Of that Ricardo felt sure.
He was trying now to make his companions visual-
ise just what he saw and understood.

"Can't you see it ? The old woman locking up

her jewels in this safe every night before the eyes
of her maid or her companion, and then, as soon as
she was alone, taking them stealthily out of the safe
and hiding them in this secret place. But I tell
you—this is human. Yes, it is interesting just
because it is so human. Then picture to yourselves
last night, the murderers opening this safe and
finding nothing—oh, but nothing!—and ransacking
the room in a deadly haste, kicking up the rugs,
forcing open the drawers, and always finding
nothing—nothing—nothing. Think of their rage,
their stupefaction, and finally their fear! They
must go, and with one pearl necklace, when they
had hoped to reap a great fortune. Oh, but this
is interesting—yes, I tell you—I, who have seen
many strange things—this is interesting."

Perrichet returned with a canvas bag, into which
Hanaud placed the jewel-cases. He sealed the bag
in the presence of the four men and handed it to
Besnard. He replaced the block of wood in the
floor, covered it over again with the rug, and rose
to his feet.

"Listen!" he said, in a low voice, and with a
gravity which impressed them all. "There is
something in this house which I do not understand.
I have told you so. I tell you something more now.
I am afraid—I am afraid." And the word startled
his hearers like a thunderclap, though it was
breathed no louder than a whisper. "Yes, my
friends," he repeated, nodding his head, "terribly
afraid." And upon the others fell a discomfort, an

awe, as though something sinister and dangerous were present in the room and close to them. So vivid was the feeling, instinctively they drew nearer together. "Now, I warn you solemnly. There must be no whisper that these jewels have been discovered; no newspaper must publish a hint of it; no one must suspect that here in this room we have found them. Is that understood?"

"Certainly," said the Commissaire.

"Yes," said Mr. Ricardo.

"To be sure, monsieur," said Perrichet.

As for Harry Wethermill, he made no reply. His burning eyes were fixed upon Hanaud's face, and that was all. Hanaud, for his part, asked for no reply from him. Indeed, he did not look towards Harry Wethermill's face at all. Ricardo understood. Hanaud did not mean to be deterred by the suffering written there.

He went down again into the little gay salon lit with flowers and August sunlight, and stood beside the couch gazing at it with troubled eyes. And, as he gazed, he closed his eyes and shivered. He shivered like a man who has taken a sudden chill. Nothing in all this morning's investigations, not even the rigid body beneath the sheet, nor the strange discovery of the jewels, had so impressed Ricardo. For there he had been confronted with facts, definite and complete; here was a suggestion of unknown horrors, a hint, not a fact, compelling the imagination to dark conjecture. Hanaud shivered. That he had no idea why Hanaud shivered made the action still more significant, still more alarming. And it was not Ricardo alone who was moved by it. A voice of despair rang through the room. The voice was Harry Wethermill's, and his face was ashy white.

"Monsieur!" he cried, "I do not know what makes you shudder; but I am remembering a few words you used this morning."

Hanaud turned round upon his heel. His face was drawn and grey and his eyes blazed.

"My friend, I also am remembering those words," he said. Thus the two men stood confronting one another, eye to eye, with awe and fear in both their faces.

Ricardo was wondering to what words they both referred, when the sound of wheels broke in upon the silence. The effect upon Hanaud was magical. He thrust his hands in his pockets.

"Héléne Vauquier's cab," he said lightly. He drew out his cigarette-case and lighted a cigarette.

"Let us see that poor woman safely off. It is a closed cab, I hope."

It was a closed landau. It drove past the open door of the salon to the front door of the house. In Hanaud's wake they all went out into the hall. The nurse came down alone carrying Héléne Vauquier's bag. She placed it in the cab and waited in the doorway.

"Perhaps Héléne Vauquier has fainted," she said anxiously: "she does not come." And she moved towards the stairs.

Hanaud took a singularly swift step forward and stopped her.

"Why should you think that?" he asked, with a queer smile upon his face, and as he spoke a door closed gently upstairs. "See," he continued, "you are wrong: she is coming."

Ricardo was puzzled. It had seemed to him that the door which had closed so gently was nearer than Héléne Vauquier's door. It seemed to him that the door was upon the first, not the second landing. But Hanaud had noticed nothing strange; so it could not be. Hanaud greeted Héléne Vauquier with a smile as she came down the stairs.

"You are better, mademoiselle," he said politely. "One can see that. There is more colour in your cheeks. A day or two, and you will be yourself again."

He held the door open while she got into the cab. The nurse took her seat beside her; Durette mounted on the box. The cab turned and went down the drive.

"Good-bye, mademoiselle," cried Hanaud, and he watched until the high shrubs hid the cab from his eyes. Then he behaved in an extraordinary way. He turned and sprang like lightning up the stairs. His agility amazed Ricardo. The others followed upon his heels. He flung himself at Celia's door and opened it. He burst into the room, stood for a second, then ran to the window. He hid behind the curtain, looking out. With his hand he waved to his companions to keep back. The sound of wheels creaking and rasping rose to their ears. The cab had just come out into the road. Durette upon the box turned and looked towards the house. Just for a moment Hanaud leaned from the window, as Besnard, the Commissaire, had done, and, like Besnard again, he waved his hand. Then he came back into the room and saw, standing in front of him, with his mouth open and his eyes starting out of his head, Perrichet—the intelligent Perrichet.

"Monsieur," cried Perrichet, "something has been taken from this room."

Hanaud looked round the room and shook his head.

"No," he said.

"But yes, monsieur," Perrichet insisted. "Oh, but yes. See! Upon this dressing-table there was a small pot of cold cream. It stood here, where my finger is, when we were in this room an hour ago. Now it is gone."

Hanaud burst into a laugh.

"My friend Perrichet," he said ironically, "I will tell you the newspaper did not do you justice. You are more than intelligent. The truth, my excellent friend, lies at the bottom of a well; but you would find it at the bottom of a pot of cold cream. Now let us go. For in this house, gentlemen, we have nothing more to do."

He passed out of the room. Perrichet stood aside, his face crimson, his attitude one of shame.

He had been rebuked by the great M. Hanaud, and justly rebuked. He knew it now. He had wished to display his intelligence—yes, at all costs he must show how intelligent he was. And he had shown himself a fool. He should have kept silence about that pot of cream.

CHAPTER VIII

THE CAPTAIN OF THE SHIP

HANAUD walked away from the Villa Rose in the company of Wethermill and Ricardo.

"We will go and lunch," he said.

"Yes; come to my hotel," said Harry Wethermill. But Hanaud shook his head.

"No; come with me to the Villa des Fleurs," he replied. "We may learn something there; and in a case like this every minute is of importance. We have to be quick."

"I may come too?" cried Mr. Ricardo eagerly.

"By all means," replied Hanaud, with a smile of extreme courtesy. "Nothing could be more delicious than monsieur's suggestions"; and with that remark he walked on silently.

Mr. Ricardo was in a little doubt as to the exact significance of the words. But he was too excited to dwell long upon them. Distressed though he sought to be at his friend's grief, he could not but assume an air of importance. All the artist in him rose joyfully to the occasion. He looked upon himself from the outside. He fancied without the slightest justification that people were pointing him out. "That man has been present at the investigation at the Villa Rose," he seemed to hear people say. "What strange things he could tell us if he would!"

And suddenly, Mr. Ricardo began to reflect. What, after all, could he have told them?

And that question he turned over in his mind while he ate his luncheon. Hanaud wrote a letter between the courses. They were sitting at a corner table, and Hanaud was in the corner with his back to the wall. He moved his plate, too, over the letter as he wrote it. It would have been impossible for either of his guests to see what he had written, even if they had wished. Ricardo, indeed, did wish. He rather resented the secrecy with which the detective, under a show of openness, shrouded his thoughts and acts. Hanaud sent the waiter out to fetch an officer in plain clothes, who was in attendance at the door, and he handed the letter to this man. Then he turned with an apology to his guests.

"It is necessary that we should find out," he explained, "as soon as possible, the whole record of Mlle. Célie."

He lighted a cigar, and over the coffee he put a question to Ricardo.

"Now tell me what you make of the case. What M. Wethermill thinks—that is clear, is it not? Héléne Vauquier is the guilty one. But you, M. Ricardo? What is your opinion?"

Ricardo took from his pocket-book a sheet of

paper and from his pocket a pencil. He was intensely flattered by the request of Hanaud, and he proposed to do himself justice. "I will make a note here of what I think the salient features of the mystery"; and he proceeded to tabulate the points in the following way:

(1) Celia Harland made her entrance into Mme. Dauvray's household under very doubtful circumstances.

(2) By methods still more doubtful she acquired an extraordinary ascendency over Mme. Dauvray's mind.

(3) If proof were needed how complete that ascendency was, a glance at Celia Harland's wardrobe would suffice; for she wore the most expensive clothes.

(4) It was Celia Harland who arranged that Servettaz, the chauffeur, should be absent at Chambéry on the Tuesday night—the night of the murder.

(5) It was Celia Harland who bought the cord with which Mme. Dauvray was strangled and Héléne Vauquier bound.

(6) The footsteps outside the salon show that Celia Harland ran from the salon to the motor-car.

(7) Celia Harland pretended that there should be a séance on the Tuesday, but she dressed as though she had in view an appointment with a lover, instead of a spiritualistic séance.

(8) Celia Harland has disappeared.

These eight points are strongly suggestive of Celia Harland's complicity in the murder. But I

have no clue which will enable me to answer the
following questions :

(*a*) Who was the man who took part in the
crime ?

(*b*) Who was the woman who came to the villa
on the evening of the murder with Mme. Dauvray
and Celia Harland ?

(*c*) What actually happened in the salon ?   How
was the murder committed ?

(*d*) Is Héléne Vauquier's story true ?

(*e*) What did the torn-up scrap of writing mean ?
(Probably spirit-writing in Celia Harland's hand.)

(*f*) Why has one cushion on the settee a small,
fresh, brown stain, which is probably blood ?   Why
is the other cushion torn ?

Mr. Ricardo had a momentary thought of putting
down yet another question. He was inclined to
ask whether or no a pot of cold cream had disappeared from Celia Harland's bedroom; but he
remembered that Hanaud had set no store upon
that incident, and he refrained. Moreover, he had
come to the end of his sheet of paper. He handed
it across the table to Hanaud, and leaned back in
his chair, watching the detective with all the eagerness of a young author submitting his first effort
to a critic.

Hanaud read it through slowly. At the end he
nodded his head in approval.

" Now we will see what M. Wethermill has to
say," he said, and he stretched out the paper to-

wards Harry Wethermill, who throughout the luncheon had not said a word.

" No, no," cried Ricardo.

But Harry Wethermill already held the written sheet in his hand. He smiled rather wistfully at his friend.

" It is best that I should know just what you both think," he said, and in his turn he began to read the paper through. He read the first eight points, and then beat with his fist upon the table.

" No no," he cried; " it is not possible! I don't blame you, Ricardo. These are facts, and, as I said, I can face facts. But there will be an explanation— if only we can discover it."

He buried his face for a moment in his hands. Then he took up the paper again.

" As for the rest, Héléne Vauquier lied," he cried violently, and he tossed the paper to Hanaud. " What do you make of it?"

Hanaud smiled and shook his head.

" Did you ever go for a voyage on a ship?" he asked.

" Yes; why?"

" Because every day at noon three officers take an observation to determine the ship's position— the captain, the first officer, and the second officer. Each writes his observation down, and the captain takes the three observations and compares them. If the first or second officer is out in his reckoning, the captain tells him so, but he does not show his own. For at times, no doubt, he is wrong too.

So, gentlemen, I criticise your observations, but I do not show you mine."

He took up Ricardo's paper and read it through again.

"Yes," he said pleasantly. "But the two questions which are most important, which alone can lead us to the truth—how do they come to be omitted from your list, Mr. Ricardo?"

Hanaud put the question with his most serious air. But Ricardo was none the less sensible of the raillery behind the solemn manner. He flushed and made no answer.

"Still," continued Hanaud, "here are undoubtedly some questions. Let us consider them! Who was the man who took a part in the crime? Ah, if we only knew that, what a lot of trouble we should save ourselves! Who was the woman? What a good thing it would be to know that too! How clearly, after all, Mr. Ricardo puts his finger on the important points! What did actually happen in the salon?" And as he quoted that question the raillery died out of his voice. He leaned his elbows on the table and bent forward.

"What did actually happen in that little pretty room, just twelve hours ago?" he repeated. "When no sunlight blazed upon the lawn, and all the birds were still, and all the windows shuttered and the world dark, what happened? What dreadful things happened? We have not much to go upon. Let us formulate what we know. We start with this. The murder was not the work of a moment. It was planned with great care and cunning, and carried out to the letter of the plan. There must be no noise, no violence. On each side of the Villa Rose there are other villas; a few yards away the road runs past. A scream, a cry, the noise of a struggle—these sounds, or any one of them, might be fatal to success. Thus the crime was planned; and there *was* no scream, there *was* no struggle. Not a chair was broken, and only a chair upset. Yes, there were brains behind that murder. We know that. But what do we know of the plan? How far can we build it up? Let us see. First, there was an accomplice in the house—perhaps two."

" No!" cried Harry Wethermill.

Hanaud took no notice of the interruption.

" Secondly, the woman came to the house with Mme. Dauvray and Mlle. Célie between nine and half-past nine. Thirdly, the man came afterwards, but before eleven, set open the gate, and was admitted into the salon, unperceived by Mme. Dauvray. That also we can safely assume. But what happened in the salon? Ah! There is the question." Then he shrugged his shoulders and said, with the note of raillery once more in his voice :

" But why should we trouble our heads to puzzle out this mystery, since M. Ricardo knows?"

" I ?" cried Ricardo in amazement.

" To be sure," replied Hanaud calmly. " For I look at another of your questions, '*What did the torn-up scrap of writing mean?*' and you add:

8

'Probably spirit-writing.' Then there was a séance held last night in the little salon! Is that so?"

Harry Wethermill started. Mr. Ricardo was at a loss.

"I had not followed my suggestion to its conclusion," he admitted humbly.

"No," said Hanaud. "But I ask myself in sober earnest, 'Was there a séance held in the salon last night?' Did the tambourine rattle in the darkness on the wall?"

"But if Hélène Vauquier's story is all untrue?" cried Wethermill, again in exasperation.

"Patience, my friend. Her story was not all untrue. I say there were brains behind this crime; yes, but brains, even the cleverest, would not have invented this queer, strange story of the séances and of Mme. de Montespan. That is truth. But yet, if there were a séance held, if the scrap of paper were spirit-writing in answer to some awkward question, why—and here I come to my first question, which M. Ricardo has omitted—why did Mlle. Célie dress herself with so much elegance last night? What Vauquier said is true. Her dress was not suited to a séance. A light-coloured, rustling frock, which would be visible in a dim light, or even in the dark, which would certainly be heard at every movement she made, however lightly she stepped, and a big hat—no, no! I tell you, gentlemen, we shall not get to the bottom of this mystery until we know why Mlle. Célie dressed herself as she did last night."

"Yes," Ricardo admitted. "I overlooked that point."

"Did she——" Hanaud broke off and bowed to Wethermill with a grace and a respect which condoned his words. "You must bear with me, my young friend, while I consider all these points. Did she expect to join that night a lover—a man with the brains to devise this crime? But if so— and here I come to the second question omitted from M. Ricardo's list—why, on the patch of grass outside the door of the salon, were the footsteps of the man and woman so carefully erased, and the footsteps of Mlle. Célie—those little footsteps so easily identified—left for all the world to see and recognise?"

Ricardo felt like a child in the presence of his schoolmaster. He was convicted of presumption. He had set down his questions with the belief that they covered the ground. And here were two of the utmost importance, not forgotten, but never even thought of.

"Did she go, before the murder, to join a lover? Or after it? At some time, you will remember, according to Vauquier's story, she must have run upstairs to fetch her coat. Was the murder committed during the interval when she was upstairs? Was the salon dark when she came down again? Did she run through it quickly, eagerly, noticing nothing amiss? And, indeed, how should she notice anything if the salon were dark, and Mme. Dauvray's body lay under the windows at the side?"

Ricardo leaned forward eagerly.

"That must be the truth," he cried; and Wethermill's voice broke hastily in:

"It is not the truth, and I will tell you why. Celia Harland was to have married me this week."

There was so much pain and misery in his voice that Ricardo was moved as he had seldom been. Wethermill buried his face in his hands. Hanaud shook his head and gazed across the table at Ricardo with an expression which the latter was at no loss to understand. Lovers were impracticable people. But he—Hanaud—he knew the world. Women had fooled men before to-day.

Wethermill snatched his hands away from before his face.

"We talk theories," he cried desperately, "of what may have happened at the villa. But we are not by one inch nearer to the man and woman who committed the crime. It is for them we have to search."

"Yes; but except by asking ourselves questions, how shall we find them, M. Wethermill?" said Hanaud. "Take the man! We know nothing of him. He has left no trace. Look at this town of Aix, where people come and go like a crowd about the baccarat-table! He may be at Marseilles to-day. He may be in this very room where we are taking our luncheon. How shall we find him?"

Wethermill nodded his head in a despairing assent.

"I know. But it is so hard to sit still and do nothing," he cried.

"Yes, but we are not sitting still," said Hanaud, and Wethermill looked up with a sudden interest. "All the time that we have been lunching here the intelligent Perrichet has been making inquiries. Mme. Dauvray and Mlle. Célie left the Villa Rose at five, and returned on foot soon after nine with the strange woman. And there I see Perrichet himself waiting to be summoned."

Hanaud beckoned towards the *sergent-de-ville*.

"Perrichet will make an excellent detective," he said; "for he looks more bovine and foolish in plain clothes than he does in uniform."

Perrichet advanced in his mufti to the table.

"Speak, my friend," said Hanaud.

"I went to the shop of M. Corval. Mlle. Célie was quite alone when she bought the cord. But a few minutes later, in the Rue du Casino, she and Mme. Dauvray were seen together, walking slowly in the direction of the villa. No other woman was with them."

"That is a pity," said Hanaud quietly, and with a gesture he dismissed Perrichet.

"You see, we shall find out nothing—nothing," said Wethermill, with a groan.

"We must not yet lose heart, for we know a little more about the woman than we do about the man," said Hanaud consolingly.

"True," exclaimed Ricardo. "We have Héléne Vauquier's description of her. We must advertise it."

Hanaud smiled.

"But that is a fine suggestion," he cried. "We must think over that," and he clapped his hand to his forehead with a gesture of self-reproach. "Why did not such a fine idea occur to me, fool that I am! However, we will call the head waiter."

The head waiter was sent for and appeared before them.

"You knew Mme. Dauvray?" Hanaud asked.

"Yes, monsieur—oh, the poor woman!" And he flung up his hands.

"And you knew her young companion?"

"Oh yes, monsieur. They generally had their meals here. See, at that little table over there! I kept it for them. But monsieur knows well"—and the waiter looked towards Harry Wethermill—"for monsieur was often with them."

"Yes," said Hanaud. "Did Mme. Dauvray dine at that little table last night?"

"No, monsieur. She was not here last night."

"Nor Mlle. Célie?"

"No, monsieur! I do not think they were in the Villa des Fleurs at all."

"We know they were not," exclaimed Ricardo. "Wethermill and I were in the rooms and we did not see them."

"But perhaps you left early," objected Hanaud.

"No," said Ricardo. "It was just ten o'clock when we reached the Majestic."

"You reached your hotel at ten," Hanaud repeated. "Did you walk straight from here?"

" Yes."

" Then you left here about a quarter to ten. And we know that Mme. Dauvray was back at the villa soon after nine. Yes—they could not have been here last night," Hanaud agreed, and sat for a moment silent. Then he turned again to the head waiter.

" Have you noticed any woman with Mme. Dauvray and her companion lately ? "

" No, monsieur. I do not think so."

" Think ! A woman, for instance, with red hair."

Harry Wethermill started forward. Mr. Ricardo stared at Hanaud in amazement. The waiter reflected.

" No, monsieur. I have seen no woman with red hair."

" Thank you," said Hanaud, and the waiter moved away.

" A woman with red hair!" cried Wethermill. " But Héléne Vauquier described her. She was sallow ; her eyes, her hair, were dark."

Hanaud turned with a smile to Harry Wethermill.

" Did Héléne Vauquier, then, speak the truth ? " he asked. " No; the woman who was in the salon last night, who returned home with Mme. Dauvray and Mlle. Célie, was not a woman with black hair and bright black eyes. Look!" And, fetching his pocket-book from his pocket, he unfolded a sheet of paper and showed them, lying upon its white surface, a long red hair.

" I picked that up on the table—the round satin-
wood table in the salon. It was easy not to see it,
but I did see it.   Now, that is not Mlle. Célie's hair,
which is fair; nor Mme. Dauvray's, which is dyed
brown; nor Héléne Vauquier's, which is black; nor
the charwoman's, which, as I have taken the trouble,
to find out, is grey   It is therefore from the head
of our unknown woman.   And I will tell you
more. This woman with the red hair—she is in
Geneva."

A startled exclamation burst from Ricardo.
Harry Wethermill sat slowly down. For the first
time that day there had come some colour into his
cheeks, a sparkle into his eye.

" But that is wonderful!" he cried. " How did
you find that out ? "

Hanaud leaned back in his chair and took a pull
at his cigar. He was obviously pleased with
Wethermill's admiration.

" Yes, how did you find it out ? " Ricardo repeated.

Hanaud smiled.

" As to that," he said, " remember I am the
captain of the ship, and I do not show you my
observation." Ricardo was disappointed. Harry
Wethermill, however, started to his feet.

" We must search Geneva, then," he cried. " It is
there that we should be, not here drinking our
coffee at the Villa des Fleurs."

Hanaud raised his hand.

" The search is not being overlooked. But
Geneva is a big city. It is not easy to search

Geneva and find, when we know nothing about the woman for whom we are searching, except that her hair is red, and that probably a young girl last night was with her. It is rather here, I think—in Aix—that we must keep our eyes wide open."

"Here!" cried Wethermill in exasperation. He stared at Hanaud as though he were mad.

"Yes, here; at the post office—at the telephone exchange. Suppose that the man is in Aix, as he may well be; some time he will wish to send a letter, or a telegram, or a message over the telephone. That, I tell you, is our chance. But here is news for us."

Hanaud pointed to a messenger who was walking towards them. The man handed Hanaud an envelope.

"From M. le Commissaire," he said; and he saluted and retired.

"From M. le Commissaire?" cried Ricardo excitedly.

But before Hanaud could open the envelope Harry Wethermill laid a hand upon his sleeve.

"Before we pass to something new, M. Hanaud," he said, "I should be very glad if you would tell me what made you shiver in the salon this morning. It has distressed me ever since. What was it that those two cushions had to tell you?"

There was a note of anguish in his voice difficult to resist. But Hanaud resisted it. He shook his head.

"Again," he said gravely, "I am to remind you

that I am the captain of the ship and do not show my observation."

He tore open the envelope and sprang up from his seat.

"Mme. Dauvray's motor-car has been found," he cried. "Let us go!"

Hanaud called for the bill and paid it. The three men left the Villa des Fleurs together.

CHAPTER IX

MME. DAUVRAY'S MOTOR-CAR

THEY got into a cab outside the door. Perrichet mounted the box, and the cab was driven along the upward-winding road past the Hôtel Bernascon. A hundred yards beyond the hotel the cab stopped opposite to a villa. A hedge separated the garden of the villa from the road, and above the hedge rose a board with the words "To Let" upon it. At the gate a gendarme was standing, and just within the gate Ricardo saw Louis Besnard, the Commissaire, and Servettaz, Mme. Dauvray's chauffeur.

"It is here," said Besnard, as the party descended from the cab, "in the coach-house of this empty villa."

"Here?" cried Ricardo in amazement.

The discovery upset all his theories. He had expected to hear that it had been found fifty leagues away; but here, within a couple of miles of the Villa Rose itself—the idea seemed absurd! Why take it away at all—unless it was taken away as a blind? That supposition found its way into

123

Ricardo's mind, and gathered strength as he thought upon it; for Hanaud had seemed to lean to the belief that one of the murderers might be still in Aix. Indeed, a glance at him showed that he was not discomposed by the discovery.

"When was it found?" Hanaud asked.

"This morning. A gardener comes to the villa on two days a week to keep the grounds in order. Fortunately Wednesday is one of his days. Fortunately, too, there was rain yesterday evening. He noticed the tracks of the wheels which you can see on the gravel, and since the villa is empty he was surprised. He found the coach-house door forced and the motor-car inside it. When he went to his luncheon he brought the news of his discovery to the depôt."

The party followed the Commissaire along the drive to the coach-house.

"We will have the car brought out," said Hanaud to Servettaz.

It was a big and powerful machine with a limousine body, luxuriously fitted and cushioned in a shade of light grey. The outside panels of the car were painted a dark grey. The car had hardly been brought out into the sunlight before a cry of stupefaction burst from the lips of Perrichet.

"Oh!" he cried, in utter abasement. "I shall never forgive myself—never, never!"

"Why?" Hanaud asked, turning sharply as he spoke.

Perrichet was standing with his round eyes staring and his mouth agape.

"Because, monsieur, I saw that car—at four o'clock this morning—at the corner of the road—not fifty yards from the Villa Rose."

"What!" cried Ricardo.

"You saw it!" exclaimed Wethermill.

Upon their faces was reflected now the stupefaction of Perrichet.

"But you must have made a mistake," said the Commissaire.

"No, no, monsieur," Perrichet insisted. "It was that car. It was that number. It was just after daylight. I was standing outside the gate of the villa on duty where M. le Commissaire had placed me. The car appeared at the corner and slackened speed. It seemed to me that it was going to turn into the road and come down past me. But instead the driver, as if he were now sure of his way, put the car at its top speed and went on into Aix."

"Was any one inside the car?" asked Hanaud.

"No, monsieur; it was empty."

"But you saw the driver!" exclaimed Wethermill.

"Yes; what was he like?" cried the Commissaire.

Perrichet shook his head mournfully.

"He wore a talc mask over the upper part of his face, and had a little black moustache, and was dressed in a heavy great-coat of blue with a white collar."

"That is my coat, monsieur," said Servettaz, and as he spoke he lifted it up from the chauffeur's seat. "It is Mme. Dauvray's livery."

Harry Wethermill groaned aloud.

"We have lost him. He was within our grasp—he,.the murderer!—and he was allowed to go!"

Perrichet's grief was pitiable.

"Monsieur," he pleaded, "a car slackens its speed and goes on again—it is not so unusual a thing. I did not know the number of Mme. Dauvray's car. I did not even know that it had disappeared"; and suddenly tears of mortification filled his eyes. "But why do I make these excuses?" he cried. "It is better, M. Hanaud, that I go back to my uniform and stand at the street corner. I am as foolish as I look."

"Nonsense, my friend," said Hanaud, clapping the disconsolate man upon the shoulder. "You remembered the car and its number. That is something—and perhaps a great deal," he added gravely. "As for the talc mask and the black moustache, that is not much to help us, it is true." He looked at Ricardo's crestfallen face and smiled. "We might arrest our good friend M. Ricardo upon that evidence, but no one else that I know."

Hanaud laughed immoderately at his joke. He alone seemed to feel no disappointment at Perrichet's oversight. Ricardo was a little touchy on the subject of his personal appearance, and bridled visibly. Hanaud turned towards Servettaz.

"Now," he said, "you know how much petrol was taken from the garage?"

"Yes, monsieur."

"Can you tell me, by the amount which has been used, how far that car was driven last night?" Hanaud asked.

Servettaz examined the tank.

"A long way, monsieur. From a hundred and thirty to a hundred and fifty kilometres, I should say."

"Yes, just about that distance, I should say," cried Hanaud.

His eyes brightened, and a smile, a rather fierce smile, came to his lips. He opened the door, and examined with a minute scrutiny the floor of the carriage, and, as he looked, the smile faded from his face. Perplexity returned to it. He took the cushions, looked them over and shook them out.

" I see no sign——" he began, and then he uttered a little shrill cry of satisfaction. From the crack of the door by the hinge he picked off a tiny piece of pale green stuff, which he spread out upon the back of his hand.

"Tell me, what is this?" he said to Ricardo.

" It is a green fabric," said Ricardo very wisely.

"It is green chiffon," said Hanaud. "And the frock in which Mlle. Célie went away was of green chiffon over satin. Yes, Mlle. Célie travelled in this car."

He hurried to the driver's seat. Upon the floor

there was some dark mould.   Hanaud cleaned it
off with his knife and held some of it in the palm
of his hand.   He turned to Servettaz.

"You drove the car on Tuesday morning before
you went to Chambéry?"

"Yes, monsieur."

"Where did you take up Mme. Dauvray and
Mlle. Célie?"

"At the front door of the Villa Rose."

"Did you get down from the seat at all?"

"No, monsieur; not after I left the garage."

Hanaud returned to his companions.

"See!" And he opened his hand. "This is
black soil—moist from last night's rain—soil like
the soil in front of Mme. Dauvray's salon. Look,
here is even a blade or two of the grass"; and
he turned the mould over in the palm of his
hand. Then he took an empty envelope from his
pocket and poured the soil into it and gummed
the flap down. He stood and frowned at the
motor-car.

"Listen," he said, "how I am puzzled! There
was a man last night at the Villa Rose. There
were a man's blurred footmarks in the mould
before the glass door. That man drove madame's
car for a hundred and fifty kilometres, and he
leaves the mould which clung to his boots upon
the floor of his seat.   Mlle. Célie and another
woman drove away inside the car. Mlle. Célie
leaves a fragment of the chiffon tunic of her frock
which caught in the hinge. But Mlle. Célie made

much clearer impressions in the mould than the man. Yet on the floor of the carriage there is no trace of her shoes. Again I say there is something here which I do not understand." And he spread out his hands with an impulsive gesture of despair.

"It looks as if they had been careful and he careless," said Mr. Ricardo, with the air of a man solving a very difficult problem.

"What a mind!" cried Hanaud, now clasping his hands together in admiration. "How quick and how profound!"

There was at times something elephantinely elfish in M. Hanaud's demeanour, which left Mr. Ricardo at a loss. But he had come to notice that these undignified manifestations usually took place when Hanaud had reached a definite opinion upon some point which had reached him.

"Yet there is, perhaps, another explanation," Hanaud continued. "For observe, M. Ricardo. We have other evidence to show that the careless one was Mlle. Célie. It was she who left her footsteps so plainly visible upon the grass, not the man. However, we will go back to M. Wethermill's room at the Hôtel Majestic and talk this matter over. We know something now. Yes, we know— what do we know, monsieur?" he asked, suddenly turning with a smile to Ricardo, and, as Ricardo paused: "Think it over while we walk down to M. Wethermill's apartment in the Hôtel Majestic."

9

"We know that the murderer has escaped," replied Ricardo hotly.

"The murderer is not now the most important object of our search. He is very likely at Marseilles by now. We shall lay our hands on him, never fear," replied Hanaud, with a superb gesture of disdain. "But it was thoughtful of you to re-mind me of him. I might so easily have clean forgotten him, and then indeed my reputation would have suffered an eclipse." He made a low, ironical bow to Ricardo and walked quickly down the road.

"For a cumbersome man he is extraordinarily active," said Mr. Ricardo to Harry Wethermill, trying to laugh, without much success. "A heavy, clever, middle-aged man, liable to become a little gutter-boy at a moment's notice."

Thus he described the great detective, and the description is quoted. For it was Ricardo's best effort in the whole of this business.

The three men went straight to Harry Wether-mill's apartment, which consisted of a sitting-room and a bedroom on the first floor. A balcony ran along outside. Hanaud stepped out on to it, looked about him, and returned.

"It is as well to know that we cannot be over-heard," he said.

Harry Wethermill meanwhile had thrown himself into a chair. The mask he had worn had slipped from its fastenings for a moment. There was a look of infinite suffering upon his face. It was the face of a man tortured by misery to the snapping-point.

Hanaud, on the other hand, was particularly alert. The discovery of the motor-car had raised his spirits. He sat at the table.

"I will tell you what we have learnt," he said, "and it is of importance. The three of them—the man, the woman with the red hair, and Mlle. Célie—all drove yesterday night to Geneva. That is only one thing we have learnt."

"Then you still cling to Geneva?" said Ricardo.

"More than ever," said Hanaud.

He turned in his chair towards Wethermill.

"Ah, my poor friend!" he said, when he saw the young man's distress.

Harry Wethermill sprang up with a gesture as though to sweep the need of sympathy away.

"What can I do for you?" he asked.

"You have a road map, perhaps?" said Hanaud.

"Yes," said Wethermill, "mine is here. There it is"; and crossing the room he brought it from a side-table and placed it in front of Hanaud.

Hanaud took a pencil from his pocket.

"One hundred and fifty kilometres was about the distance which the car had travelled. Measure the distances here, and you will see that Geneva is the likely place. It is a good city to hide in. Moreover the car appears at the corner at daylight. How does it appear there? What road is it which comes out at that corner? The road from Geneva. I am not sorry that it is

Geneva, for the Chef de la Sûreté is a friend of mine."

"And what else do we know?" asked Ricardo.

"This," said Hanaud. He paused impressively. "Bring up your chair to the table, M. Wethermill, and consider whether I am right or wrong"; and he waited until Harry Wethermill had obeyed. Then he laughed in a friendly way at himself.

"I cannot help it," he said; "I have an eye for dramatic effects. I must prepare for them when I know they are coming. And one, I tell you, is coming now."

He shook his finger at his companions. Ricardo shifted and shuffled in his chair. Harry Wethermill kept his eyes fixed on Hanaud's face, but he was quiet, as he had been throughout the long inquiry.

Hanaud lit a cigarette and took his time.

"What I think is this. The man who drove the car into Geneva drove it back, because—he meant to leave it again in the garage of the Villa Rose."

"Good heavens!" cried Ricardo, flinging himself back. The theory so calmly enunciated took his breath away.

"Would he have dared?" asked Harry Wethermill.

Hanaud leaned across and tapped his fingers on the table to emphasise his answer.

"All through this crime there are two things visible—brains and daring; clever brains and extraordinary daring. Would he have dared? He dared to be at the corner close to the Villa Rose at day-

light.   Why else should he have returned except to
put back the car?   Consider!   The petrol is taken
from tins which Servettaz might never have touched
for a fortnight, and by that time he might, as he
said, have forgotten whether he had not used them
himself.   I had this possibility in my mind when
I put the questions to Servettaz about the petrol
which the Commissaire thought so stupid.   The
utmost care is taken that there shall be no mould
left on the floor of the carriage.   The scrap of
chiffon was torn off, no doubt, when the women
finally left the car, and therefore not noticed, or
that, too, would have been removed.   That the
exterior of the car was dirty betrayed nothing, for
Servettaz had left it uncleaned."

Hanaud leaned back and, step by step, related the
journey of the car

"The man leaves the gate open; he drives into
Geneva the two women, who are careful that their
shoes shall leave no marks upon the floor.   At
Geneva they get out.   The man returns.   If he can
only leave the car in the garage he covers all traces
of the course he and his friends have taken.   No
one would suspect that the car had ever left the
garage.   At the corner of the road, just as he is
turning down to the villa, he sees a *sergent-de-ville*
at the gate.   He knows that the murder is discovered.   He puts on full speed and goes straight
out of the town.   What is he to do?   He is driving
a car for which the police in an hour or two, if not
now already, will be surely watching.   He is driving

it in broad daylight. He must get rid of it, and
at once, before people are about to see it, and to
see him in it. Imagine his feelings! It is almost
enough to make one pity him. Here he is in a car
which convicts him as a murderer, and he has
nowhere to leave it. He drives through Aix. Then
on the outskirts of the town he finds an empty villa.
He drives in at the gate, forces the door of the
coach-house, and leaves his car there. Now, observe!
It is no longer any use for him to pretend that he
and his friends did not disappear in that car. The
murder is already discovered, and with the murder
the disappearance of the car. So he no longer
troubles his head about it. He does not remove
the traces of mould from the place where his feet
rested, which otherwise, no doubt, he would have
done. It no longer matters. He has to run to
earth now before he is seen. That is all his business.
And so the state of the car is explained. It was a
bold step to bring that car back—yes, a bold and
desperate step. But a clever one. For, if it had
succeeded, we should have known nothing of their
movements—oh, but nothing—nothing. Ah! I tell
you this is no ordinary blundering affair. They are
clever people who devised this crime—clever, and
of an audacity which is surprising."

Then Hanaud lit another cigarette.

Mr. Ricardo, on the other hand, could hardly continue to smoke for excitement.

"I cannot understand your calmness," he exclaimed.

"No?" said Hanaud. "Yet it is so obvious. You are the amateur, I am the professional—that is all."

He looked at his watch and rose to his feet.

"I must go," he said, and as he turned towards the door a cry sprang from Mr. Ricardo's lips.

"It is true; I am the amateur. Yet I have knowledge, M. Hanaud, which the professional would do well to obtain."

Hanaud turned a guarded face towards Ricardo. There was no longer any raillery in his manner. He spoke slowly and coldly.

"Let me have it, then!"

"I have driven in my motor-car from Geneva into France," said Ricardo excitedly. "A bridge crosses a ravine among the hills. At the bridge there is a Customs House. There—at the Pont de la Caille, your car is stopped. It is searched. You must sign your name in a book. And there is no way round. You would find certain proof whether or no the car travelled last night to Geneva. Not so many travellers pass along that road at night. You would find certain proof, too, of how many travelled in the car, for they search carefully at the Pont de la Caille."

A dark flush of colour overspread Hanaud's face. Ricardo was in the seventh heaven. He had at last contributed something to the history of this crime. He had supplied knowledge to the omniscient.

Wethermill looked up.

"Yes, you must not neglect that clue," he said eagerly.

Hanaud replied testily.

"It is not a clue. M. Ricardo tells us that he travelled from Geneva into France, and that his car was searched. Well, we know already that the officers are particular at the Customs Houses of France. But travelling from France into Switzerland is a very different affair. In Switzerland, hardly a glance, hardly a word."

That was true. Mr. Ricardo recognised the truth. But his spirits rose again at once.

"But the car came back from Geneva into France!" he cried.

"Yes, but when the car came back," Hanaud replied, "the man was alone in it. I have more important things to attend to. For instance, I must find out whether by any chance they have caught our man at Marseilles." He laid his hand on Wethermill's shoulder. "And you, my friend, I should counsel you to get some sleep. We may need all our strength to-morrow. I hope so." He was speaking very gravely. "Yes, I hope so."

Wethermill nodded.

"I shall try," he said.

"That's better," said Hanaud cheerfully. "You will both stay here this evening; for if I have news, I can then ring you up."

Both men agreed, and Hanaud went away. He left Mr. Ricardo greatly dissatisfied.

"That man will take advice from no one," he

cried; "his vanity is colossal. It is true they are not particular at the Swiss frontier. Still, the car would have to stop there. At the Customs House they would know. Hanaud ought to make inquiries."

But neither Ricardo nor Harry Wethermill heard a word more from Hanaud that night.

CHAPTER X

NEWS FROM GENEVA

THE next morning, however, before Mr. Ricardo was out of his bed, M. Hanaud was announced. He came stepping gaily into the room, more elephantinely elfish than ever.

"Send your valet away," he said. And as soon as they were alone he produced a newspaper, which he flourished in Mr. Ricardo's face and then dropped into his hands.

Ricardo saw staring him in the face a full description of Celia Harland, of her appearance and her dress, of everything except her name, coupled with an intimation that a reward of four thousand francs would be paid to any one who could give information leading to the discovery of her whereabouts to Mr. Ricardo, the Hôtel Majestic, Aix-les-Bains!

Mr. Ricardo sat up in his bed with a sense of outrage.

"You have done this?" he asked.

"Yes."

"Why have you done it?" Mr. Ricardo cried.

Hanaud advanced to the bed mysteriously on the tips of his toes.

" I will tell you," he said, in his most confidential tones. " Only it must remain a secret between you and me. I did it—because I have a sense of humour."

" I hate publicity," said Mr. Ricardo acidly.

" On the other hand, you have four thousand francs," protested the detective. " Besides, what else should I do ? If I name myself, the very people we are seeking to catch—who, you may be sure, will be the first to read this advertisement—will know that I, the great, the incomparable Hanaud, am after them ; and I do not want them to know that. Besides "—and he spoke now in a gentle and most serious voice—" why should we make life more difficult for Mlle. Célie by telling the world that the police want her ? It will be time enough for that when she appears before the Juge d'Instruction."

Mr. Ricardo grumbled inarticulately, and read through the advertisement again.

" Besides, your description is incomplete," he said. " There is no mention of the diamond earrings which Celia Harland was wearing when she went away."

" Ah ! so you noticed that ! " exclaimed Hanaud. " A little more experience and I should be looking very closely to my laurels. But as for the earrings —I will tell you. Mlle. Célie was not wearing them when she went away from the Villa Rose."

" But—but," stammered Ricardo, " the case upon the dressing-room table was empty."

"Still, she was not wearing them, I know," said Hanaud decisively.

"How do you know?" cried Ricardo, gazing at Hanaud with awe in his eyes. "How could you know?"

"Because"—and Hanaud struck a majestic attitude, like a king in a play—"because I am the captain of the ship."

Upon that Mr. Ricardo suffered a return of his ill-humour.

"I do not like to be trifled with," he remarked, with as much dignity as his ruffled hair and the bed-clothes allowed him. He looked sternly at the newspaper, turning it over, and then he uttered a cry of surprise.

"But this is yesterday's paper!" he said.

"Yesterday evening's paper," Hanaud corrected.

"Printed at Geneva!"

"Printed and published and sold at Geneva," said Hanaud.

"When did you send the advertisement in, then?"

"I wrote a letter while we were taking our luncheon," Hanaud explained. "The letter was to Besnard, asking him to telegraph the advertisement at once."

"But you said never a word about it to us," Ricardo grumbled.

"No. And was I not wise?" said Hanaud, with complacency. "For you would have forbidden me to use your name."

"Oh, I don't go so far as that," said Ricardo reluctantly. His indignation was rapidly evaporating. For there was growing up in his mind a pleasant perception that the advertisement placed him in the limelight.

He rose from his bed.

"You will make yourself comfortable in the sitting-room while I have my bath."

"I will, indeed," replied Hanaud cheerily. "I have already ordered my morning chocolate. I have hopes that you may have a telegram very soon. This paper was cried last night through the streets of Geneva."

Ricardo dressed for once in a way with some approach to ordinary celerity, and joined Hanaud.

"Has nothing come?" he asked.

"No. This chocolate is very good; it is better than that which I get in my hotel."

"Good heavens!" cried Ricardo, who was fairly twittering with excitement. "You sit there talking about chocolate while my cup shakes in my fingers."

"Again I must remind you that you are the amateur, I the professional, my friend."

As the morning drew on, however, Hanaud's professional quietude deserted him. He began to start at the sound of footsteps in the corridor, to glance every other moment from the window, to eat his cigarettes rather than to smoke them. At eleven o'clock Ricardo's valet brought a telegram into the room. Ricardo seized it.

" Calmly, my friend," said Hanaud.

With trembling fingers Ricardo tore it open. He jumped in his chair. Speechless, he handed the telegram to Hanaud. It had been sent from Geneva, and it ran thus:

" Expect me soon after three.—MARTHE GOBIN."

Hanaud nodded his head.

" I told you I had hopes." All his levity had gone in an instant from his manner. He spoke very quietly.

" I had better send for Wethermill?" asked Ricardo.

Hanaud shrugged his shoulders.

" As you like. But why raise hopes in that poor man's breast which an hour or two may dash for ever to the ground? Consider! Marthe Gobin has something to tell us. Think over those eight points of evidence which you drew up yesterday in the Villa des Fleurs, and say whether what she has to tell us is more likely to prove Mlle. Célie's innocence than her guilt. Think well, for I will be guided by you, M. Ricardo," said Hanaud solemnly " If you think it better that your friend should live in torture until Marthe Gobin comes, and then perhaps suffer worse torture from the news she brings, be it so. You shall decide. If, on the other hand, you think it will be best to leave M. Wethermill in peace until we know her story, be it so. You shall decide."

Ricardo moved uneasily. The solemnity of

Hanaud's manner impressed him. He had no wish to take the responsibility of the decision upon himself. But Hanaud sat with his eyes strangely fixed upon Ricardo, waiting for his answer.

"Well," said Ricardo, at length, "good news will be none the worse for waiting a few hours. Bad news will be a little the better."

"Yes," said Hanaud; "so I thought you would decide." He took up a Continental Bradshaw from a bookshelf in the room. "From Geneva she will come through Culoz. Let us see!" He turned over the pages. "There is a train from Culoz which reaches Aix at seven minutes past three. It is by that train she will come. You have a motor-car?"

"Yes."

"Very well. Will you pick me up in it at three at my hotel? We will drive down to the station and see the arrivals by that train. It may help us to get some idea of the person with whom we have to deal. That is always an advantage. Now I will leave you, for I have much to do. But I will look in upon M. Wethermill as I go down and tell him that there is as yet no news."

He took up his hat and stick, and stood for a moment staring out of the window. Then he roused himself from his reverie with a start.

"You look out upon Mont Revard, I see. I think M. Wethermill's view over the garden and the town is the better one," he said, and went out of the room.

At three o'clock Ricardo called in his car, which was an open car of high power, at Hanaud's hotel, and the two men went to the station. They waited outside the exit while the passengers gave up their tickets. Amongst them a middle-aged, short woman, of a plethoric tendency, attracted their notice. She was neatly but shabbily dressed in black; her gloves were darned, and she was obviously in a hurry. As she came out she asked a commissionaire:

"How far is it to the Hôtel Majestic?"

The man told her the hotel was at the very top of the town, and the way was steep.

"But madame can go up in the omnibus of the hotel," he suggested.

Madame, however, was in too much of a hurry. The omnibus would have to wait for luggage. She hailed a closed cab and drove off inside it.

"Now, if we go back in the car, we shall be all ready for her when she arrives," said Hanaud.

They passed the cab, indeed, a few yards up the steep hill which leads from the station. The cab was moving at a walk.

"She looks honest," said Hanaud, with a sigh of relief. "She is some good bourgeoise anxious to earn four thousand francs."

They reached the hotel in a few minutes.

"We may need your car again the moment Marthe Gobin has gone," said Hanaud.

"It shall wait here," said Ricardo.

"No," said Hanaud; "let it wait in the little street

at the back of my hotel. It will not be so noticeable there. You have petrol for a long journey?"

Ricardo gave the order quietly to his chauffeur, and followed Hanaud into the hotel. Through a glass window they could see Wethermill smoking a cigar over his coffee.

"He looks as if he had not slept," said Ricardo.

Hanaud nodded sympathetically, and beckoned Ricardo past the window.

"But we are nearing the end. These two days have been for him days of great trouble; one can see that very clearly. And he has done nothing to embarrass us. Men in distress are apt to be a nuisance. I am grateful to M. Wethermill. But we are nearing the end. Who knows? Within an hour or two we may have news for him."

He spoke with great feeling, and the two men ascended the stairs to Ricardo's rooms. For the second time that day Hanaud's professional calm deserted him. The window overlooked the main entrance to the hotel. Hanaud arranged the room, and, even while he arranged it, ran every other second and leaned from the window to watch for the coming of the cab.

"Put the bank-notes upon the table," he said hurriedly. "They will persuade her to tell us all that she has to tell. Yes, that will do. She is not in sight yet? No."

"She could not be. It is a long way from the station," said Ricardo, "and the whole distance is uphill."

"Yes, that is true," Hanaud replied. "We will not embarrass her by sitting round the table like a tribunal. You will sit in that arm-chair."

Ricardo took his seat, crossed his knees, and joined the tips of his fingers.

"So! Not too judicial!" said Hanaud. "I will sit here at the table. Whatever you do, do not frighten her." Hanaud sat down in the chair which he had placed for himself. "Marthe Gobin shall sit opposite, with the light upon her face. So!" And, springing up, he arranged a chair for her. "Whatever you do, do not frighten her," he repeated. "I am nervous. So much depends upon this interview." And in a second he was back at the window.

Ricardo did not move. He arranged in his mind the interrogatory which was to take place. He was to conduct it. He was the master of the situation. All the limelight was to be his. Startling facts would come to light elicited by his deft questions. Hanaud need not fear. He would not frighten her. He would be gentle, he would be cunning. Softly and delicately he would turn this good woman inside out, like a glove. Every artistic fibre in his body vibrated to the dramatic situation.

Suddenly Hanaud leaned out of the window.

"It comes! it comes!" he said in a quick, feverish whisper. "I can see the cab between the shrubs of the drive."

"Let it come!" said Mr. Ricardo superbly.

Even as he sat he could hear the grating of

wheels upon the drive. He saw Hanaud lean farther from the window and stamp impatiently upon the floor.

"There it is at the door," he said; and for a few seconds he spoke no more. He stood looking downwards, craning his head, with his back towards Ricardo.

Then, with a wild and startled cry, he staggered back into the room. His face was white as wax, his eyes full of horror, his mouth open.

"What is the matter?" exclaimed Ricardo, springing to his feet.

"They are lifting her out! She doesn't move! They are lifting her out!"

For a moment he stared into Ricardo's face—paralysed by fear. Then he sprang down the stairs. Ricardo followed him.

There was confusion in the corridor. Men were running, voices were crying questions. As they passed the window they saw Wethermill start up, aroused from his lethargy. They knew the truth before they reached the entrance of the hotel. A cab had driven up to the door from the station; in the cab was an unknown woman stabbed to the heart.

"She should have come by the omnibus," Hanaud repeated and repeated stupidly. For the moment he was off his balance.

CHAPTER XI

THE UNOPENED LETTER

THE hall of the hotel had been cleared of people. At the entrance from the corridor a porter barred the way.

"No one can pass," said he.

"I think that I can," said Hanaud, and he produced his card. "From the Sûreté at Paris."

He was allowed to enter, with Ricardo at his heels. On the ground lay Marthe Gobin; the manager of the hotel stood at her side; a doctor was on his knees. Hanaud gave his card to the manager.

"You have sent word to the police?"

"Yes," said the manager.

"And the wound?" asked Hanaud, kneeling on the ground beside the doctor. It was a very small wound, round and neat and clean, and there was very little blood. "It was made by a bullet," said Hanaud—"some tiny bullet from an air-pistol."

"No," answered the doctor.

"No knife made it," Hanaud asserted.

"That is true," said the doctor. "Look!" and he took up from the floor by his knee the weapon which had caused Marthe Gobin's death. It was nothing but an ordinary skewer with a ring at one end and a sharp point at the other, and a piece of common white firewood for a handle. The wood had been split, the ring inserted and spliced in position with strong twine. It was a rough enough weapon, but an effective one. The proof of its effect- iveness lay stretched upon the floor beside them.

Hanaud gave it to the manager of the hotel.

"You must be very careful of this, and give it as it is to the police."

Then he bent once more over Marthe Gobin.

"Did she suffer?" he asked in a low voice.

"No; death must have been instantaneous," said the doctor.

"I am glad of that," said Hanaud, as he rose again to his feet.

In the doorway the driver of the cab was standing.

"What has he to say?" Hanaud asked.

The man stepped forward instantly. He was an old, red-faced, stout man, with a shiny white tall hat, like a thousand drivers of cabs.

"What have I to say, monsieur?" he grumbled in a husky voice. "I take up the poor woman at the station and I drive her where she bids me, and I find her dead, and my day is lost. Who will pay my fare, monsieur?"

"I will," said Hanaud. "There it is," and he handed the man a five-franc piece. "Now, answer me! Do you tell me that this woman was murdered

in your cab and that you knew nothing about
it ? "

"But what should I know? I take her up at
the station, and all the way up the hill her head is
every moment out of the window, crying, ' Faster,
faster!' Oh, the good woman was in a hurry!
But for me I take no notice. The more she shouts,
the less I hear; I bury my head between my
shoulders, and I look ahead of me and I take no
notice. One cannot expect cab-horses to run up
these hills; it is not reasonable."

"So you went at a walk," said Hanaud. He
beckoned to Ricardo, and said to the manager:
" M. Besnard will, no doubt, be here in a few
minutes, and he will send for the Juge d'Instruction.
There is nothing that we can do."

He went back to Ricardo's sitting-room and flung
himself into a chair. He had been calm enough
downstairs in the presence of the doctor and the
body of the victim. Now, with only Ricardo for a
witness, he gave way to distress.

"It is terrible," he said. " The poor woman! It
was I who brought her to Aix. It was through my
carelessness. But who would have thought——?"
He snatched his hands from his face and stood up.
"*I* should have thought," he said solemnly.
"Extraordinary daring—that was one of the qualities of my criminal. I knew it, and I disregarded
it. Now we have a second crime."

" The skewer may lead you to the criminal," said
Mr. Ricardo.

"The skewer!" cried Hanaud. "How will that help us? A knife, yes—perhaps. But a skewer!"

"At the shops—there will not be so many in Aix at which you can buy skewers—they may remember to whom they sold one within the last day or so."

"How do we know it was bought in the last day or so?" cried Hanaud scornfully. "We have not to do with a man who walks into a shop and buys a single skewer to commit a murder with, and so hands himself over to the police. How often must I say it!"

The violence of his contempt nettled Ricardo.

"If the murderer did not buy it, how did he obtain it?" he asked obstinately.

"Oh, my friend, could he not have stolen it? From this or from any hotel in Aix? Would the loss of a skewer be noticed, do you think? How many people in Aix to-day have had rognons à la brochette for their luncheon! Besides, it is not merely the death of this poor woman which troubles me. We have lost the evidence which she was going to bring to us. She had something to tell us about Célie Harland which now we shall never hear. We have to begin all over again, and I tell you we have not the time to begin all over again. No, we have not the time. Time will be lost, and we have no time to lose." He buried his face again in his hands and groaned aloud. His grief was so violent and so sincere that Ricardo, shocked as he was by the murder of Marthe Gobin, set himself to console him.

"But you could not have foreseen that at three o'clock in the afternoon at Aix——"

Hanaud brushed the excuse aside.

"It is no extenuation. I *ought* to have foreseen. Oh; but I will have no pity now," he cried, and as he ended the words abruptly his face changed. He lifted a trembling forefinger and pointed. There came a sudden look of life into his dull and despairing eyes.

He was pointing to a side-table on which were piled Mr. Ricardo's letters.

"You have not opened them this morning?" he asked.

"No. You came while I was still in bed. I have not thought of them till now."

Hanaud crossed to the table, and, looking down at the letters, uttered a cry.

"There's one, the big envelope," he said, his voice shaking like his hand. "It has a Swiss stamp."

He swallowed to moisten his throat. Ricardo sprang across the room and tore open the envelope. There was a long letter enclosed in a handwriting unknown to him. He read aloud the first lines of the letter

"I write what I saw and post it to-night, so that no one may be before me with the news. I will come over to-morrow for the money."

A low exclamation from Hanaud interrupted the words.

"The signature! Quick!"

Ricardo turned to the end of the letter.

"Marthe Gobin."

"She speaks, then! After all she speaks!" Hanaud whispered in a voice of awe. He ran to the door of the room, opened it suddenly, and, shutting it again, locked it. "Quick! We cannot bring that poor woman back to life; but we may still——" He did not finish his sentence. He took the letter unceremoniously from Ricardo's hand and seated himself at the table. Over his shoulder Mr. Ricardo, too, read Marthe Gobin's letter.

It was just the sort of letter, which in Ricardo's view, Marthe Gobin would have written—a long, straggling letter which never kept to the point, which exasperated them one moment by its folly and fired them to excitement the next.

It was dated from a small suburb of Geneva, on the western side of the lake, and it ran as follows :

"The suburb is but a street close to the lake-side, and a tram runs into the city. It is quite respectable, you understand, monsieur, with an hotel at the end of it, and really some very good houses. But I do not wish to deceive you about the social position of myself or my husband. Our house is on the wrong side of the street—definitely—yes. It is a small house, and we do not see the water from any of the windows because of the better houses opposite. M. Gobin, my husband, who was a clerk in one of the great banks in Geneva, broke down in health in the spring, and for the last three

months has been compelled to keep indoors. Of
course, money has not been plentiful, and I could
not afford a nurse. Consequently I myself have
been compelled to nurse hin. Monsieur, if you
were a woman, you would know what men are
when they are ill—how fretful, how difficult.
There is not much distraction for the woman who
nurses them. So, as I am in the house most of the
day, I find what amusement I can in watching the
doings of my neighbours. You will not blame me.

"A month ago the house almost directly opposite
to us was taken furnished for the summer by a
Mme. Rossignol. She is a widow, but during the
last fortnight a young gentleman has come several
times in the afternoon to see her, and it is said in
the street that he is going to marry her. But I
cannot believe it myself. Monsieur is a young man
of perhaps thirty, with smooth, black hair. He
wears a moustache, a little black moustache, and is
altogether captivating. Mme. Rossignol is five or
six years older, I should think—a tall woman, with
red hair and a bold sort of coarse beauty. I was
not attracted by her. She seemed not quite of the
same world as that charming monsieur who was
said to be going to marry her. No; I was not
attracted by Adéle Rossignol."

And when he had come to that point Hanaud
looked up with a start.

"So the name was Adéle," he whispered.

"Yes," said Ricardo. "Héléne Vauquier spoke
the truth."

Hanaud nodded with a queer smile upon his lips.

"Yes, there she spoke the truth. I thought she did."

"But she said Adéle's hair was black," interposed Mr. Ricardo.

"Yes, there she didn't," said Hanaud drily, and his eyes dropped again to the paper.

"I knew her name was Adéle, for often I have heard her servant calling her so, and without any 'Madame' in front of the name. That is strange, is it not, to hear an elderly servant-woman calling after her mistress, 'Adéle,' just simple 'Adéle'? It was that which made me think monsieur and madame were not of the same world. But I do not believe that they are going to be married. I have an instinct about it. Of course, one never knows with what extraordinary women the nicest men will fall in love. So that after all these two may get married. But if they do, I do not think they will be happy.

"Besides the old woman there was another servant, a man, Hippolyte, who served in the house and drove the carriage when it was wanted—a respectable man. He always touched his hat when Mme. Rossignol came out of the house. He slept in the house at night, although the stable was at the end of the street. I thought he was probably the son of Jeanne, the servant-woman. He was young, and his hair was plastered down upon his forehead, and he was altogether satisfied with himself and a great favourite amongst the servants

in the street. The carriage and the horse were
hired from Geneva. That is the household of
Mme. Rossignol."

So far, Mr. Ricardo read in silence. Then he
broke out again.

"But we have them! The red-haired woman
called Adéle; the man with the little black moustache. It was he who drove the motor-car!"

Hanaud held up his hand to check the flow of
words, and both read on again:

"At three o'clock on Tuesday afternoon madame
was driven away in the carriage, and I did not see
it return all that evening. Of course, it may have
returned to the stables by another road. But it
was not unusual for the carriage to take her into
Geneva and wait a long time. I went to bed at
eleven, but in the night M. Gobin was restless,
and I rose to get him some medicine. We slept
in the front of the house, monsieur, and while I
was searching for the matches upon the table in
the middle of the room I heard the sound of carriage wheels in the silent street. I went to the
window, and, raising a corner of the curtains,
looked out. M. Gobin called to me fretfully from
the bed to know why I did not light the candle and
get him what he wanted. I have already told you
how fretful sick men can be, always complaining if
just for a minute one distracts oneself by looking
out of the window. But there! One can do nothing to please them. Yet how right I was to raise
the blind and look out of the window! For if I

had obeyed my husband I might have lost four thousand francs. And four thousand francs are not to be sneezed at by a poor woman whose husband lies in bed.

"I saw the carriage stop at Mme. Rossignol's house. Almost at once the house door was opened by the old servant, although the hall of the house and all the windows in the front were dark. That was the first thing that surprised me. For when madame came home late and the house was dark, she used to let herself in with a latchkey. Now, in the dark house, in the early morning, a servant was watching for them. It was strange.

"As soon as the door of the house was opened the door of the carriage opened too, and a young lady stepped quickly out on to the pavement. The train of her dress caught in the door, and she turned round, stooped, freed it with her hand, and held it up off the ground. The night was clear, and there was a lamp in the street close by the door of Mme. Rossignol's house. As she turned I saw her face under the big green hat. It was very pretty and young, and the hair was fair. She wore a white coat, but it was open in front and showed her evening frock of pale green. When she lifted her skirt I saw the buckles sparkling on her satin shoes. It was the young lady for whom you are advertising, I am sure. She remained standing just for a moment without moving, while Mme. Rossignol got out. I was surprised to see a young lady of such distinction in Mme. Rossignol's company.

Then, still holding her skirt up, she ran very lightly and quickly across the pavement into the dark house. I thought, monsieur, that she was very anxious not to be seen. So when I saw your advertisement I was certain that this was the young lady for whom you are searching.

." I waited for a few moments and saw the carriage drive off towards the stable at the end of the street. But no light went up in any of the rooms in front of the house. And M. Gobin was so fretful that I dropped the corner of the blind, lit the candle, and gave him his cooling drink. His watch was on the table at the bedside, and I saw that it was five minutes to three. I will send you a telegram to-morrow, as soon as I am sure at what hour I can leave my husband. Accept, monsieur, I beg you, my most distinguished salutations.

" MARTHE GOBIN."

Hanaud leant back with an extraordinary look of perplexity upon his face. But to Ricardo the whole story was now clear. Here was an independent witness, without the jealousy or rancours of Héléne Vauquier. Nothing could be more damning than her statement; it corroborated those footmarks upon the soil in front of the glass door of the salon. There was nothing to be done except to set about arresting Mlle. Célie at once.

" The facts work with your theory, M. Hanaud. The young man with the black moustache did not return to the house at Geneva. For somewhere upon the road he met the carriage close to Geneva. He was driving back the car to Aix——" And then another thought struck him : "But no!" he cried. "We are altogether wrong. See! They did not reach home until five minutes to three."

Five minutes to three! But this demolished the whole of Hanaud's theory about the motor-car. The murderers had left the villa between eleven and twelve, probably before half-past eleven. The car was a machine of sixty horse-power, and the roads were certain to be clear. Yet the travellers only reached their home at three. Moreover, the car was back in Aix at four. It was evident they did not travel by the car.

"Geneva time is an hour later than French time," said Hanaud shortly. It seemed as if the corroboration of this letter disappointed him. "A quarter to three in Mme. Gobin's house would be a quarter to two by our watches here."

Hanaud folded up the letter, and rose to his feet.

"We will go now, and we will take this letter with us." Hanaud looked about the room, and picked up a glove lying upon a table. "I left this behind me," he said, putting it into his pocket. "By the way, where is the telegram from Marthe Gobin ?"

"You put it in your letter-case."

"Oh, did I ?"

Hanaud took out his letter-case and found the telegram within it. His face lightened.

"Good!" he said emphatically. "For, since we

have this telegram, there must have been another message sent from Adéle Rossignol to Aix saying that Marthe Gobin, that busybody, that inquisitive neighbour, who had no doubt seen M. Ricardo's advertisement, was on her way hither. Oh, it will not be put as crudely as that, but that is what the message will mean. We shall have him." And suddenly his face grew very stern. " I *must* catch him, for Marthe Gobin's death I cannot forgive. A poor woman meaning no harm, and murdered like a sheep under our noses. No, that I cannot forgive."

Ricardo wondered whether it was the actual murder of Marthe Gobin or the fact that he had been beaten and outwitted which Hanaud could not forgive. But discretion kept him silent.

" Let us go," said Hanaud. " By the lift, if you please ; it will save time."

They descended into the hall close by the main door. The body of Marthe Gobin had been removed to the mortuary of the town. The life of the hotel had resumed its course.

" M. Besnard has gone, I suppose ? " Hanaud asked of the porter ; and, receiving an assent, he walked quickly out of the front door.

" But there is a shorter way," said Ricardo, running after him : " across the garden at the back and down the steps."

" It will make no difference now," said Hanaud.

They hurried along the drive and down the road which circled round the hotel and dipped to the town. Behind Hanaud's hotel Ricardo's car was waiting.

"We must go first to Besnard's office. The poor man will be at his wits' end to know who was Mme. Gobin and what brought her to Aix. Besides, I wish to send a message over the telephone."

Hanaud descended and spent a quarter of an hour with the Commissaire. As he came out he looked at his watch.

"We shall be in time, I think," he said. He climbed into the car. "The murder of Marthe Gobin on her way from the station will put our friends at their ease. It will be published, no doubt, in the evening papers, and those good people over there in Geneva will read it with amusement. They do not know that Marthe Gobin wrote a letter yesterday night. Come, let us go!"

"Where to?" asked Ricardo.

"Where to?" exclaimed Hanaud. "Why, of course, to Geneva."

CHAPTER XII

THE ALUMINIUM FLASK

"I HAVE telephoned to Lemerre, the Chef de la Sûreté at Geneva," said Hanaud, as the car sped out of Aix along the road to Annecy. "He will have the house watched. We shall be in time. They will do nothing until dark."

But though he spoke confidently there was a note of anxiety in his voice, and he sat forward in the car, as though he were already straining his eyes to see Geneva.

Ricardo was a trifle disappointed. They were on the great journey to Geneva. They were going to arrest Mlle. Célie and her accomplices. And Hanaud had not come disguised. Hanaud, in Ricardo's eyes, was hardly living up to the dramatic expedition on which they had set out. It seemed to him that there was something incorrect in the great detective coming out on the chase without a false beard.

"But, my dear friend, why should I?" pleaded Hanaud. "We are going to dine together at the Restaurant du Nord, over the lake, until it grows dark. It is not pleasant to eat one's soup in a false beard. Have you tried it? Besides, everybody stares so, seeing perfectly well that it is false. Now, I do not want to-night that people should know me for a detective; so I do not go disguised."

"Humorist!" said Mr. Ricardo.

"There! you have found me out!" cried Hanaud, in mock alarm. "Besides, I told you this morning that that is precisely what I am."

Beyond Annecy they came to the bridge over the ravine. At the far end of it the car was stopped. A question, a hurried glance into the body of the car, and the officers of the Customs stood aside.

"You see how perfunctory it is," said Hanaud, and with a jerk the car moved on. The jerk threw Hanaud against Mr. Ricardo. Something hard in the detective's pocket knocked against his companion.

"You have got them?" he whispered.

"What?"

"The handcuffs."

Another disappointment awaited Ricardo. A detective without a false beard was bad enough, but that was nothing to a detective without handcuffs. The paraphernalia of justice were sadly lacking. However, Hanaud consoled Mr. Ricardo by showing him the hard thing; it was almost as thrilling as the handcuffs, for it was a loaded revolver.

"There will be danger, then?" said Ricardo, with a tremor of excitement. "I should have brought mine."

"There would have been danger, my friend,"

Hanaud objected gravely, "if you had brought yours."

They reached Geneva as the dusk was falling, and drove straight to the restaurant by the side of the lake and mounted to the balcony on the first floor. A small, stout man sat at a table alone in a corner of the balcony. He rose and held out his hands.

"My friend, M. Lemerre, the Chef de la Sûreté of Geneva," said Hanaud, presenting the little man to his companion.

There were as yet only two couples dining in the restaurant, and Hanaud spoke so that neither could overhear him. He sat down at the table.

"What news?" he asked.

"None," said Lemerre. "No one has come out of the house, no one has gone in."

"And if anything happens while we dine?"

"We shall know," said Lemerre. "Look, there is a man loitering under the trees there. He will strike a match to light his pipe."

The hurried conversation was ended.

"Good," said Hanaud. "We will dine, then, and be gay."

He called to the waiter and ordered dinner. It was after seven when they sat down to dinner, and they dined while the dusk deepened. In the street below the lights flashed out, throwing a sheen on the foliage of the trees at the water's side. Upon the dark lake the reflections of lamps rippled and shook. A boat, in which musicians sang to music, passed by with a cool splash of oars. The green and red lights of the launches glided backwards and forwards. Hanaud alone of the party on the balcony tried to keep the conversation upon a light and general level. But it was plain that even he was overdoing his gaiety. There were moments when a sudden contraction of the muscles would clench his hands and give a spasmodic jerk to his shoulders. He was waiting uneasily, uncomfortably, until darkness should come.

"Eat," he cried—"eat, my friends," playing with his own barely tasted food.

And then, at a sentence from Lemerre, his knife and fork clattered on his plate, and he sat with a face suddenly grown white.

For Lemerre said, as though it was no more than a matter of ordinary comment:

"So Mme. Dauvray's jewels were, after all, never stolen?"

Hanaud started.

"You know that? How did you know it?"

"It was in this evening's paper. I bought one on the way here. They were found under the floor of the bedroom."

And even as he spoke a newsboy's voice rang out in the street below them. Lemerre was alarmed by the look upon his friend's face.

"Does it matter, Hanaud?" he asked, with some solicitude.

"It matters——" and Hanaud rose up abruptly.

The boy's voice sounded louder in the street

below. The words became distinct to all upon that balcony.

"The Aix murder! Discovery of the jewels!"

"We must go," Hanaud whispered hoarsely. "Here are life and death in the balance, as I believe, and there"—he pointed down to the little group gathering about the newsboy under the trees —"there is the command which way to tip the scales."

"It was not I who sent it," said Ricardo eagerly.

He had no precise idea what Hanaud meant by his words; but he realised that the sooner he exculpated himself from the charge the better.

"Of course it was not you. I know that very well," said Hanaud. He called for the bill. "When is that paper published?"

"At seven," said Lemerre.

"They have been crying it in the streets of Geneva, then, for more than half an hour."

He sat drumming impatiently upon the table until the bill should be brought.

"By Heaven, that's clever!" he muttered savagely. "There's a man who gets ahead of me at every turn. See, Lemerre, I take every care, every precaution, that no message shall be sent. I let it be known, I take careful pains to let it be known, that no message can be sent without detection following, and here's the message sent by the one channel I never thought to guard against and stop. Look!"

The murder at the Villa Rose and the mystery

which hid its perpetration had aroused interest. This new development had quickened it. From the balcony Hanaud could see the groups thickening about the boy and the white sheets of the newspapers in the hands of passers-by.

" Every one in Geneva or near Geneva will know of this message by now."

" Who could have told ? " asked Ricardo blankly, and Hanaud laughed in his face, but laughed without any merriment.

" At last ! " he cried, as the waiter brought the bill, and just as he had paid it the light of a match flared up under the trees.

" The signal ! " said Lemerre.

" Not too quickly," whispered Hanaud.

With as much unconcern as each could counterfeit, the three men descended the stairs and crossed the road. Under the trees a fourth man joined them—he who had lighted his pipe.

" The coachman, Hippolyte," he whispered, " bought an evening paper at the front door of the house from a boy who came down the street shouting the news. The coachman ran back into the house."

" When was this ? " asked Lemerre.

The man pointed to a lad who leaned against the balustrade above the lake, hot and panting for breath.

" He came on his bicycle. He has just arrived."

" Follow me," said Lemerre.

Six yards from where they stood a couple

of steps led down from the embankment on
to a wooden landing-stage, where boats were
moored. Lemerre, followed by the others, walked
briskly down on to the landing-stage. An electric
launch was waiting. It had an awning and was
of the usual type which one hires at Geneva.
There were two sergeants in plain clothes on board,
and a third man, whom Ricardo recognised.

"That is the man who found out in whose shop
the cord was bought," he said to Hanaud.

"Yes, it is Durette. He has been here since
yesterday."

Lemerre and the three who followed him stepped
into it, and it backed away from the stage and,
turning, sped swiftly outwards from Geneva. The
gay lights of the shops and the restaurants were
left behind, the cool darkness enveloped them;
a light breeze blew over the lake, a trail of white
and tumbled water lengthened out behind, and overhead, in a sky of deepest blue, the bright stars
shone like gold.

"If only we are in time!" said Hanaud, catching
his breath.

"Yes," answered Lemerre; and in both their
voices there was a strange note of gravity.

Lemerre gave a signal after a while, and the boat
turned to the shore and reduced its speed. They
had passed the big villas. On the bank the gardens
of houses—narrow, long gardens of a street of small
houses—reached down to the lake, and to almost
each garden there was a rickety landing-stage of

wood projecting into the lake. Again Lemerre gave a signal, and the boat's speed was so much reduced that not a sound of its coming could be heard. It moved over the water like a shadow, with not so much as a curl of white at its bows.

Lemerre touched Hanaud on the shoulder and pointed to a house in a row of houses. All the windows except two upon the second floor and one upon the ground floor were in absolute darkness, and over those upper two the wooden shutters were closed. But in the shutters there were diamond-shaped holes, and from these holes two yellow beams of light, like glowing eyes upon the watch, streamed out and melted in the air.

"You are sure that the front of the house is guarded?" asked Hanaud anxiously.

"Yes," replied Lemerre.

Ricardo shivered with excitement. The launch slid noiselessly into the bank and lay hidden under its shadow. Hanaud turned to his associates with his finger to his lips. Something gleamed darkly in his hand. It was the barrel of his revolver. Cautiously the men disembarked and crept up the bank. First came Lemerre, then Hanaud; Ricardo followed him, and the fourth man, who had struck the match under the trees, brought up the rear. The other three officers remained in the boat.

Stooping under the shadow of the side wall of the garden, the invaders stole towards the house. When a bush rustled or a tree whispered in the

light wind, Ricardo's heart jumped to his throat.
Once Lemerre stopped, as though his ears heard
a sound which warned him of danger. Then
cautiously he crept on again. The garden was a
ragged place of unmown lawn and straggling bushes.
Behind each one Mr. Ricardo seemed to feel an
enemy. Never had he been in so strait a predicament. He, the cultured host of Grosvenor
Square, was creeping along under a wall with
Continental policemen; he was going to raid a
sinister house by the Lake of Geneva. It was
thrilling. Fear and excitement gripped him in turn
and let him go, but always he was sustained by
the pride of the man doing an out-of-the-way thing.
"If only my friends could see me now!" The
ancient vanity was loud in his bosom. Poor fellows,
they were upon yachts in the Solent or on grouse-
moors in Scotland, or on golf-links at North
Berwick. He alone of them all was tracking male-
factors to their doom by Leman's Lake.

From these agreeable reflections Ricardo was
shaken. Lemerre stopped. The raiders had reached
the angle made by the side wall of the garden and
the house. A whisper was exchanged, and the
party turned and moved along the house wall
towards the lighted window on the ground floor.
As Lemerre reached it he stooped. Then slowly
his forehead and his eyes rose above the sill and
glanced this way and that into the room. Mr.
Ricardo could see his eyes gleaming as the light
from the window caught them. His face rose

completely over the sill. He stared into the room without care or apprehension, and then dropped again out of the reach of the light. He turned to Hanaud.

"The room is empty," he whispered.

Hanaud turned to Ricardo.

"Pass under the sill, or the light from the window will throw your shadow upon the lawn."

The party came to the back door of the house. Lemerre tried the handle of the door, and to his surprise it yielded. They crept into the passage. The last man closed the door noiselessly, locked it, and removed the key. A panel of light shone upon the wall a few paces ahead. The door of the lighted room was open. As Ricardo stepped silently past it, he looked in. It was a parlour meanly furnished. Hanaud touched him on the arm and pointed to the table.

Ricardo had seen the objects at which Hanaud pointed often enough without uneasiness ; but now, in this silent house of crime, they had the most sinister and appalling aspect. There was a tiny phial half full of a dark-brown liquid, beside it a little leather case lay open, and across the case, ready for use or waiting to be filled, was a bright morphia needle. Ricardo felt the cold creep along his spine, and shivered.

"Come," whispered Hanaud.

They reached the foot of a flight of stairs, and cautiously mounted it. They came out in a passage which ran along the side of the house from the

back to the front. It was unlighted, but they were
now on the level of the street, and a fan-shaped
glass window over the front door admitted a pale
light. There was a street lamp near to the door,
Ricardo remembered. For by the light of it Marthe
Gobin had seen Celia Harland run so nimbly into
this house.

For a moment the men in the passage held their
breath. Some one strode heavily by on the pavement outside—to Mr. Ricardo's ear a most com-
panionable sound. Then a clock upon a church
struck the half-hour musically, distantly. It was
half-past eight. And a second afterwards a tiny
bright light shone. Hanaud was directing the light
of a pocket electric torch to the next flight of stairs.

Here the steps were carpeted, and once more the
men crept up. One after another they came out
upon the next landing. It ran, like those below it,
along the side of the house from the back to the
front, and the doors were all upon their left hand.
From beneath the door nearest to them a yellow
line of light streamed out.

They stood in the darkness listening. But not a
sound came from behind the door. Was this room
empty, too? In each one's mind was the fear that
the birds had flown. Lemerre carefully took the
handle of the door and turned it. Very slowly and
cautiously he opened the door. A strong light
beat out through the widening gap upon his face.
And then, though his feet did not move, his
shoulders and his face drew back. The action was

significant enough.   This room, at all events, was
not empty.   But of what Lemerre saw in the room
his face gave no hint.   He opened the door wider,
and now Hanaud saw.   Ricardo, trembling with
excitement, watched him.   But again there was no
expression of surprise, consternation, or delight.
He stood stolidly and watched.   Then he turned
to Ricardo, placed a finger on his lips, and made
room.   Ricardo crept on tiptoe to his side.   And
now he too could look in.   He saw a brightly lit
bedroom with a made bed.   On his left were the
shuttered windows overlooking the lake.   On his
right in the partition wall a door stood open.
Through the door he could see a dark, windowless
closet, with a small bed from which the bedclothes
hung and trailed upon the floor, as though some
one had been but now roughly dragged from it.
On a table, close by the door, lay a big green hat
with a brown ostrich feather, and a white cloak.
But the amazing spectacle which kept him riveted
was just in front of him.   An old hag of a woman
was sitting in a chair with her back towards them.
She was mending with a big needle the holes in an
old sack, and while she bent over her work she
crooned to herself some French song.   Every now
and then she raised her eyes, for in front of her,
under her charge, Mlle. Célie, the girl of whom
Hanaud was in search, lay helpless upon a sofa.
The train of her delicate green frock swept the
floor.   She was dressed as Héléne Vauquier had
described.   Her gloved hands were tightly bound

behind her back, her feet were crossed so that she could not have stood, and her ankles were cruelly strapped together. Over her face and eyes a piece of coarse sacking was stretched like a mask, and the ends were roughly sewn together at the back of her head. She lay so still that, but for the labouring of her bosom and a tremor which now and again shook her limbs, the watchers would have thought her dead. She made no struggle of resistance; she lay quiet and still. Once she writhed, but it was with the uneasiness of one in pain, and the moment she stirred the old woman's hand went out to a bright aluminium flask which stood on a little table at her side.

"Keep quiet, little one!" she ordered in a careless, chiding voice, and she rapped with the flask peremptorily upon the table. Immediately, as though the tapping had some strange message of terror for the girl's ear, she stiffened her whole body and lay rigid.

"I am not ready for you yet, little fool," said the old woman, and she bent again to her work.

Ricardo's brain whirled. Here was the girl whom they had come to arrest, who had sprung from the salon with so much activity of youth across the stretch of grass, who had run so quickly and lightly across the pavement into this very house, so that she should not be seen. And now she was lying in her fine and delicate attire a captive, at the mercy of the very people who were her accomplices.

Suddenly a scream rang out in the garden—a shrill, loud scream, close beneath the windows. The old woman sprang to her feet. The girl on the sofa raised her head. The old woman took a step towards the window, and then she swiftly turned towards the door. She saw the men upon the threshold. She uttered a bellow of rage. There is no other word to describe the sound. It was not a human cry; it was the bellow of an angry animal. She reached out her hand towards the flask, but before she could grasp it Hanaud seized her. She burst into a torrent of foul oaths. Hanaud flung her across to Lemerre's officer, who dragged her from the room.

"Quick!" said Hanaud, pointing to the girl, who was now struggling helplessly upon the sofa. "Mlle. Célie!"

Ricardo cut the stitches of the sacking. Hanaud unstrapped her hands and feet. They helped her to sit up. She shook her hands in the air as though they tortured her, and then, in a piteous, whimpering voice, like a child's, she babbled incoherently and whispered prayers. Suddenly the prayers ceased. She sat stiff, with eyes fixed and staring. She was watching Lemerre, and she was watching him fascinated with terror. He was holding in his hand the large, bright aluminium flask. He poured a little of the contents very carefully on to a piece of the sack; and then with an exclamation of anger he turned towards Hanaud. But Hanaud was supporting Celia; and so, as Lemerre turned abruptly towards him with the flask in his hand, he turned abruptly towards Celia too. She wrenched herself from Hanaud's arms, she shrank violently away. Her white face flushed scarlet and grew white again. She screamed loudly, terribly; and after the scream she uttered a strange, weak sigh, and so fell sideways in a swoon. Hanaud caught her as she fell. A light broke over his face.

"Now I understand!" he cried. "Good God! That's horrible."

CHAPTER XIII

IN THE HOUSE AT GENEVA

IT was well, Mr. Ricardo thought, that some one understood. For himself, he frankly admitted that he did not. Indeed, in his view the first principles of reasoning seemed to be set at naught. It was obvious from the solicitude with which Celia Harland was surrounded that every one except himself was convinced of her innocence. Yet it was equally obvious that any one who bore in mind the eight points he had tabulated against her must be convinced of her guilt. Yet again, if she were guilty, how did it happen that she had been so mishandled by her accomplices? He was not allowed, however, to reflect upon these remarkable problems. He had too busy a time of it. At one moment he was running to fetch water wherewith to bathe Celia's forehead. At another, when he had returned with the water, he was distracted by the appearance of Durette, the inspector from Aix, in the doorway.

"We have them both," he said—" Hippolyte and the woman. They were hiding in the garden."

"So I thought," said Hanaud, "when I saw the

door open downstairs, and the morphia-needle on the table."

Lemerre turned to one of the officers.

"Let them be taken with old Jeanne in cabs to the depôt."

And when the man had gone upon his errand Lemerre spoke to Hanaud.

"You will stay here to-night to arrange for their transfer to Aix?

"I will leave Durette behind," answered Hanaud. "I am needed in Aix. We shall make a formal application for the prisoners."

He was kneeling by Celia's side and awkwardly dabbing her forehead with a wet handkerchief. He raised a warning hand. Celia Harland moved and opened her eyes. She sat up on the sofa, shivering, and looked with dazed and wondering eyes from one to another of the strangers who surrounded her. She searched in vain for a familiar face.

"You are amongst good friends, Mlle. Célie," said Hanaud, with great gentleness.

"Oh, I wonder! I wonder!" she cried piteously.

"Be very sure of it," he said heartily, and she clung to the sleeve of his coat with desperate hands.

"I suppose you *are* friends," she said; "else why——?" and she moved her numbed limbs to make certain that she was free. She looked about the room. Her eyes fell upon the sack and widened with terror.

"They came to me a little while ago in that

cupboard there—Adéle and the old woman Jeanne.
They made me get up. They told me they were
going to take me away. They brought my clothes
and dressed me in everything I wore when I came,
so that no single trace of me might be left behind.
Then they tied me." She tore off her gloves and
showed them her lacerated wrists. "I think they
meant to kill me—horribly." And she caught her
breath and whimpered like a child. Her spirit
was broken.

"My poor girl, all that is over," said Hanaud.
And he stood up.

But at the first movement he made she cried
incisively, "No," and tightened the clutch of her
fingers upon his sleeve.

"But, mademoiselle, you are safe," he said, with
a smile. She stared at him stupidly. It seemed
the words had no meaning for her. She would not
let him go. It was only the feel of his coat within
the clutch of her fingers which gave her any comfort.

"I want to be sure that I am safe," she said, with
a wan little smile.

"Tell me, mademoiselle, what have you had to
eat and drink during the last two days?"

"Is it two days?" she asked. "I was in the dark
there. I did not know. A little bread, a little
water."

"That's what is wrong," said Hanaud. "Come,
let us go from here!"

"Yes, yes!" Celia cried eagerly. She rose to
her feet, and tottered. Hanaud put his arm about

her. "You are very kind," she said in a low voice, and again doubt looked out from her face and disappeared. "I am sure that I can trust you."

Ricardo fetched her cloak and slipped it on her shoulders. Then he brought her hat, and she pinned it on. She turned to Hanaud; unconsciously familiar words rose to her lips.

"Is it straight?" she asked. And Hanaud laughed outright, and in a moment Celia smiled herself.

Supported by Hanaud she stumbled down the stairs to the garden. As they passed the open door of the lighted parlour at the back of the house Hanaud turned back to Lemerre and pointed silently to the morphia-needle and the phial. Lemerre nodded his head, and going into the room took them away. They went out again into the garden. Celia Harland threw back her head to the stars and drew in a deep breath of the cool night air.

" I did not think," she said in a low voice, "to see the stars again."

They walked slowly down the length of the garden, and Hanaud lifted her into the launch. She turned and caught his coat.

"You must come too," she said stubbornly.

Hanaud sprang in beside her.

" For to-night," he said gaily, " I am your papa! "

Ricardo and the others followed, and the launch moved out over the lake under the stars. The bow was turned towards Geneva, the water tumbled behind them like white fire, the night breeze blew fresh upon their faces. They disembarked at the landing-stage, and then Lemerre bowed to Celia and took his leave. Hanaud led Celia up on to the balcony of the restaurant and ordered supper. There were people still dining at the tables.

One party indeed sitting late over their coffee Ricardo recognised with a kind of shock. They had taken their places, the very places in which they now sat, before he and Hanaud and Lemerre had left the restaurant upon their expedition of rescue. Into that short interval of time so much that was eventful had been crowded.

Hanaud leaned across the table to Celia and said in a low voice:

"Mademoiselle, if I may suggest it, it would be as well if you put on your gloves; otherwise they may notice your wrists."

Celia followed his advice. She ate some food and drank a glass of champagne. A little colour returned to her cheeks.

"You are very kind to me, you and monsieur your friend," she said, with a smile towards Ricardo. "But for you——" and her voice shook.

"Hush!" said Hanaud—"all that is over; we will not speak of it."

Celia looked out across the road on to the trees, of which the dark foliage was brightened and made pale by the lights of the restaurant. Out on the water some one was singing.

"It seems impossible to me," she said in a low voice, "that I am here, in the open air, and free."

Hanaud looked at his watch.

" Mlle. Célie, it is past ten o'clock. M. Ricardo's car is waiting there under the trees. I want you to drive back to Aix. I have taken rooms for you at an hotel, and there will be a nurse from the hospital to look after you."

" Thank you, monsieur," she said ; " you have thought ol everything. But I shall not need a nurse."

" But you will have a nurse," said Hanaud firmly. "You feel stronger now—yes, but when you lay your head upon your pillow, mademoiselle, it will be a comfort to you to know that you have her within call. And in a day or two," he added gently, "you will perhaps be able to tell us what happened on Tuesday night at the Villa Rose ?"

Celia covered her face with her hands for a few moments. Then she drew them away and said simply :

" Yes, monsieur, I will tell you."

Hanaud bowed to her with a genuine deference.

" Thank you, mademoiselle," he said, and in his voice there was a strong ring of sympathy.

They went downstairs and entered Ricardo's motor-car.

" I want to send a telephone message," said Hanaud, " if you will wait here."

"No!" cried Celia decisively, and she again laid hold of his coat, with a pretty imperiousness, as though he belonged to her.

" But I must," said Hanaud, with a laugh.

"Then I will come too," said Celia, and she opened the door and set a foot upon the step.

"You will not, mademoiselle," said Hanaud, with a laugh. "Will you take your foot back into that car? That is better. Now you will sit with your friend, M. Ricardo, whom, by the way, I have not yet introduced to you. He is a very good friend of yours, mademoiselle, and will in the future be a still better one."

Ricardo felt his conscience rather heavy within him, for he had come out to Geneva with the fixed intention of arresting her as a most dangerous criminal. Even now he could not understand how she could be innocent of a share in Mme. Dauvray's murder. But Hanaud evidently thought she was. And since Hanaud thought so, why, it was better to say nothing if one was sensitive to gibes. So Ricardo sat and talked with her while Hanaud ran back into the restaurant. It mattered very little, however, what he said, for Celia's eyes were fixed upon the doorway through which Hanaud had disappeared. And when he came back she was quick to turn the handle of the door.

"Now, mademoiselle, we will wrap you up in M. Ricardo's spare motor-coat and cover your knees with a rug and put you between us, and then you can go to sleep."

The car sped through the streets of Geneva. Celia Harland, with a little sigh of relief, nestled down between the two men.

"If I knew you better," she said to Hanaud, "I

should tell you—what, of course, I do not tell you now—that I feel as if I had a big Newfoundland dog with me."

"Mlle. Célie," said Hanaud, and his voice told her that he was moved, "that is a very pretty thing which you have said to me."

The lights of the city fell away behind them. Now only a glow in the sky spoke of Geneva; now even that was gone, and with a smooth continuous purr the car glided along the cool, dark road. The great head-lamps threw a bright circle of light before them, and the road slipped away beneath the wheels like a running tide. Celia fell asleep. Even when the càr stopped at the Pont de la Caille she did not waken. The door was opened, a search for contraband was made, the book was signed. Still she did not wake. The car sped onwards.

"You see coming into France *is* a different affair," said Hanaud.

"Yes," replied Ricardo.

"Still—I will own it—you caught me napping yesterday."

"I did?" cried Ricardo joyfully.

"You did," returned Hanaud. "I had never heard of the Pont de la Caille. But you will not mention it? You will not ruin me?"

"I will not," said Mr. Ricardo, superb in his magnanimity. "You are a good detective."

"Thank you! thank you!" cried Hanaud in a voice which shook—surely with emotion. He wrung Ricardo's hand. He wiped an imaginary tear from his eye.

And still Celia slept. Mr. Ricardo looked at her. He bent to Hanaud and said in a whisper:

"Yet I do not understand. The car, though no serious search was made, must still have stopped on the Swiss side of the Pont de la Caille. Why did she not cry for help then? One cry and she was safe. A movement even was enough. Do you understand?"

"I think so," Hanaud answered, with a very gentle look at Celia. "Poor girl, I think so."

When Celia was aroused she found that the car had stopped before the door of an hotel, and that a woman in the dress of a nurse was standing in the doorway.

"You can trust Marie," said Hanaud. And Celia turned as she stood upon the ground and gave her hands to the two men.

"Thank you! Thank you both!" she said in a trembling voice. She looked at Hanaud and nodded her head. "You understand why I thank you so very much?"

"Yes," said Hanaud. "But, mademoiselle"—and he bent over the car and spoke to her quietly, holding her hand—"there is *always* a big New-foundland dog in the worst of troubles—if only you will look for him. I tell you so—I, who belong to the Sûreté in Paris. Do not lose heart!" And in his mind he added: "God forgive me for the lie." He shook her hand and let it go; and gathering up her skirt she went into the hall of the hotel.

Hanaud watched her as she went. She was to him a lonely and pathetic creature, in spite of the nurse who bore her company.

"You must be a good friend to that young girl, M. Ricardo," he said. " Let us drive to your hotel."

"Yes," said Ricardo. And as they went the curiosity which all the way from Geneva had been smouldering within him burst into flame.

" Will you explain to me one thing?" he asked. " When the scream came from the garden you were not surprised. Indeed, you said that when you saw the open door and the morphia-needle on the table of the little room downstairs you thought Adèle and the man Hippolyte were hiding in the garden."

" Yes, I did think so."

"Why? And why did the publication that the jewels had been discovered so alarm you?"

" Ah!" said Hanaud. " Did not you understand that? Yet it is surely clear and obvious, if you once grant that the girl was innocent, was a witness of the crime, and was now in the hands of the criminals. Grant me those premisses, M. Ricardo, for a moment, and you will see that we had just one chance of finding the girl alive in Geneva. From the first I was sure of that. What was the one chance? Why, this! She might be kept alive on the chance that she could be forced to tell what, by the way, she did not know, namely, the place where Mme. Dauvray's valuable jewels were secreted. Now, follow this. We, the police, find the jewels and take charge of them. Let that news reach the house in Geneva, and on the same night Mlle. Célie loses her life, and not—very pleasantly. They have no further use for her. She is merely a danger to them. So I take my pre-cautions—never mind for the moment what they were. I take care that if the murderer is in Aix and gets wind of our discovery he shall not be able to communicate his news."

"The Post Office would have stopped letters or telegrams," said Ricardo. "I understand."

"On the contrary," replied Hanaud. "No, I took my precautions, which were of quite a different kind, before I knew the house in Geneva or the name of Rossignol. But one way of communication I did not think of. I did not think of the possibility that the news might be sent to a newspaper, which of course would publish it and cry it through the streets of Geneva. The moment I heard the news I knew we must hurry. The garden of the house ran down to the lake. A means of disposing of Mlle. Célie was close at hand. And the night had fallen. As it was, we arrived just in time, and no earlier than just in time. The paper had been bought, the message had reached the house, Mlle. Célie was no longer of any use, and every hour she stayed in that house was of course an hour of danger to her captors."

"What were they going to do ?" asked Ricardo.

Hanaud shrugged his shoulders.

"It is not pretty—what they were going to do. We reach the garden in our launch. At that moment Hippolyte and Adéle, who is most likely Hippolyte's wife, are in the lighted parlour on the basement floor. Adéle is preparing her morphia-needle. Hippolyte is going to get ready the rowing-boat which was tied at the end of the landing-stage. Quietly as we came into the bank, they heard or saw us. They ran out and hid in the garden, having no time to lock the garden door, or perhaps not daring to lock it lest the sound of the key should reach our ears. We find that door upon the latch, the door of the room open; on the table lies the morphia-needle. Upstairs lies Mlle. Célie— she is helpless, she cannot see what they are meaning to do."

"But she could cry out," exclaimed Ricardo. "She did not even do that!"

"No, my friend, she could not cry out," replied Hanaud very seriously. "I know why. She could not. No living man or woman could. Rest assured of that!"

Ricardo was mystified; but since the captain of the ship would not show his observation, he knew it would be in vain to press him.

"Well, while Adéle was preparing her morphia-needle and Hippolyte was about to prepare the boat, Jeanne upstairs was making her preparation too. She was mending a sack. Did you see Mlle. Célie's eyes and face when first she saw that sack? Ah! she understood! They meant to give her a dose of morphia, and, as soon as she became unconscious, they were going, perhaps, to take some terrible precaution." Hanaud paused for a second. "I only say perhaps as to that. Certainly they were going to sew her up in that sack, row her well out across the lake, fix a weight to her feet, and drop her quietly overboard. She was to wear everything which she had brought with her to the house. Mlle. Célie would have disappeared for ever, and left not even a ripple upon the water to trace her by!"

Ricardo clenched his hands.

"But that's horrible!" he cried; and as he uttered the words the car swerved into the drive and stopped before the door of the Hôtel Majestic.

Ricardo sprang out. A feeling of remorse seized hold of him. All through that evening he had not given one thought to Harry Wethermill, so utterly had the excitement of each moment engrossed his mind.

"He will be glad to know!" cried Ricardo. "To-night, at all events, he shall sleep. I ought to have telegraphed to him from Geneva that we and Miss Celia were coming back." He ran up the steps into the hotel.

"I took care that he should know," said Hanaud, as he followed in Ricardo's steps.

"Then the message could not have reached him, else he would have been expecting us," replied Ricardo, as he hurried into the office, where a clerk sat at his books.

"Is Mr. Wethermill in?" he asked.

The clerk eyed him strangely.

"Mr. Wethermill was arrested this evening," he said.

Ricardo stepped back.

"Arrested! When?"

"At twenty-five minutes past ten," replied the clerk shortly.

"Ah," said Hanaud quietly. "That was my telephone message."

Ricardo stared in stupefaction at his companion.

"Arrested!" he cried. "Arrested! But what for?"

"For the murders of Marthe Gobin and Mme. Dauvray," said Hanaud. "Good-night."

CHAPTER XIV

MR. RICARDO IS BEWILDERED

RICARDO passed a most tempestuous night. He was tossed amongst dark problems. Now it was Harry Wethermill who beset him. He repeated and repeated the name, trying to grasp the new and sinister suggestion which, if Hanaud were right, its sound must henceforth bear. Of course Hanaud might be wrong. Only, if he were wrong, how had he come to suspect Harry Wethermill? What had first directed his thoughts to that seemingly heart-broken man? And when? Certain recollections became vivid in Mr. Ricardo's mind —the luncheon at the Villa Rose, for instance. Hanaud had been so insistent that the woman with the red hair was to be found in Geneva, had so clearly laid it down that a message, a telegram, a letter from Aix to Geneva, would enable him to lay his hands upon the murderer in Aix. He was isolating the house in Geneva even so early in the history of his investigations, even so soon he suspected Harry Wethermill. Brains and audacity—yes, these two qualities he had stipulated in the criminal. Ricardo now for the first time

understood the trend of all Hanaud's talk at that
luncheon.   He was putting Harry Wethermill upon
his guard, he was immobilising him, he was fettering
him in precautions; with a subtle skill he was
forcing him to isolate himself.   And he was doing
it deliberately to save the life of Celia Harland in
Geneva.   Once Ricardo lifted himself up with the
hair stirring on his scalp.   He himself had been
with Wethermill in the baccarat-rooms on the
very night of the murder.   They had walked
together up the hill to the hotel.   It could not
be that Harry Wethermill was guilty.   And yet,
he suddenly remembered, they had together left
the rooms at an early hour.   It was only ten
o'clock when they had separated in the hall, when
they had gone each to his own room.   There
would have been time for Wethermill to reach
the Villa Rose and do his dreadful work upon
that night before twelve, if all had been arranged
beforehand, if all went as it had been arranged.
And as he thought upon the careful planning of
that crime, and remembered Wethermill's easy
chatter as they had strolled from table to table in
the Villa des Fleurs, Ricardo shuddered.   Though
he encouraged a taste for the bizarre, it was with an
effort.   He was naturally of an orderly mind, and
to touch the eerie or inhuman caused him a physical
discomfort.   So now he marvelled in a great uneasiness at the calm placidity with which Wethermill had talked, his arm in his, while the load of
so dark a crime to be committed within the hour

lay upon his mind.   Each minute he must have
been thinking, with a swift spasm of the heart,
" Should such a precaution fail—should such or
such an unforeseen thing intervene," yet there had
been never a sign of disturbance, never a hint of
any disquietude.

Then Ricardo's thoughts turned, as he tossed upon
his bed, to Celia Harland, a tragic and a lonely
figure.   He recalled the look of tenderness upon her
face when her eyes had met Harry Wethermill's
across the baccarat-table in the Villa des Fleurs.
He gained some insight into the reason why she had
clung so desperately to Hanaud's coat-sleeve
yesterday.   Not merely had he saved her life.   She
was lying with all her world of trust and illusion
broken about her, and Hanaud had raised her up.
She had found some one whom she trusted—the
big Newfoundland dog, as she expressed it.   Mr.
Ricardo was still thinking of Celia Harland when
the morning came.   He fell asleep, and awoke to
find Hanaud by his bed.

" You will be wanted to-day," said Hanaud.

Ricardo got up and walked down from the hotel
with the detective.   The front door faces the hill-
side of Mont Revard, and on this side Mr. Ricardo's
rooms looked out.   The drive from the front door
curves round the end of the long building and joins
the road, which then winds down towards the town
past the garden at the back of the hotel.   Down
this road the two men walked, while the supporting
wall of the garden upon their right hand grew

higher and higher above their heads. They came
to a steep flight of steps which makes a short cut
from the hotel to the road, and at the steps Hanaud
stopped.

"Do you see?" he said. "On the opposite side
there are no houses; there is only a wall. Behind
the wall there are climbing gardens and the ground
falls steeply to the turn of the road below. There's
a flight of steps leading down which corresponds
with the flight of steps from the garden. Very
often there's a *serjent-de-ville* stationed on the top
of the steps. But there was not one there yesterday afternoon at three. Behind us is the supporting
wall of the hotel garden. Well, look about you.
We cannot be seen from the hotel. There's not
a soul in sight—yes, there's some one coming up
the hill, but we have been standing here quite
long enough for you to stab me and get back to
your coffee on the verandah of the hotel."

Ricardo started back.

"Marthe Gobin!" he cried. "It was here,
then?"

Hanaud nodded.

"When we returned from the station in your
motor-car and went up to your rooms we passed
Harry Wethermill sitting upon the verandah over
the garden drinking his coffee. He had the news
then that Marthe Gobin was on her way."

"But you had isolated the house in Geneva.
How could he have the news?" exclaimed Ricardo,
whose brain was whirling.

" I had isolated the house from him, in the sense that he dared not communicate with his accomplices. That is what you have to remember. He could not even let them know that they must not communicate with him. So he received a telegram. It was carefully worded. No doubt he had arranged the wording of any message with the care which was used in all the preparations. It ran like this "— and Hanaud took a scrap of paper from his pocket and read out from it a copy of the telegram : " ' Agent arrives Aix 3.7 to negotiate purchase of your patent.' The telegram was handed in at Geneva station at 12.45, five minutes after the train had left which carried Marthe Gobin to Aix. And more, it was handed in by a man strongly resembling Hippolyte Tacé—that we know."

" That was madness," said Ricardo.

" But what else could they do over there in Geneva ? They did not know that Harry Wethermill was suspected. Harry Wethermill had no idea of it himself. But, even if they had known, they must take the risk. Put yourself into their place for a moment. They had seen my advertisement about Célie Harland in the Geneva paper. Marthe Gobin, that busybody who was always watching her neighbours, was no doubt watched the next day herself. They see her leave the house, an unusual proceeding for her with her husband ill, as her own letter tells us. Hippolyte follows her to the station, sees her take her ticket to Aix and mount into the train. He must guess at once that she saw Célie Harland enter their house, that she is travelling to Aix with the information of her whereabouts. At all costs she must be prevented from giving that information. At all risks, there-fore, the warning telegram must be sent to Harry Wethermill."

Ricardo recognised the force of the argument.

"If only you had heard of the telegram yesterday in time!" he cried.

"Ah, yes!" Hanaud agreed. "But it was only sent off at a quarter to one. It was delivered to Wethermill and a copy was sent to the Prefecture, but the telegram was delivered first."

"When was it delivered to Wethermill?" asked Ricardo.

"At three. We had already left for the station. Wethermill was sitting on the verandah. The telegram was brought to him there. It was brought by a waiter in the hotel who remembers the incident very well. Wethermill has seven minutes and the time it will take for Marthe Gobin to drive from the station to the Majestic. What does he do? He runs up first to your rooms, very likely not yet knowing what he must do. He runs up to verify his telegram."

"Are you sure of that?" cried Ricardo. "How can you be? You were at the station with me. What makes you sure?"

Hanaud produced a brown kid glove from his pocket.

"This."

"That is your glove ; you told me so yesterday."

"I told you so," replied Hanaud calmly; "but it is not my glove. It is Wethermill's ; there are his initials stamped upon the lining—see? I picked up that glove in your room, after we had returned from the station. It was not there before. He went to your rooms. No doubt he searched for a telegram. Fortunately he did not examine your letters, or Marthe Gobin would never have spoken to us as she did after she was dead."

"Then what did he do?" asked Ricardo eagerly; and, though Hanaud had been with him at the entrance to the station all this while, he asked the question in absolute confidence that the true answer would be given to him.

"He returned to the verandah wondering what he should do. He saw us come back from the station in the motor-car and go up to your room. We were alone. Marthe Gobin, then, was following. There was his chance. Marthe Gobin must not reach us, must not tell her news to us. He ran down the garden steps to the gate. No one could see him from the hotel. Very likely he hid behind the trees, whence he could watch the road. A cab comes up the hill; there's a woman in it—not quite the kind of woman who stays at your hotel, M. Ricardo. Yet she must be going to your hotel, for the road ends. The driver is nodding on his box, refusing to pay any heed to his fare lest again she should bid him hurry. His horse is moving at a walk. Wethermill puts his head in at the window and asks if she has come to see M. Ricardo. Anxious for her four thousand francs, she answers 'Yes.' Perhaps he steps into the cab, perhaps as he walks by the side he strikes, and strikes hard and strikes surely. Long before the cab reaches the hotel he is back again on the verandah."

" Yes," said Ricardo, " it's the daring of which you spoke which made the crime possible—the same daring which made him seek your help. That was unexampled."

"No," replied Hanaud. "There's an historic crime in your own country, monsieur. Cries for help were heard in a by-street of a town. When people ran to answer them, a man was found kneeling by a corpse. It was the kneeling man who cried for help, but it was also the kneeling man who did the murder. I remembered that when I first began to suspect Harry Wethermill."

Ricardo turned eagerly.

" And when—when did you first begin to suspect Harry Wethermill ? "

Hanaud smiled and shook his head.

"That you shall know in good time. I am the captain of the ship." His voice took on a deeper note. " But I prepare you. Listen! Daring and brains, those were the property of Harry Wethermill—yes. But it is not he who is the chief actor in the crime. Of that I am sure. He was no more than one of the instruments."

" One of the instruments ? Used, then, by whom ? " asked Ricardo.

"By my Normandy peasant-woman, M. Ricardo," said Hanaud. "Yes, there's the dominating figure— cruel, masterful, relentless—that strange woman, Héléne Vauquier. You are surprised? You will see! It is not the man of intellect and daring; it's my peasant-woman who is at the bottom of it all."

"But she's free!" exclaimed Ricardo. "You let her go free!"

"Free!" repeated Ricardo. "She was driven straight from the Villà Rose to the depôt. She has been kept *au secret* ever since."

Ricardo stared in amazement.

"Already you knew of her guilt?"

"Already she had lied to me in her description of Adéle Rossignol. Do you remember what she said—a black-haired woman with beady eyes; and I only five minutes before had picked up from the table—this."

He opened his pocket-book, and took from an envelope a long strand of red hair.

"But it was not only because she lied that I had her taken to the depôt. A pot of cold cream had disappeared from the room of Mlle. Célie."

"Then Perrichet after all was right."

"Perrichet after all was quite wrong—not to hold his tongue. For in that pot of cold cream, as I was sure, were hidden those valuable diamond earrings which Mlle. Célie habitually wore."

The two men had reached the square in front of the Établissement des Bains. Ricardo dropped on to a bench and wiped his forehead.

"But I am in a maze," he cried. "My head turns
round. I don't know where I am."

Hanaud stood in front of Ricardo, smiling. He
was not displeased with his companion's bewilder-
ment; it was all so much of tribute to himself.

"I am the captain of the ship," he said.

·His smile irritated Ricardo, who spoke impatiently.

"I should be very glad," he said, "if you would
tell me how you discovered all these things. And
what it was that the little salon on the first morning
had to tell to you? And why Célia Harland ran
from the glass doors across the grass to the motor-
car and again from the carriage into the house on
the lake? Why she did not resist yesterday
evening? Why she did not cry for help? How
much of Héléne Vauquier's evidence was true and
how much false? For what reason Wethermill
concerned himself in this affair? Oh! and a
thousand things which I don't understand."

"Ah, the cushions, and the scrap of paper, and
the aluminium flask," said Hanaud; and the triumph
faded from his face. He spoke now to Ricardo
with a genuine friendliness. "You must not be
angry with me if I keep you in the dark for a little
while. I, too, M. Ricardo, have artistic inclinations.
I will not spoil the remarkable story which I think
Mlle. Célie will be ready to tell us. Afterwards I
will willingly explain to you what I read in the
evidences of the room, and what so greatly puzzled
me then. But it is not the puzzle or its solution,"

he said modestly, "which is most interesting here. Consider the people. Mme. Dauvray, the old, rich, ignorant woman, with her superstitions and her generosity, her desire to converse with Mme. de Montespan and the great ladies of the past, and her love of a young, fresh face about her; Héléne Vauquier, the maid with her seven years of confidential service, who finds herself suddenly supplanted and made to tend and dress in dainty frocks the girl who has supplanted her; the young girl herself, that poor child, with her love of fine clothes; the Bohemian who, brought up amidst trickeries and practising them as a profession, looking upon them and upon misery and starvation and despair as the commonplaces of life, keeps a simplicity and a delicacy and a freshness which would have withered in a day had she been brought up otherwise; Harry Wethermill, the courted and successful man of genius. Just imagine, if you can, what his feelings must have been when in Mme. Dauvray's bedroom, with the woman he had uselessly murdered lying rigid beneath the sheet, he saw me raise the block of wood from the inlaid floor and take out one by one those jewel-cases for which, less than twelve hours before, he had been ransacking that very room. But what he must have felt! And to show no sign! Oh, these people are the interesting problems in this story. Let us hear what happened on that terrible night. The puzzle—that can wait."

In Mr. Ricardo's view Hanaud was proved right. The extraordinary and appalling story which was gradually unrolled of what had happened on that night of Tuesday in the Villa Rose exceeded in its grim interest all the mystery of the puzzle. But it was not told at once.

The trouble at first with Mlle. Célie was a fear of sleep. She dared not sleep—even with a light in the room and a nurse at her bedside. When her eyes were actually closing she would force herself desperately back into the living world. For when she slept she dreamed through again that dark and dreadful night of Tuesday and the two days which followed it, until at some moment endurance snapped and she woke up screaming. But youth, a good constitution, and a healthy appetite had their way with her in the end.

She told her share of the story—she told what happened. There was apparently one terrible scene when she was confronted with Harry Wethermill in the office of Monsieur Fleuriot, the Juge d'Instruction, and on her knees, with the tears streaming down her face, besought him to confess the truth. For a long while he held out. And then there came a strange and human turn to the affair. Adéle Rossignol—or, to give her real name, Adéle Tacé, the wife of Hippolyte—had conceived a veritable passion for Harry Wethermill. He was of a not uncommon type, cold and callous in himself, yet with the power to provoke passion in women. And Adéle Tacé, as the story was told of how Harry Wethermill had paid his court to Celia Harland, was seized with a vindictive jealousy.

Hanaud was not surprised. He knew the woman-criminal of his country—brutal, passionate, treacherous. The anonymous letters in a woman's handwriting which descend upon the Rue de Jerusalem, and betray the men who have committed thefts, had left him no illusions upon that figure in the history of crime. Adéle Rossignol ran forward to confess, so that Harry Wethermill might suffer to the last possible point of suffering. Then at last Wethermill gave in and, broken down by the ceaseless interrogations of the magistrate, confessed in his turn too. The one, and the only one, who stood firmly throughout and denied the crime was Héléne Vauquier. Her thin lips were kept contemptuously closed, whatever the others might admit. With a white, hard face, quietly and respectfully she faced the magistrate week after week. She was the perfect picture of a servant who knew her place. And nothing was wrung from her. But without her help the story became complete. And Ricardo was at pains to write it out.

CHAPTER XV

CELIA'S STORY

THE story begins with the explanation of that circumstance which had greatly puzzled Mr. Ricardo—Celia's entry into the household of Mme. Dauvray.

Celia's father was a Captain Harland, of a marching regiment, who had little beyond good looks and excellent manners wherewith to support his position. He was extravagant in his tastes, and of an easy mind in the presence of embarrassments. To his other disadvantages he added that of falling in love with a pretty girl no better off than himself. They married, and Celia was born. For nine years they managed, through the wife's constant devotion, to struggle along and to give their daughter an education. Then, however, Celia's mother broke down under the strain and died. Captain Harland, a couple of years later, went out of the service with discredit, passed through the bankruptcy court, and turned showman. His line was thought-reading; he enlisted the services of his daughter, taught her the tricks of his trade, and became " The Great Fortinbras " of the music-halls. Captain Harland would move amongst the audience, asking the spectators in a whisper to think of a number or of an article in their pockets, after the usual fashion, while the child, in her short frock, with her long fair hair tied back with a ribbon, would stand blind-folded upon the platform and reel off the answers with astonishing rapidity. She was singularly quick, singularly receptive.

The undoubted cleverness of the performance, and the beauty of the child, brought to them a temporary prosperity. The Great Fortinbras rose from the music-halls to the assembly rooms of provincial towns. The performance became genteel, and ladies flocked to the *matinées*.

The Great Fortinbras dropped his pseudonym and became once more Captain Harland.

As Celia grew up, he tried a yet higher flight— he became a spiritualist, with Celia for his medium. The thought-reading entertainments became thrilling séances, and the beautiful child, now grown into a beautiful girl of seventeen, created a greater sensation as a medium in a trance than she had done as a lightning thought-reader.

"I saw no harm in it," Celia explained to M. Fleuriot, without any attempt at extenuation. "I never understood that we might be doing any hurt to any one. People were interested. They were to find us out if they could, and they tried to and they couldn't. I looked upon it quite simply in that way. It was just my profession. I accepted it without any question. I was not troubled about it until I came to Aix."

A startling exposure, however, at Cambridge discredited the craze for spiritualism, and Captain Harland's fortunes declined. He crossed with his daughter to France and made a disastrous tour in that country, wasted the last of his resources in the Casino at Dieppe, and died in that town, leaving Celia just enough money to bury him and to pay her third-class fare to Paris.

There she lived honestly but miserably. The slimness of her figure and a grace of movement which was particularly hers obtained her at last a situation as a *mannequin* in the show-rooms of a modiste. She took a room on the top floor of a house in the Rue St. Honoré and settled down to a hard and penurious life.

"I was not happy or contented—no," said Celia frankly and decisively. "The long hours in the close rooms gave me headaches and made me nervous. I had not the temperament. And I was very lonely—my life had been so different. I had had fresh air, good clothes, and freedom. Now all was changed. I used to cry myself to sleep up in my little room, wondering whether I would ever have friends. You see, I was quite young—only eighteen—and I wanted to live."

A change came in a few months, but a disastrous change. The modiste failed. Celia was thrown out of work, and could get nothing to do. Gradually she pawned what clothes she could spare; and then there came a morning when she had a single five-franc piece in the world and owed a month's rent for her room. She kept the five-franc piece all day and went hungry, seeking for work. In the evening she went to a provision shop to buy food, and the man behind the counter took the five-franc piece. He looked at it, rung it on the counter, and, with a laugh, bent it easily in half.

"See here, my little one," he said, tossing the coin back to her, "one does not buy good food with lead."

Celia dragged herself out of the shop in despair. She was starving. She dared not go back to her room. The thought of the concierge at the bottom of the stairs, insistent for the rent, frightened her. She stood on the pavement and burst into tears. A few people stopped and watched her curiously, and went on again. Finally a *sergent-de-ville* told her to go away.

The girl moved on with the tears running down her cheeks. She was desperate, she was lonely.

"I thought of throwing myself into the Seine," said Celia simply, in telling her story to the Juge d'Instruction. "Indeed, I went to the river. But the water looked so cold, so terrible, and I was young. I wanted so much to live. And then—the night came, and the lights made the city bright, and I was very tired and—and——"

And, in a word, the young girl went up to Montmartre in desperation, as quickly as her tired legs would carry her. She walked once or twice timidly past the restaurants, and, finally, entered one of them, hoping that some one would take pity on her and give her some supper. She stood just within the door of the supper-room. People pushed past her—men in evening dress, women in bright frocks and jewels. No one noticed her. She had shrunk into a corner, rather hoping not to be noticed, now that she had come. But the novelty of her surroundings wore off. She knew that for want of food she was almost fainting. There were two girls engaged by the management to dance amongst the tables while people had supper—one dressed as a page in blue satin, and the other as a Spanish dancer. Both girls were kind. They spoke to Celia between their dances. They let her waltz with them. Still no one noticed her. She had no jewels, no fine clothes, no *chic*— the three indispensable things. She had only youth and a pretty face.

"But," said Celia, "without jewels and fine clothes and *chic* these go for nothing in Paris. At last, however, Mme. Dauvray came in with a party of friends from a theatre, and she saw how unhappy I was, and gave me some supper. She asked me about myself, and I told her. She was very kind, and took me home with her, and I cried all the way in the carriage. She kept me a few days, and then she told me that I was to live with her, for often she was lonely too, and that if I would she would some day find me a nice, comfortable husband and give me a marriage portion. So all my troubles seemed to be at an end," said Celia, with a smile.

Within a fortnight Mme. Dauvray confided to

Celia that there was a new fortune-teller come to Paris, who, by looking into a crystal, could tell the most wonderful things about the future. The old woman's eyes kindled as she spoke. She took Celia to the fortune-teller's rooms next day, and the girl quickly understood the ruling passion of the woman who had befriended her. It took very little time then for Celia to notice how easily Mme. Dauvray was duped, how perpetually she was robbed. Celia turned the problem over in her mind.

" Madame had been very good to me. She was kind and simple," said Celia, with a very genuine affection in her voice. " The people whom we knew laughed at her, and were ungenerous. But there are many women whom the world respects who are worse than ever was poor Mme. Dauvray. I was very fond of her, so I proposed to her that we should hold a séance, and I would bring people from the spirit world. I knew that I could amuse her with something much more clever and more interesting than the fortune-tellers. And at the same time I could save her from being plundered. That was all I thought about."

That was all she thought about, yes. She left Héléne Vauquier out of her calculations, and she did not foresee the effect of her séances upon Mme. Dauvray. Celia had no suspicions of Héléne Vauquier. She would have laughed if any one had told her that this respectable and respectful middle-aged woman, who was so attentive, so neat,

so grateful for any kindness, was really nursing a
rancorous hatred against her. Celia had sprung
from Montmartre suddenly; therefore Héléne
Vauquier despised her. Celia had taken her place
in Mme. Dauvray's confidence, had deposed her
unwittingly, had turned the confidential friend into
a mere servant; therefore Héléne Vauquier hated
her. And her hatred reached out beyond the girl,
and embraced the old, superstitious, foolish woman,
whom a young and pretty face could so easily
beguile. Héléne Vauquier despised them both,
hated them both, and yet must nurse her rancour
in silence and futility. Then came the séances,
and at once, to add fuel to her hatred, she found
herself stripped of those gifts and commissions
which she had exacted from the herd of common
tricksters who had been wont to make their harvest
out of Mme. Dauvray. Héléne Vauquier was
avaricious and greedy, like so many of her class.
Her hatred of Celia, her contempt for Mme.
Dauvray, grew into a very delirium. But it was
a delirium she had the cunning to conceal. She
lived at white heat, but to all the world she had
lost nothing of her calm.

Celia did not foresee the hatred she was arousing;
nor, on the other hand, did she foresee the overwhelming effect of these spiritualistic séances on
Mme. Dauvray. Celia had never been brought
quite close to the credulous before.

"There had always been the row of footlights,"
she said. "I was on the platform; the audience

was in the hall; or, if it was at a house, my father made the arrangements. I only came in at the last moment, played my part, and went away. It was never brought home to me that some amongst these people really and truly believed. I did not think about it. Now, however, when I saw Mme. Dauvray so feverish, so excited, so firmly convinced that great ladies from the spirit world came and spoke to her, I became terrified. I had aroused a passion which I had not suspected. I tried to stop the séances, but I was not allowed. I had aroused a passion which I could not control. I was afraid that Mme. Dauvray's whole life—it seems absurd to those who did not know her, but those who did will understand—yes, her whole life and happiness would be spoilt if she discovered that what she believed in was all a trick."

She spoke with a simplicity and a remorse which it was difficult to disbelieve. M. Fleuriot, the judge, now at last convinced that the Dreyfus affair was for nothing in the history of this crime, listened to her with sympathy.

"That is your explanation, mademoiselle," he said gently. "But I must tell you that we have another."

"Yes, monsieur?" Celia asked.

"Given by Héléne Vauquier," said Fleuriot.

Even after these days Celia could not hear that woman's name without a shudder of fear and a flinching of her whole body. Her face grew white, her lips dry.

"I know, monsieur, that Héléne Vauquier is not my friend," she said. "I was taught that very cruelly."

"Listen, mademoiselle, to what she says," said the judge, and he read out to Celia an extract or two from Hanaud's report of his first interview with Héléne Vauquier in her bedroom at the Villa Rose.

"You hear what she says. 'Mme. Dauvray would have had séances all day, but Mlle. Célie pleaded that she was left exhausted at the end of them. But Mlle. Célie was of an address.' And again, speaking of Mme. Dauvray's queer craze that the spirit of Mme. de Montespan should be called up, Héléne Vauquier says : 'She was never gratified. Always she hoped. Always Mlle. Célie tantalised her with the hope. She would not spoil her fine affairs by making these treats too common.' Thus she attributes your reluctance to multiply your experiments to a desire to make the most profit possible out of your wares, like a good business woman."

"It is not true, monsieur," cried Celia earnestly. "I tried to stop the séances because now for the first time I recognised that I had been playing with a dangerous thing. It was a revelation to me. I did not know what to do. Mme. Dauvray would promise me everything, give me everything, if only I would consent when I refused. I was terribly frightened of what would happen. I did not want power over people. I knew it was not good for her that she should suffer so much excitement. No, I did not know what to do. And so we all moved to Aix."

And there she met Harry Wethermill on the second day after her arrival, and proceeded straightway for the first time to fall in love. To Celia it seemed that at last that had happened for which she had so longed. She began really to live as she understood life at this time. The day, until she met Harry Wethermill, was one flash of joyous expectation; the hours when they were together a time of contentment which thrilled with some chance meeting of the hands into an exquisite happiness. Mme. Dauvray understood quickly what was the matter, and laughed at her affectionately.

"Célie, my dear," she said, "your friend, M. Wethermill—'Arry, is it not? See, I pronounce your tongue—will not be as comfortable as the nice, fat, bourgeois gentleman I meant to find for you. But, since you are young, naturally you want storms. And there will be storms, Célie," she concluded, with a laugh.

Celia blushed.

"I suppose there will," she said regretfully. There were, indeed, moments when she was frightened of Harry Wethermill, but frightened with a delicious thrill of knowledge that he was only stern because he cared so much.

But in a day or two there began to intrude upon her happiness a stinging dissatisfaction with her

past life. At times she fell into melancholy, com-
paring her career with that of the man who loved
her. At times she came near to an extreme irri-
tation with Héléne Vauquier. Her lover was in
her thoughts. As she put it herself:

"I wanted always to look my best, and always
to be very good."

Good in the essentials of life, that is to be understood. She had lived in a lax world. She was
not particularly troubled by the character of her
associates; she was untouched by them; she liked
her fling at the baccarat-tables. These were details, and did not distress her. Love had not turned
her into a Puritan. But certain recollections
plagued her soul. The visit to the restaurant at
Montmartre, for instance, and the séances. Of
these, indeed, she thought to have made an end.
There were the baccarat-rooms, the beauty of the
town and the neighbourhood to distract Mme.
Dauvray. Celia kept her thoughts away from
séances. There was no séance as yet held in the
Villa Rose. And there would have been none but
for Héléne Vauquier.

One evening, however, as Harry Wethermill
walked down from the Cercle to the Villa des
Fleurs, a woman's voice spoke to him from behind.

"Monsieur!"

He turned and saw Mme. Dauvray's maid. He
stopped under a street lamp, and said:

"Well, what can I do for you?"

The woman hesitated.

"I hope monsieur will pardon me," she said
humbly. "I am committing a great impertinence.
But I think monsieur is not very kind to Mlle.
Célie."

Wethermill stared at her.

"What on earth do you mean?" he asked
angrily.

Héléne Vauquier looked him quietly in the face.

"It is plain, monsieur, that Mlle. Célie loves
monsieur. Monsieur has led her on to love him.
But it is also plain to a woman with quick eyes
that monsieur himself cares no more for mademoiselle than for the button on his coat. It is
not very kind to spoil the happiness of a young
and pretty girl, monsieur."

Nothing could have been more respectful than
the manner in which these words were uttered.
Wethermill was taken in by it. He protested
earnestly, fearing lest the maid should become an
enemy.

"Héléne, it is not true that I am playing with
Mlle. Célie. Why should I not care for her?"

Héléne Vauquier shrugged her shoulders. The
question needed no answer.

"Why should I seek her so often if I did not
care?"

And to this question Héléne Vauquier smiled—
a quiet, slow, confidential smile.

"What does monsieur want of Mme. Dauvray?"
she asked. And the question was her answer.

Wethermill stood silent. Then he said abruptly:

"Nothing, of course; nothing." And he walked away.

But the smile remained on Hélène Vauquier's face. What did they all want of Mme. Dauvray? She knew very well. It was what she herself wanted—with other things. It was money—always money. Wethermill was not the first to seek the good graces of Mme. Dauvray through her pretty companion. Hélène Vauquier went home. She was not discontented with her conversation. Wethermill had paused long enough before he denied the suggestion of her words. She approached him a few days later a second time and more openly. She was shopping in the Rue du Casino when he passed her. He stopped of his own accord and spoke to her. Hélène Vauquier kept a grave and respectful face. But there was a pulse of joy at her heart. He was coming to her hand.

"Monsieur," she said, "you do not go the right way." And again her strange smile illuminated her face. "Mlle. Célie sets a guard about Mme. Dauvray. She will not give to people the opportunity to find madame generous."

"Oh," said Wethermill slowly. "Is that so?" And he turned and walked by Hélène Vauquier's side.

"Never speak of Mme. Dauvray's wealth, monsieur, if you would keep the favour of Mlle. Célie. She is young, but she knows her world."

"I have not spoken of money to her," replied

Wethermill; and then he burst out laughing. "But why should you think that I—I, of all men—want money?" he asked.

And Héléne answered him again enigmatically.

"If I am wrong, monsieur, I am sorry, but you can help me too," she said, in her submissive voice. And she passed on, leaving Wethermill rooted to the ground.

It was a bargain she proposed—the impertinence of it! It was a bargain she proposed—the value of it! In that shape ran Harry Wethermill's thoughts. He was in desperate straits, though to the world's eye he was a man of wealth. A gambler, with no inexpensive tastes, he had been always in need of money. The rights in his patent he had mortgaged long ago. He was not an idler; he was no sham foisted as a great man on an ignorant public. He had really some touch of genius, and he cultivated it assiduously. But the harder he worked, the greater was his need of gaiety and extravagance. Gifted with good looks and a charm of manner, he was popular alike in the great world and the world of Bohemia. He kept and wanted to keep a foot in each. That he was in desperate straits now, probably Héléne Vauquier alone in Aix had recognised. She had drawn her inference from one simple fact. Wethermill asked her at a later time, when they were better acquainted, how she had guessed his need.

"Monsieur," she replied, "you were in Aix without a valet, and it seemed to me that you were of the class of men who would never move without a valet so long as there was money to pay his wages. That was my first thought. Then, when I saw you pursue your friendship with Mlle. Célie— you who so clearly to my eyes did not love her—I felt sure."

· On the next occasion that the two met, it was again Harry Wethermill who sought Hélène Vauquier. He talked for a minute or two upon indifferent subjects, and then he said quickly :

" I suppose Mme. Dauvray is very rich ? "

" She has a great fortune in jewels," said Héléne Vauquier.

Wethermill started. He was agitated that evening, the woman saw. His hands shook, his face twitched. Clearly he was hard put to it. For he seldom betrayed himself. She thought it time to strike.

" Jewels which she keeps in the safe in her bedroom," she added.

" Then why don't you——? " he began, and stopped.

" I said that I too needed help," replied Héléne, without a ruffle of her composure.

It was nine o'clock at night. Héléne Vauquier had come down to the Casino with a wrap for Mme. Dauvray. The two people were walking down the little street of which the Casino blocks the end. And it happened that an attendant at the Casino, named Alphonse Ruel, passed them, recognised them both, and—smiled to himself with some amusement. What was Wethermill doing in company with Mme. Dauvray's maid? Ruel had no doubt. Ruel had seen Wethermill often enough these recent days with Mme. Dauvray's pretty companion. Ruel had all a Frenchman's sympathy with lovers. He wished them well, those two young and attractive people, and hoped that the maid would help their plans.

But as he passed he caught a sentence spoken suddenly by Wethermill.

"Well, it is true; I must have money." And the agitated voice and words remained fixed in his memory. He heard, too, a warning "Hush!" from the maid. Then they passed out of his hearing. But he turned and saw that Wethermill was talking volubly. What Harry Wethermill was saying he was saying in a foolish burst of confidence.

"You have guessed it, Héléne—you alone." He had mortgaged his patent twice over—once in France, once in England—and the second time had been a month ago. He had received a large sum down, which went to pay his pressing creditors. He had hoped to pay the sum back from a new invention.

"But, Héléne, I tell you," he said, "I have a conscience." And when she smiled he explained. "Oh, not what the priests would call a conscience; that I know. But none the less I have a conscience—a conscience about the things which really matter, at all events to me. There is a flaw in that new invention. It can be improved; I know that. But

as yet I do not see how, and—I cannot help it
—I must get it right; I cannot let it go imperfect when I know that it's imperfect, when I know
that it can be improved, when I am sure that I
shall sooner or later hit upon the needed improve-
ment. That is what I mean when I say I have a
conscience."

Héléne Vauquier smiled indulgently. Men were
queer fish. Things which were really of no account
troubled and perplexed them and gave them sleep-
less nights. But it was not for her to object, since
it was one of these queer anomalies which was
giving her her chance.

"And the people are finding out that you have
sold your rights twice over," she said sympathetically. "That is a pity, monsieur."

"They know," he answered; "those in England
know."

"And they are very angry ?"

"They threaten me," said Wethermill. "They
give me a month to restore the money. Otherwise
there will be disgrace, imprisonment, penal servi-
tude."

Héléne Vauquier walked calmly on. No sign of
the intense joy which she felt was visible in her
face, and only a trace of it in her voice.

"Monsieur will, perhaps, meet me to-morrow in
Geneva," she said. And she named a small café in
a back street. "I can get a holiday for the afternoon." And as they were near to the villa and the
lights, she walked on ahead.

Wethermill loitered behind. He had tried his luck at the tables and had failed. And—and—he must have the money.

He travelled, accordingly, the next day to Geneva, and was there presented to Adéle Tacé and Hippolyte.

"They are trusted friends of mine," said Héléne Vauquier to Wethermill, who was not inspired to confidence by the sight of the young man with the big ears and the plastered hair. As a matter of fact, she had never met them before they came this year to Aix.

The Tacé family, which consisted of Adéle and her husband and Jeanne, her mother, were practised criminals. They had taken the house in Geneva deliberately in order to carry out some robberies from the great villas on the lake-side. But they had not been fortunate; and a description of Mme. Dauvray's jewellery in the woman's column of a Geneva newspaper had drawn Adéle Tacé over to Aix. She had set about the task of seducing Mme. Dauvray's maid, and found a master, not an instrument.

In the small café on that afternoon of July Héléne Vauquier instructed her accomplices, quietly and methodically, as though what she proposed was the most ordinary stroke of business. Once or twice subsequently Wethermill, who was the only safe go-between, went to the house in Geneva, altering his hair and wearing a moustache, to complete the arrangements. He maintained firmly at his trial that at none of these meetings was there any talk of murder.

"To be sure," said the judge, with a savage sarcasm. "In decent conversation there is always a reticence. Something is left to be understood."

And it is difficult to understand how murder could not have been an essential part of their plan, since—— But let us see what happened.

CHAPTER XVI

THE FIRST MOVE

On the Friday before the crime was committed Mme. Dauvray and Celia dined at the Villa des Fleurs. While they were drinking their coffee Harry Wethermill joined them. He stayed with them until Mme. Dauvray was ready to move, and then all three walked into the baccarat rooms together. But there, in the throng of people, they were separated.

Harry Wethermill was looking carefully after Celia, as a good lover should. He had, it seemed, no eyes for any one else; and it was not until a minute or two had passed that the girl herself noticed that Mme. Dauvray was not with them.

"We will find her easily," said Harry.

"Of course," replied Celia.

"There is, after all, no hurry," said Wethermill, with a laugh; "and perhaps she was not unwilling to leave us together."

Celia dimpled to a smile.

"Mme. Dauvray is kind to me," she said, with a very pretty timidity.

"And yet more kind to me," said Wethermill in a

low voice which brought the blood into Celia's cheeks.

But even while he spoke he soon caught sight of Madame Dauvray standing by one of the tables; and near to her was Adéle Tacé. Adéle had not yet made Madame Dauvray's acquaintance; that was evident. She was apparently unaware of her; but she was gradually edging towards her. Wethermill smiled, and Celia caught the smile.

"What is it?" she asked, and her head began to turn in the direction of Mme. Dauvray.

"Why, I like your frock—that's all," said Wethermill at once; and Celia's eyes went down to it.

"Do you?" she said, with a pleased smile. It was a dress of dark blue, which suited her well. "I am glad. I think it is pretty." And they passed on.

Wethermill stayed by the girl's side throughout the evening. Once again he saw Mme. Dauvray and Adéle Tacé. But now they were together; now they were talking. The first step had been taken. Adéle Tacé had scraped acquaintance with Mme. Dauvray. Celia saw them almost at the same moment.

"Oh, there is Mme. Dauvray," she cried, taking a step towards her.

Wethermill detained the girl.

"She seems quite happy," he said; and, indeed, Mme. Dauvray was talking volubly and with the utmost interest, the jewels sparkling about her neck. She raised her head, saw Celia, nodded

to her affectionately, and then pointed her out to
her companion. Adéle Tacé looked the girl over
with interest and smiled contentedly. There was
nothing to be feared from her. Her youth, her
very daintiness, seemed to offer her as the easiest
of victims.

"You see Mme. Dauvray does not want you,"
said Harry Wethermill. "Let us go and play
chemin-de-fer"; and they did, moving off into one
of the further rooms.

It was not until another hour had passed that
Celia rose and went in search of Mme. Dauvray.
She found her still talking earnestly to Adéle
Tacé. Mme. Dauvray got up at once.

"Are you ready to go, dear?" she asked, and
she turned to Adéle Tacé. "This is Célie, Mme.
Rossignol," she said, and she spoke with a marked
significance and a note of actual exultation in her
voice.

Celia, however, was not unused to this tone.
Madame Dauvray was proud of her companion,
and had a habit of showing her off, to the
girl's discomfort. The three women spoke a few
words, and then Mme. Dauvray and Celia left the
rooms and walked to the entrance-doors. But as
they walked Celia became alarmed.

She was by nature extraordinarily sensitive to
impressions. It was to that quick receptivity that
the success of "The Great Fortinbras" had been
chiefly due. She had a gift of rapid comprehension.
It was not that she argued, or deducted, or inferred.

15

But she felt. To take a metaphor from the work of the man she loved, she was a natural receiver. So now, although no word was spoken, she was aware that Mme. Dauvray was greatly excited—greatly disturbed; and she dreaded the reason of that excitement and disturbance.

While they were driving home in the motor-car she said apprehensively:

"You met a friend then, to-night, madame?"

"No," said Mme. Dauvray; "I made a friend. I had not met Mme. Rossignol before. A bracelet of hers came undone, and I helped her to fasten it. We talked afterwards. She lives in Geneva."

Mme. Dauvray was silent for a moment or two. Then she turned impulsively and spoke in a voice of appeal.

"Célie, we talked of things"; and the girl moved impatiently. She understood very well what were the things of which Mme. Dauvray and her new friend had talked. "And she laughed. . . . I could not bear it."

Celia was silent, and Mme. Dauvray went on in a voice of awe:

"I told her of the wonderful things which happened when I sat with Hélène in the dark—how the room filled with strange sounds, how ghostly fingers touched my forehead and my eyes. She laughed—Adéle Rossignol laughed, Célie. I told her of the spirits with whom we held converse. She would not believe. Do you remember the evening, Célie, when Mme. de Castiglione came back an old, old woman, and told us how, when she had grown old and had lost her beauty and was very lonely, she would no longer live in the great house which was so full of torturing memories, but took a small *appartement* near by, where no one knew her; and how she used to walk out late at night, and watch, with her eyes full of tears, the dark windows which had been once so bright with light? Adéle Rossignol would not believe. I told her that I had found the story afterwards in a volume of memoirs. Adéle Rossignol laughed and said no doubt you had read that volume yourself before the séance."

Celia stirred guiltily.

"She had no faith in you, Célie. It made me angry, dear. She said that you invented your own tests. She sneered at them. A string across a cupboard! A child, she said, could manage that; much more, then, a clever young lady. Oh, she admitted that you were clever! Indeed, she urged that you were far too clever to submit to the tests of some one you did not know. I replied that you would. I was right, Célie, was I not?"

And again the appeal sounded rather piteously in Mme. Dauvray's voice.

"Tests!" said Celia, with a contemptuous laugh. And, in truth, she was not afraid of them. Mme. Dauvray's voice at once took courage.

"There!" she cried triumphantly. "I was sure. I told her so. Célie, I arranged with her that next Tuesday——"

And Celia interrupted quickly.

"No! Oh, no!"

Again there was silence; and then Mme. Dauvray said gently, but very seriously:

"Célie, you are not kind."

Celia was moved by the reproach.

· "Oh, madame!" she cried eagerly. "Please don't think that. How could I be anything else to you who are so kind to me?"

"Then prove it, Célie. On Tuesday I have asked Mme. Rossignol to come; and——" The old woman's voice became tremulous with excitement. "And perhaps—who knows?—perhaps *she* will appear to us."

Celia had no doubt who "she" was. She was Mme. de Montespan.

"Oh, no, madame!" she stammered. "Here, at Aix, we are not in the spirit for such things."

And then, in a voice of dread, Mme. Dauvray asked:

"Is it true, then, what Adéle said?"

And Celia started violently. Mme. Dauvray doubted.

"I believe it would break my heart, my dear, if I were to think that; if I were to know that you had tricked me," she said, with a trembling voice.

Celia covered her face with her hands. It would be true. She had no doubt of it. Mme. Dauvray would never forgive herself—would never forgive Celia. Her infatuation had grown so to engross her that the rest of her life would surely be embittered. It was not merely a passion—it was a creed as well. Celia shrank from the renewal of these séances. Every fibre in her was in revolt. They were so unworthy—so unworthy of Harry Wethermill, and of herself as she now herself wished to be. But she had to pay now; the moment for payment had come.

"Célie," said Mme. Dauvray, "it isn't true! Surely it isn't true?"

Celia drew her hands away from her face.

"Let Mme. Rossignol come on Tuesday!" she cried, and the old woman caught the girl's hand and pressed it with affection.

"Oh, thank you! thank you!" she cried. "Adéle Rossignol laughs to-night; we shall convince her on Tuesday, Célie! Célie, I am so glad!" And her voice sank into a solemn whisper, pathetically ludicrous. "It is not right that she should laugh! To bring people back through the gates of the spirit-world—that is wonderful."

To Celia the sound of the jargon learnt from her own lips, used by herself so thoughtlessly in past times, was odious. "For the last time," she pleaded to herself. All her life was going to change; though no word had yet been spoken by Harry Wethermill, she was sure of it. Just for this one last time, then, so that she might leave Mme. Dauvray the colours of her belief, she would hold a séance at the Villa Rose.

Mme. Dauvray told the news to Héléne Vauquier when they reached the villa.

"You will be present, Héléne,' she cried excitedly. "It will be Tuesday. There will be the three of us."

"Certainly, if madame wishes," said Héléne submissively. She looked round the room. "Mlle. Célie can be placed on a chair in that recess and the curtains drawn, whilst we—madame and madame's friend and I—can sit round this table under the side windows."

"Yes," said Celia, "that will do very well."

It was Madame Dauvray's habit when she was particularly pleased with Celia to dismiss her maid quickly, and to send her to brush the girl's hair at night; and in a little while on this night Héléne went to Celia's room. While she brushed Celia's hair she told her that Servettaz's parents lived at Chambéry, and that he would like to see them.

"But the poor man is afraid to ask for a day," she said. "He has been so short a time with madame."

"Of course madame will give him a holiday if he asks," replied Celia with a smile. "I will speak to her myself to-morrow."

"It would be kind of mademoiselle," said Héléne Vauquier. "But perhaps——" She stopped.

"Well," said Celia.

"Perhaps mademoiselle would do better still to speak to Servettaz himself and encourage him to ask with his own lips. Madame has her moods, is it not so? She does not always like it to be forgotten that she is the mistress."

On the next day accordingly Celia did speak to Servettaz, and Servettaz asked for his holiday.

" But of course," Mme. Dauvray at once replied. " We must decide upon a day."

It was then that Héléne Vauquier ventured humbly upon a suggestion.

" Since madame has a friend coming here on Tuesday, perhaps that would be the best day for him to go. Madame would not be likely to take a long drive that afternoon."

" No, indeed," replied Mme. Dauvray. " We shall all three dine together early in Aix and return here."

" Then I will tell him he may go to-morrow," said Celia.

For this conversation took place on the Monday, and in the evening Mme. Dauvray and Celia went as usual to the Villa des Fleurs and dined there.

" I was in a bad mind," said Celia, when asked by the Juge d'Instruction to explain that attack of nerves in the garden which Ricardo had witnessed. " I hated more and more the thought of the séance which was to take place on the morrow. I felt that I was disloyal to Harry. My nerves were all tingling. I was not nice that night at all," she added quaintly. " But at dinner I determined that if I met Harry after dinner, as I was sure to do, I would tell him the whole truth about myself. However, when I did meet him I was frightened. I knew how stern he could suddenly look. I dreaded what he would

think.   I was too afraid that I should lose him. No,
I could not speak; I had not the courage. That
made me still more angry with myself, and so I—
I quarrelled at once with Harry. He was surprised;
but it was natural, wasn't it?   What else should
one do under such circumstances, except quarrel
with the man one loved? Yes, I really quarrelled
with him, and said things which I thought and
hoped would hurt.   Then I ran away from him lest
I should break down and cry.   I went to the tables
and lost at once all the money I had except one note
of five louis. But that did not console me. And I
ran out into the garden, very unhappy. There I
behaved like a child, and Mr. Ricardo saw me.   But
it was not the little money I had lost which troubled
me; no, it was the thought of what a coward I was.
Afterwards Harry and I made it up, and I thought,
like the little fool I was, that he wanted to ask me
to marry him.   But I would not let him that night.
Oh! I wanted him to ask me—I was longing for him
to ask me—but not that night.   Somehow I felt that
the séance and the tricks must be all over and done
with before I could listen or answer."

The quiet and simple confession touched the
magistrate who listened to it to a profound pity.
He shaded his eyes with his hand.   The girl's sense
of her unworthiness, the love she had given so
unstintingly to Harry Wethermill, the deep pride
she had felt in the delusion that he loved her too,
had in it an irony too bitter. But he was aroused
to anger against the man.

" Go on, mademoiselle," he said. But in spite of himself his voice trembled.

" So I arranged with him that we should meet on Wednesday, as Mr. Ricardo heard."

" You told him that you would 'want him' on Wednesday ? " said the judge, quoting Mr. Richard's words.

" Yes," replied Celia. " I meant that the last word of all these deceptions would have been spoken. I should be free to hear what he had to say to me. You see, monsieur, I was so sure that I knew what it was he had to say to me——" and her voice broke upon the words. She recovered herself with an effort. " Then I went home with Mme. Dauvray."

On the morning of Tuesday, however, there came a letter from Adéle Tacé, of which no trace was afterwards discovered. The letter invited Mme. Dauvray and Celia to come out to Annecy and dine with her at an hotel there. They could then return together to Aix. The proposal fitted well with Mme. Dauvray's inclinations. She was in a feverish mood of excitement.

"Yes, it will be better that we dine quietly together in a place where there is no noise and no crowd, and where no one knows us," she said ; and she looked up the time-table. " There is a train back which reaches Aix at nine o'clock," she said, " so we need not spoil Servettaz' holiday."

" His parents will be expecting him," Héléne Vauquier added.

Accordingly Servettaz left for Chambéry by the

1.50 train from Aix; and later on in the afternoon Mme. Dauvray and Celia went by train to Annecy. In the one woman's mind was the queer longing that "she" should appear and speak to-night; in the girl's there was a wish passionate as a cry. "This shall be the last time," she said to herself again and again—"the very last."

Meanwhile, Héléne Vauquier, it must be held, burnt carefully Adéle Tacé's letter. She was left in the Villa Rose with the charwoman to keep her company. The charwoman bore testimony that Héléne Vauquier certainly did burn a letter in the kitchen-stove, and that after she had burned it she sat for a long time rocking herself in a chair, with a smile of great pleasure upon her face, and now and then moistening her lips with her tongue. But Hélène Vauquier kept her mouth sealed.

CHAPTER XVII

THE AFTERNOON OF TUESDAY

MME. DAUVRAY and Celia found Adéle Rossignol, to give Adéle Tacé the name which she assumed, waiting for them impatiently in the garden of an hotel at Annecy, on the Promenade du Paquier. She was a tall, lithe woman, and she was dressed, by the purse and wish of Héléne Vauquier, in a robe and a long coat of sapphire velvet, which toned down the coarseness of her good looks and lent something of elegance to her figure.

"So it is mademoiselle," Adéle began, with a smile of raillery, " who is so remarkably clever."

" Clever ? " answered Celia, looking straight at Adéle, as though through her she saw mysteries beyond. She took up her part at once. Since for the last time it had got to be played, there must be no fault in the playing. For her own sake, for the sake of Mme. Dauvray's happiness, she must carry it off to-night with success. The suspicions of Adéle Rossignol must obtain no verification. She spoke in a quiet and most serious voice. " Under spirit-control no one is clever. One does the bidding of the spirit which controls."

"Perfectly," said Adéle in a malicious tone. "I only hope you will see to it, mademoiselle, that some amusing spirits control you this evening and appear before us."

"I am only the living gate by which the spirit forms pass from the realm of mind into the world of matter," Celia replied.

"Quite so," said Adéle comfortably. "Now let us be sensible and dine. We can amuse ourselves with mademoiselle's rigmaroles afterwards."

Mme. Dauvray was indignant. Celia, for her part, felt humiliated and small. They sat down to their dinner in the garden, but the rain began to fall and drove them indoors. There were a few people dining at the same hour, but none near enough to overhear them. Alike in the garden and the dining-room, Adéle Tacé kept up the same note of ridicule and disbelief. She had been carefully tutored for her work. She was able to cite the stock cases of exposure—"les frères Davenport," as she called them, Eusapia Palladino and Dr. Slade. She knew the precautions which had been taken to prevent trickery and where those precautions had failed. Her whole conversation was carefully planned to one end, and to one end alone. She wished to produce in the minds of her companions so complete an impression of her scepticism that it would seem the most natural thing in the world to both of them that she should insist upon subjecting Celia to the severest tests. The rain ceased, and they took their coffee on the terrace of the hotel. Mme.

Dauvray had been really pained by the conversation of Adéle Tacé. She had all the missionary zeal of a fanatic.

"I do hope, Adéle, that we shall make you believe. But we shall. Oh, I am confident we shall." And her voice was feverish.

Adéle dropped for the moment her tone of raillery.

"I am not unwilling to believe," she said, " but I cannot. I am interested—yes. You see how much I have studied the subject. But I cannot believe. I have heard stories of how these manifestations are produced—stories which make me laugh. I cannot help it. The tricks are so easy. A young girl wearing a black frock which does not rustle—it is always a black frock, is it not, because a black frock cannot be seen in the dark ?— carrying a scarf or veil, with which she can make any sort of headdress if only she is a little clever, and shod in a pair of felt-soled slippers, is shut up in a cabinet or placed behind a screen, and the lights are turned down or out——" Adéle broke off with a comic shrug of the shoulders. "Bah ! It ought not to deceive a child."

Celia sat with a face which *would* grow red. She did not look, but none the less she was aware that Mme. Dauvray was gazing at her with a perplexed frown and some return of her suspicion showing in her eyes. Adéle Tacé was not content to leave the subject there.

"Perhaps," she said, with a smile, " Mlle. Célie dresses in that way for a séance ? "

"Madame shall see to-night," Celia stammered, and Camille Dauvray rather sternly repeated her words.

"Yes, Adéle shall see to-night. I myself will decide what you shall wear, Célie."

Adéle Tacé casually suggested the kind of dress which she would prefer.

"Something light in colour with a train, something which will hiss and whisper if mademoiselle moves about the room—yes, and I think one of mademoiselle's big hats," she said. "We will have mademoiselle as modern as possible, so that, when the great ladies of the past appear in the coiffure of their day, we may be sure it is not Mlle. Célie who represents them."

"I will speak to Héléne," said Mme. Dauvray, and Adéle Tacé was content.

There was a particular new dress of which she knew, and it was very desirable that Mlle. Célie should wear it to-night. For one thing, if Celia wore it, it would help the theory that she had put it on because she expected that night a lover; for another, with that dress there went a pair of satin slippers which had just come home from a shoemaker at Aix, and which would leave upon soft mould precisely the same imprints as the grey suéde shoes which the girl was wearing now.

Celia was not greatly disconcerted by Mme. Rossignol's precautions. She would have to be a little more careful, and Mme. de Montespan would be a little longer in responding to the call of Mme.

Dauvray than most of the other dead ladies of the past had been. But that was all. She was, however, really troubled in another way. All through dinner, at every word of the conversation, she had felt her reluctance towards this séance swelling into a positive disgust. More than once she had felt driven by some uncontrollable power to rise up at the table and cry out to Adéle:

"You are right! It *is* trickery. There is no truth in it."

But she had mastered herself. For opposite to her sat her patroness, her good friend, the woman who had saved her. The flush upon Mme. Dauvray's cheeks and the agitation of her manner warned Celia how much hung upon the success of this last séance. How much for both of them!

And in the fullness of that knowledge a great fear assailed her. She began to be afraid, so strong was her reluctance, that she would not bring her heart into the task. "Suppose I failed to-night because I could not force myself to wish not to fail!" she thought, and she steeled herself against the thought. To-night she must not fail. For apart altogether from Mme. Dauvray's happiness, her own, it seemed, was at stake too.

"It must be from my lips that Harry learns what I have been," she said to herself, and with the resolve she strengthened herself.

"I will wear what you please," she said, with a smile. "I only wish Mme. Rossignol to be satisfied."

"And I shall be," said Adéle, "if——" She leaned

forward in anxiety.   She had come to the real
necessity of Héléne Vauquier's plan.   "If we
abandon as quite laughable the cupboard door and
the string across it; if, in a word, mademoiselle
consents that we tie her hand and foot and fasten
her securely in a chair.   Such restraints are usual
in the experiments of which I have read.   Was
there not a medium called Mlle. Cook who was
secured in this way, and then remarkable things,
which I could not believe, were supposed to have
happened ? "

"Certainly I permit it," said Celia, with indifference ; and Mme. Dauvray cried enthusiastically :

" Ah, you shall believe to-night in those wonderful things ! "

Adéle Tacé leaned back. She drew a breath. It
was a breath of relief.

"Then we will buy the cord in Aix," she said.

"We have some, no doubt, in the house," said
Mme. Dauvray.

Adéle shook her head and smiled.

" My dear madame, you are dealing with a sceptic.
I should not be content."

Celia shrugged her shoulders.

" Let us satisfy Mme. Rossignol," she said.

Celia, indeed, was not alarmed by this last precaution.   For her it was a test less difficult than the
light-coloured rustling robe. She had appeared
upon so many platforms, had experienced too often
the bungling efforts of spectators called up from
the audience, to be in any fear.   There were very

few knots from which her small hands and supple fingers had not learnt long since to extricate themselves. She was aware how much in all these matters the personal equation counted. Men who might, perhaps, have been able to tie knots from which she could not get free were always too uncomfortable and self-conscious, or too afraid of hurting her white arms and wrists, to do it. Women, on the other hand, who had no compunctions of that kind, did not know how.

It was now nearly eight o'clock; the rain still held off.

"We must go," said Mme. Dauvray, who for the last half-hour had been continually looking at her watch.

They drove to the station and took the train. Once more the rain came down, but it had stopped again before the train steamed into Aix at nine o'clock.

"We will take a cab," said Mme. Dauvray: "it will save time."

"It will do us good to walk, madame," pleaded Adéle. The train was full. Adéle passed quickly out from the lights of the station in the throng of passengers and waited in the dark square for the others to join her. "It is barely nine. A friend has promised to call at the Villa Rose for me after eleven and drive me back in a motor-car to Geneva, so we have plenty of time."

They walked accordingly up the hill, Mme. Dauvray slowly, since she was stout, and Celia

keeping pace with her. Thus it seemed natural
that Adéle Tacé should walk ahead, though a passer-
by would not have thought she was of their
company. At the corner of the Rue du Casino
Adéle waited for them and said quickly:

"Mademoiselle, you can get some cord, I think, at
the shop there," and she pointed to the shop of
M. Corval. "Madame and I will go slowly on; you,
who are the youngest, will easily catch us up."
Celia went into the shop, bought the cord, and
caught Madame Dauvray up before she reached the
villa.

"Where is Mme. Rossignol?" she asked.

"She went on," said Camille Dauvray. "She
walks faster than I do."

They passed no one whom they knew, although
they did pass one who recognised them, as Perrichet
had discovered. They came upon Adéle, waiting
for them at the corner of the road, where it turns
down toward the villa.

"It is near here—the Villa Rose?" she asked.

"A minute more and we are there."

They turned in at the drive, closed the gate
behind them, and walked up to the villa.

The windows and the glass doors were closed,
the latticed shutters fastened. A light burned in
the hall.

"Héléne is expecting us," said Mme. Dauvray,
for as they approached she saw the front door open
to admit them, and Héléne Vauquier in the doorway.
The three women went straight into the little salon,

which was ready with the lights up and a small fire burning. Celia noticed the fire with a trifle of dismay. She moved a fire-screen in front of it.

" I can understand why you do that, mademoiselle," said Adéle Rossignol, with a satirical smile. But Mme. Dauvray came to the girl's help.

" She is right, Adéle. Light is the great barrier between us and the spirit-world," she said solemnly.

Meanwhile, in the hall Héléne Vauquier locked and bolted the front door. Then she stood motionless, with a smile upon her face and a heart beating high. All through that afternoon she had been afraid that some accident at the last moment would spoil her plan, that Adéle Tacé had not learned her lesson, that Célie would take fright, that she would not return. Now all those fears were over. She had her victims safe within the villa. The charwoman had been sent home. She had them to herself. She was still standing in the hall when Mme. Dauvray called aloud impatiently:

" Héléne! Héléne!"

And when she entered the salon there was still, as Celia was able to recall, some trace of her smile lingering upon her face.

Adéle Rossignol had removed her hat and was taking off her gloves. Mme. Dauvray was speaking impatiently to Celia.

" We will arrange the room, dear, while Héléne helps you to dress. It will be quite easy. We shall use the recess."

And Celia, as she ran up the stairs, heard Mme. Dauvray discussing with her maid what frock she should wear. She was hot, and she took a hurried bath. When she came from her bathroom she saw with dismay that it was her new pale-green evening gown which had been laid out. It was the last which she would have chosen. But she dared not refuse it. She must still any suspicion. She must succeed. She gave herself into Héléne's hands. Celia remembered afterwards one or two points which passed barely heeded at the time. Once while Héléne was dressing her hair she looked up at the maid in the mirror and noticed a strange and rather horrible grin upon her face, which disappeared the moment their eyes met. Then again, Héléne was extraordinarily slow and extraordinarily fastidious that evening. Nothing satisfied her, neither the hang of the girl's skirt, the folds of her sash, nor the arrangement of her hair.

"Come, Héléne, be quick," said Celia. "You know how madame hates to be kept waiting at these times. You might be dressing me to go to meet my lover," she added, with a blush and a smile at her own pretty reflection in the glass; and a queer look came upon Héléne Vauquier's face. For it was at creating just this very impression that she aimed.

"Very well, mademoiselle," said Héléne. And even as she spoke Mme. Dauvray's voice rang shrill and irritable up the stairs.

"Célie! Célie!"

" Quick, Hélène," said Celia. For she herself was now anxious to have the séance over and done with.

But Hélène did not hurry. The more irritable Mme. Dauvray became, the more impatient with Mlle. Célie, the less would Mlle. Célie dare to refuse the tests Adéle wished to impose upon her. But that was not all. She took a subtle and ironic pleasure to-night in decking out her victim's natural loveliness. Her face, her slender throat, her white shoulders, should look their prettiest, her grace of limb and figure should be more alluring than ever before. The same words, indeed, were running through both women's minds.

" For the last time," said Celia to herself, thinking of these horrible séances, of which to-night should see the end.

" For the last time," said Hélène Vauquier too. For the last time she laced the girl's dress. There would be no more patient and careful service for Mlle. Célie after to-night. But she should have it and to spare to-night. She should be conscious that her beauty had never made so strong an appeal ; that she was never so fit for life as at the moment when the end had come. One thing Hélène regretted. She would have liked Celia—Celia, smiling at herself in the glass—to know suddenly what was in store for her ! She saw in imagination the colour die from the cheeks, the eyes stare wide with terror.

" Célie ! Célie ! "

Again the impatient voice rang up the stairs, as

Héléne pinned the girl's hat upon her fair head.
Célie sprang up, took a quick step or two towards
the door, and stopped in dismay. The swish of her
long satin train must betray her. She caught up
the dress and tried again. Even so, the rustle of it
was heard.

"I shall have to be very careful. You will help
me, Héléne?"

"Of course, mademoiselle. I will sit underneath
the switch of the light in the salon. If madame,
your visitor, makes the experiment too difficult, I
will find a way to help you," said Héléne Vauquier,
and as she spoke she handed Celia a long pair of
white gloves.

"I shall not want them," said Celia.

"Mme. Dauvray ordered me to give them to
you," replied Héléne.

Celia took them hurriedly, picked up a white scarf
of tulle, and ran down the stairs. Héléne Vauquier
listened at the door and heard madame's voice in
feverish anger,

"We have been waiting for you, Célie. You have
been an age."

Héléne Vauquier laughed softly to herself, took
out Celia's white cloak from the wardrobe, turned
off the lights, and followed her down to the hall.
She placed the cloak just outside the door of the
salon. Then she carefully turned out all the lights
in the hall and in the kitchen, and went into the
salon. The rest of the house was in darkness. This
room was brightly lit ; and it had been made ready.

CHAPTER XVIII

THE SÉANCE

HÉLÈNE VAUQUIER locked the door of the salon upon the inside and placed the key upon the mantel-shelf, as she had always done whenever a séance had been held. The curtains had been loosened at the sides of the arched recess in front of the glass doors, ready to be drawn across. Inside the recess, against one of the pillars which supported the arch, a high stool without a back, taken from the hall, had been placed, and the back legs of the stool had been lashed with cord firmly to the pillar, so that it could not be moved. The round table had been put in position, with three chairs about it. Mme. Dauvray waited impatiently. Celia stood apparently unconcerned, apparently lost to all that was going on. Her eyes saw no one. Adéle looked up at Celia, and laughed maliciously.

"Mademoiselle, I see, is in the very mood to produce the most wonderful phenomena. But it will be better, I think, madame," she said, turning to Mme. Dauvray, "that Mlle. Célie should put on those gloves which I see she has thrown on to a chair. It will be a little more difficult for mademoiselle to loosen these cords, should she wish to do so."

The argument silenced Celia. If she refused this condition now she would excite Mme. Dauvray to a terrible suspicion. She drew on her gloves rue-fully and slowly, smoothed them over her elbows, and buttoned them. To free her hands with her fingers and wrists already hampered in gloves would not be so easy a task. But there was no escape. Adéle Rossignol was watching her with a satiric smile. Mme. Dauvray was urging her to be quick. Obeying a second order the girl raised her skirt and extended a slim foot in a pale-green silk stocking and a satin slipper to match. Adéle was content. Celia was wearing the shoes she was meant to wear. They were made upon the very same last as those which Celia had just kicked off upstairs. An almost imperceptible nod from Héléne Vauquier, moreover, assured her.

She took up a length of the thin cord.

"Now, how are we to begin?" she said awk-wardly. "I think I will ask you, mademoiselle, to put your hands behind you."

Celia turned her back and crossed her wrists. She stood in her satin frock, with her white arms and shoulders bare, her slender throat supporting her small head with its heavy curls, her big hat—a picture of young grace and beauty. She would have had an easy task that night had there been men instead of women to put her to the test. But the women were intent upon their own ends: Mme.

Dauvray eager for her séance, Adéle Tacé and Héléne Vauquier for the climax of their plot.

Celia clenched her hands to make the muscles of her wrists rigid to resist the pressure of the cord. Adéle quietly unclasped them and placed them palm to palm. And at once Celia became uneasy. It was not merely the action, significant though it was of Adéle's alertness to thwart her, which troubled Celia. But she was extraordinarily receptive of impressions, extraordinarily quick to feel, from a touch, some dim sensation of the thought of the one who touched her. So now the touch of Adéle's swift, strong, nervous hands caused her a queer, vague shock of discomfort. It was no more than that at the moment, but it was quite definite as that.

"Keep your hands so, please, mademoiselle," said Adéle; "your fingers loose."

And the next moment Celia winced and had to bite her lip to prevent a cry. The thin cord was wound twice about her wrists, drawn cruelly tight and then cunningly knotted. For one second Celia was thankful for her gloves; the next, more than ever she regretted that she wore them. It would have been difficult enough for her to free her hands now, even without them. And upon that a worse thing befell her.

"I beg mademoiselle's pardon if I hurt her," said Adéle.

And she tied the girl's thumbs and little fingers. To slacken the knots she must have the use of her fingers, even though her gloves made them fumble. Now she had lost the use of them altogether. She began to feel that she was in master-hands. She was sure of it the next instant. For Adéle stood up, and, passing a cord round the upper part of her arms, drew her elbows back. To bring any strength to help her in wriggling her hands free she must be able to raise her elbows. With them trussed in the small of her back she was robbed entirely of her strength. And all the time her strange uneasiness grew. She made a movement of revolt, and at once the cord was loosened.

"Mlle. Célie objects to my tests," said Adéle, with a laugh, to Mme. Dauvray. "And I do not wonder."

Celia saw upon the old woman's foolish and excited face a look of veritable consternation.

"Are you afraid, Célie?" she asked.

There was anger, there was menace in the voice, but above all these there was fear—fear that her illusions were to tumble about her. Celia heard that note and was quelled by it. This folly of belief, these séances, were the one touch of colour in Mme. Dauvray's life. And it was just that instinctive need of colour which had made her so easy to delude. How strong the need is, how seductive the proposal to supply it, Celia knew well. She knew it from the experience of her life when the Great Fortinbras was at the climax of his fortunes. She had travelled much amongst monotonous, drab towns without character or amusements. She had kept her eyes open. She had seen that it was from the denizens of the dull streets in these towns that the quack religions won their recruits. Mme. Dauvray's life had been a featureless sort of affair until these experiments had come to colour it. Madame Dauvray must at any rate preserve the memory of that colour.

"No," she said boldly; "I am not afraid," and after that she moved no more.

Her elbows were drawn firmly back and tightly bound. She was sure she could not free them. She glanced in despair at Héléne Vauquier, and then some glimmer of hope sprang up. For Héléne Vauquier gave her a look, a smile of reassurance. It was as if she said, "I will come to your help." Then, to make security still more sure, Adéle turned the girl about as unceremoniously as if she had been a doll, and, passing a cord at the back of her arms, drew both ends round in front and knotted them at her waist.

"Now, Célie," said Adéle, with a vibration in her voice which Celia had not remarked before.

Excitement was gaining upon her, as upon Mme. Dauvray. Her face was flushed and shiny, her manner peremptory and quick. Celia's uneasiness grew into fear. She could have used the words which Hanaud spoke the next day in that very room—"There is something here which I do not understand." The touch of Adéle Tacé's hands communicated something to her—something which filled her with a vague alarm. She could not have formulated it if she would; she dared not if she could. She had but to stand and submit.

"Now," said Adéle.

She took the girl by the shoulders and set her in a clear space in the middle of the room, her back to the recess, her face to the mirror, where all could see her.

"Now, Célie"—she had dropped the "Mlle." and the ironic suavity of her manner—"try to free yourself."

For a moment the girl's shoulders worked, her hands fluttered. But they remained helplessly bound.

"Ah, you will be content, Adéle, to-night," cried Mme. Dauvray eagerly.

But even in the midst of her eagerness—so thoroughly had she been prepared—there lingered a flavour of doubt, of suspicion. In Celia's mind there was still the one desperate resolve.

"I must succeed to-night," she said to herself—"I must!"

Adéle Rossignol kneeled on the floor behind her. She gathered in carefully the girl's frock. Then she picked up the long train, wound it tightly round her limbs, pinioning and swathing them in the folds of satin, and secured the folds with a cord about the knees.

She stood up again.

"Can you walk, Célie?" she asked. "Try!"

With Héléne Vauquier to support her if she fell, Célia took a tiny shuffling step forward, feeling supremely ridiculous. No one, however, of her

audience was inclined to laugh. To Mme. Dauvray
the whole business was as serious as the most
solemn ceremonial. Adéle was intent upon making
her knots secure. Héléne Vauquier was the well-
bred servant who knew her place. It was not for
her to laugh at her young mistress, in however
ludicrous a situation she might be.

"Now," said Adéle, "we will tie mademoiselle's
ankles, and then we shall be ready for Mme. de
Montespan."

The raillery in her voice had a note of savagery
in it now. Celia's vague terror grew. She had a
feeling that a beast was waking in the woman, and
with it came a growing premonition of failure.
Vainly she cried to herself, "I must not fail to-
night." But she felt instinctively that there was a
stronger personality than her own in that room,
taming her, condemning her to failure, influencing
the others.

She was placed in a chair. Adéle passed a cord
round her ankles, and the mere touch of it quickened
Celia to a spasm of revolt. Her last little remnant
of liberty was being taken from her. She raised
herself, or rather would have raised herself. But
Héléne with gentle hands held her in the chair, and
whispered under her breath:

"Have no fear! Madame is watching."

Adéle looked fiercely up into the girl's face.

"Keep still, *hein, la petite!*" she cried. And the
epithet—"little one"—was a light to Celia. Till
now, upon these occasions, with her black ceremonial

dress, her air of aloofness, her vague eyes, and the
dignity of her carriage, she had already produced
some part of her effect before the séance had begun.
She had been wont to sail into the room, distant,
mystical. She had her audience already expectant
of mysteries, prepared for marvels. Her work was
already half done. But now of all that help she
was deprived. She was no longer a person aloof, a
prophetess, a seer of visions; she was simply a
smartly-dressed girl of to-day, trussed up in a
ridiculous and painful position—that was all. The
dignity was gone. And the more she realised that,
the more she was hindered from influencing her
audience, the less able she was to concentrate her
mind upon them, to will them to favour her. Mme.
Dauvray's suspicions, she was sure, were still awake.
She could not quell them. There was a stronger
personality than hers at work in the room. The
cord bit through her thin stockings into her ankles.
She dared not complain. It was savagely tied. She
made no remonstrance. And then Héléne Vauquier
raised her up from the chair and lifted her easily off
the ground. For a moment she held her so. If
Celia had felt ridiculous before, she knew that she
was ten times more so now. She could see herself
as she hung in Héléne Vauquier's arms, with her
delicate frock ludicrously swathed and swaddled
about her legs. But, again, of those who watched
her no one smiled.

"We have had no such tests as these," Mme.
Dauvray exclaimed, half in fear, half in hope.

Adéle Rossignol looked the girl over and nodded her head with satisfaction. She had no animosity towards Celia; she had really no feeling of any kind for her or against her. Fortunately she was unaware at this time that Harry Wethermill had been paying his court to her or it would have gone worse with Mlle. Célie before the night was out. Mlle. Célie was just a pawn in a very dangerous game which she happened to be playing, and she had succeeded in engineering her pawn into the desired condition of helplessness. She was content.

" Mademoiselle," she said, with a smile, " you wish me to believe. You have now your opportunity."

Opportunity! And she was helpless. She knew very well that she could never free herself from these cords without Héléne's help. She would fail, miserably and shamefully fail.

"It was madame who wished you to believe," she stammered.

And Adéle Rossignol laughed suddenly—a short, loud, harsh laugh, which jarred upon the quiet of the room. It turned Celia's vague alarm into a definite terror. Some magnetic current brought her grave messages of fear. The air about her seemed to tingle with strange menaces. She looked at Adéle. Did they emanate from her? And her terror answered her " Yes." She made her mistake in that. The strong personality in the room was not Adéle Rossignol, but Héléne Vauquier, who held her like a child in her arms. But she was definitely aware of danger, and too late aware of it.

She struggled vainly. From her head to her feet
she was powerless. She cried out hysterically to
her patron:

"Madame! Madame! There is something—a
presence here—some one who means harm! I
know it!"

And upon the old woman's face there came a look,
not of alarm, but of extraordinary relief. The
genuine, heartfelt cry restored her confidence in
Celia.

"Some one—who means harm!" she whispered,
trembling with excitement.

"Ah, mademoiselle is already under control," said
Héléne, using the jargon which she had learnt from
Celia's lips.

Adéle Rossignol grinned.

"Yes, *la petite* is under control," she repeated,
with a sneer; and all the elegance of her velvet
gown was unable to hide her any longer from
Celia's knowledge. Her grin had betrayed her.
She was of the dregs. But Héléne Vauquier
whispered:

"Keep still, mademoiselle. I shall help you."

Vauquier carried the girl into the recess and
placed her upon the stool. With a long cord Adéle
bound her by the arms and the waist to the pillar,
and her ankles she fastened to the rung of the stool,
so that they could not touch the ground.

"Thus we shall be sure that when we hear rapping
it will be the spirits, and not the heels, which rap,"
she said. "Yes, I am contented now." And she

added, with a smile, "Célie may even have her
scarf," and, picking up a white scarf of tulle which
Celia had brought down with her, she placed it
carelessly round her shoulders.

"Wait!" Héléne Vauquier whispered in Celia's
ear.

To the cord about Celia's waist Adèle was fasten-
ing a longer line.

"I shall keep my foot on the other end of this,"
she said, "when the lights are out, and I shall know
then if our little one frees herself."

The three women went out of the recess. And
the next moment the heavy silk curtains swung
across the opening, leaving Celia in darkness.
Quickly and noiselessly the poor girl began to twist
and work her hands. But she only bruised her
wrists. This was to be the last of the séances.
But it must succeed! So much of Mme. Dauvray's
happiness, so much of her own, hung upon its
success. Let her fail to-night, she would be surely
turned from the door. The story of her trickery
and her exposure would run through Aix. And
she had not told Harry! It would reach his ears
from others. He would never forgive her. To face
the old, difficult life of poverty and perhaps starvation again, and again alone, would be hard enough;
but to face it with Harry Wethermill's contempt
added to its burdens—as the poor girl believed she
surely would have to do—no, that would be impossible! Not this time would she turn away from
the Seine, because it was so terrible and cold. If

she had had the courage to tell him yesterday, he
would have forgiven, surely he would! The tears
gathered in her eyes and rolled down her cheeks.
What would become of her now? She was in pain
besides. The cords about her arms and ankles
tortured her. And she feared—yes, desperately she
feared the effect of the exposure upon Mme. Dauvray.
She had been treated as a daughter; now she was
in return to rob Mme. Dauvray of the belief which
had become the passion of her life.

"Let us take our seats at the table," she heard
Mme. Dauvray say. "Héléne, you are by the switch
of the electric light. "Will you turn it off?"
And upon that Héléne whispered, yet so that the
whisper reached to Celia and awakened hope:

"Wait! I will see what she is doing."

The curtains opened, and Héléne Vauquier slipped
to the girl's side.

Celia checked her tears. She smiled imploringly,
gratefully.

"What shall I do?" asked Héléne, in a voice so
low that the movement of her mouth rather than
the words made the question clear.

Celia raised her head to answer. And then a
thing incomprehensible to her happened. As she
opened her lips Héléne Vauquier swiftly forced a
handkerchief in between the girl's teeth, and lifting
the scarf from her shoulders wound it tightly twice
across her mouth, binding her lips, and made it fast
under the brim of her hat behind her head. Celia
tried to scream; she could not utter a sound. She

stared at Hélène with incredulous, horror-stricken
eyes. Hélène nodded at her with a cruel grin of
satisfaction, and Celia realised, though she did not
understand, something of the rancour and the hatred
which seethed against her in the heart of the woman
whom she had supplanted. Hélène Vauquier meant
to expose her to-night; Celia had not a doubt of it.
That was her explanation of Hélène Vauquier's
treachery; and believing that error, she believed
yet another—that she had reached the terrible
climax of her troubles. She was only at the beginning of them.

"Hélène!" cried Mme. Dauvray sharply. "What
are you doing?"

The maid instantly slid back into the room.

"Mademoiselle has not moved," she said.

Celia heard the women settle in their chairs about
the table.

"Is madame ready?" asked Hélène; and then
there was the sound of the snap of a switch. In the
salon darkness had come.

If only she had not been wearing her gloves,
Celia thought, she might possibly have just been
able to free her fingers and her supple hands from
their bonds. But as it was she was helpless. She
could only sit and wait until the audience in the
salon grew tired of waiting and came to her. She
closed her eyes, pondering if by any chance she
could excuse her failure. But her heart sank within
her as she thought of Mme. Rossignol's raillery.
No, it was all over for her. . . .

She opened her eyes, and she wondered. It seemed to her that there was more light in the recess than there had been when she closed them. Very likely her eyes were growing used to the darkness. Yet—yet—she ought not to be able to distinguish quite so clearly the white pillar opposite to her. She looked towards the glass doors and understood. The wooden shutters outside the doors were not quite closed. They had been carelessly left unbolted. A chink from lintel to floor let in a grey thread of light. Celia heard the women whispering in the salon, and turned her head to catch the words.

" Do you hear any sound ? "

" No."

" Was that a hand which touched me ? "

" No."

" We must wait."

And so silence came again, and suddenly there was quite a rush of light into the recess. Celia was startled. She turned her head back again towards the window. The wooden door had swung a little more open. There was a wider chink to let the twilight of that starlit darkness through. And as she looked, the chink slowly broadened and broadened, the door swung slowly back on hinges which were strangely silent. Celia stared at the widening panel of grey light with a vague terror. It was strange that she could hear no whisper of wind in the garden. Why, oh, why was that latticed door opening so noiselessly ? Almost she believed

that the spirits after all . . . And suddenly the
recess darkened again, and Celia sat with her heart
leaping and shivering in her breast. There was
something black against the glass doors—a man.
He had appeared as silently, as suddenly, as any
apparition. He stood blocking out the light,
pressing his face against the glass, peering into
the room. For a moment the shock of horror
stunned her. Then she tore frantically at the
cords. All thought of failure, of exposure, of
dismissal had fled from her The three poor
women—that was her thought—were sitting un-
warned, unsuspecting, defenceless in the pitch-
blackness of the salon. A few feet away a man,
a thief, was peering in. They were waiting for
strange things to happen in the darkness. Strange
and terrible things would happen unless she could
free herself, unless she could warn them. And she
could not. Her struggles were mere efforts to
struggle, futile, a shiver from head to foot, and
noiseless as a shiver. Adéle Rossignol had done
her work well and thoroughly. Celia's arms, her
waist, her ankles were pinioned; only the bandage
over her mouth seemed to be loosening. Then
upon horror, horror was added. The man touched
the glass doors, and they swung silently inwards.
They, too, had been carelessly left unbolted. The
man stepped without a sound over the sill into
the room. And, as he stepped, fear for herself
drove out for the moment from Celia's thoughts
fear for the three women in the black room. If

only he did not see her! She pressed herself
against the pillar. He might overlook her, perhaps!
His eyes would not be so accustomed to the darkness of the recess as hers. He might pass her
unnoticed—if only he did not touch some fold of
her dress.

·And then, in the midst of her terror, she experienced so great a revulsion from despair to joy
that a faintness came upon her, and she almost
swooned. She saw who the intruder was. For
when he stepped into the recess he turned towards
her, and the dim light struck upon him and showed
her the contour of his face. It was her lover,
Harry Wethermill. Why he had come at this
hour, and in this strange way, she did not consider. Now she must attract his eyes, now her
fear was lest he should not see her.

But he came at once straight towards her. He
stood in front of her, looking into her eyes. But
he uttered no cry. He made no movement of
surprise. Celia did not understand it. His face
was in the shadow now and she could not see it.
Of course, he was stunned, amazed. But—but—
he stood almost as if he had expected to find her
there and just in that helpless attitude. It was
absurd, of course, but he seemed to look upon her
helplessness as nothing out of the ordinary way.
And he raised no hand to set her free. A chill
struck through her. But the next moment he did
raise his hand and the blood flowed again at her
heart. Of course, she was in the darkness. He

had not seen her plight. Even now he was only
beginning to be aware of it. For his hand touched
the bandage over her mouth—tentatively. He felt
for the knot under the broad brim of her hat at
the back of her head. He found it. In a moment
she would be free. She kept her head quite still,
and then—why was he so long? she asked herself.
Oh, it was not possible! But her heart seemed to
stop, and she knew that it was not only possible—
it was true: he was tightening the scarf, not
loosening it. The folds bound her lips more surely.
She felt the ends drawn close at the back of her
head. In a frenzy she tried to shake her head free.
But he held her face firmly and finished his work.
He was wearing gloves, she noticed with horror,
just as thieves do. Then his hands slid down her
trembling arms and tested the cord about her
wrists. There was something horribly deliberate
about his movements. Celia, even at that moment,
even with him, had the sensation which had pos-
sessed her in the salon. It was the personal
equation on which she was used to rely. But
neither Adéle nor this—this *stranger* was consider-
ing her as even a human being. She was a pawn
in their game, and they used her, careless of her
terror, her beauty, her pain. Then he freed from
her waist the long cord which ran beneath the
curtain to Adéle Rossignol's foot. Celia's first
thought was one of relief. He would jerk the
cord unwittingly. They would come into the recess and see him. And then the real truth flashed

in upon her blindingly. He had jerked the cord, but he had jerked it deliberately. He was already winding it up in a coil as it slid noiselessly across the polished floor beneath the curtains towards him. He had given a signal to Adéle Rossignol. All that woman's scepticism and precaution against trickery had been a mere blind, under cover of which she had been able to pack the girl away securely without arousing her suspicions. Héléne Vauquier was in the plot, too. The scarf at Celia's mouth was proof of that. As if to add proof to proof, she heard Adéle Rossignol speak in answer to the signal.

"Are we all ready? Have you got Mme. Dauvray's left hand, Héléne?"

"Yes, madame," answered the maid.

"And I have her right hand. Now give me yours, and thus we are in a circle about the table."

Celia, in her mind, could see them sitting about the round table in the darkness, Mme. Dauvray between the two women, securely held by them. And she herself could not utter a cry—could not move a muscle to help her.

Wethermill crept back on noiseless feet to the window, closed the wooden doors, and slid the bolts into their sockets. Yes, Héléne Vauquier was in the plot. The bolts and the hinges would not have worked so smoothly but for her. Darkness again filled the recess instead of the grey twilight. But in a moment a faint breath of wind played upon Celia's forehead, and **she** knew that the man had parted the curtains and slipped into the room. Celia let her head fall towards her shoulder. She was sick and faint with terror. Her lover was in this plot—the lover in whom she had felt so much pride, for whose sake she had taken herself so bitterly to task. He was the associate of Adéle Rossignol, of Héléne Vauquier. He had used her, Celia, as an instrument for his crime. All their hours together at the Villa des Fleurs—here to-night was their culmination. The blood buzzed in her ears and hammered in the veins of her temples. In front of her eyes the darkness whirled, flecked with fire. She would have fallen, but she could not fall. Then, in the silence, a tambourine jangled. There was to be a séance to-night, then, and the séance had begun. In a dreadful suspense she heard Mme. Dauvray speak.

CHAPTER XIX

HÉLÈNE EXPLAINS

AND what she heard made her blood run cold.

Mme. Dauvray spoke in a hushed, awestruck voice.

"There is a presence in the room."

It was horrible to Celia that the poor woman was speaking the jargon which she herself had taught to her.

"I will speak to it," said Mme. Dauvray, and, raising her voice a little, she asked, "Who are you that come to us from the spirit-world?"

No answer came, but all the while Celia knew that Wethermill was stealing noiselessly across the floor towards that voice which spoke this professional patter with so simple a solemnity.

"Answer!" she said. And the next moment she uttered a little shrill cry—a cry of enthusiasm. "Fingers touch my forehead—now they touch my cheek—now they touch my throat!"

And upon that the voice ceased. But a dry, choking sound was heard, and a horrible scuffling and tapping of feet upon the polished floor, a sound most dreadful. They were murdering her—murdering an old, kind woman silently and methodically in the darkness. The girl strained and twisted against the pillar furiously, like an animal in a trap. But the coils of rope held her; the scarf suffocated her. The scuffling became a spasmodic sound, with intervals between, and then ceased altogether. A voice spoke—a man's voice—Wethermill's. But Celia would never have recognised it—it had so shrill and fearful an intonation.

" That's horrible," he said, and his voice suddenly rose to a scream.

" Hush !" Héléne Vauquier whispered sharply. " What's the matter ? "

" She fell against me—her whole weight. Oh ! "

" You are afraid of her ! "

" Yes, yes ! " And in the darkness Wethermill's voice came querulously between long breaths. " Yes, *now* I am afraid of her ! "

Héléne Vauquier replied again contemptuously. She spoke aloud and quite indifferently. Nothing of any importance whatever, one would have gathered, had occurred.

" I will turn on the light," she said. And through the chinks in the curtain the bright light shone. Celia heard a loud rattle upon the table, and then fainter sounds of the same kind. And as a kind of horrible accompaniment there ran the laboured breathing of the man, which broke now and then with a sobbing sound. They were stripping Mme. Dauvray of her pearl necklace, her bracelets, and her rings. Celia had a sudden importunate vision of the old woman's fat, podgy hands loaded with brilliants. A jingle of keys followed.

"That's all," Héléne Vauquier said. She might have just turned out the pocket of an old dress.

There was the sound of something heavy and inert falling with a dull crash upon the floor. A woman laughed, and again it was Héléne Vauquier.

"Which is the key of the safe?" asked Adéle. And Héléne Vauquier replied :—

" That one."

Celia heard some one drop heavily into a chair. It was Wethermill, and he buried his face in his hands. Héléne went over to him and laid her hand upon his shoulder and shook him.

" Do you go and get her jewels out of the safe," she said, and she spoke with a rough friendliness.

" You promised you would blindfold the girl," he cried hoarsely.

Héléne Vauquier laughed.

" Did I ?" she said. " Well, what does it matter ?"

"There would have been no need to——" And his voice broke off shudderingly.

"Wouldn't there ? And what of us—Adéle and me ? She knows certainly that we are here. Come, go and get the jewels. The key of the door's on the mantelshelf. While you are away we two will arrange the pretty baby in there."

She pointed to the recess; her voice rang with contempt. Wethermill staggered across the room like a drunkard, and picked up the key in trembling fingers. Celia heard it turn in the lock, and the door bang. Wethermill had gone upstairs.

Celia leaned back, her heart fainting within her. Arrange! It was her turn now. She was to be "arranged." She had no doubt what sinister meaning that innocent word concealed. The dry, choking sound, the horrid scuffling of feet upon the floor, were in her ears. And it had taken so long—so terribly long!

She heard the door open again and shut again. Then steps approached the recess. The curtains were flung back, and the two women stood in front of her—the tall Adéle Rossignol with her red hair and her coarse good looks and her sapphire dress, and the hard-featured, sallow maid. The maid was carrying Celia's white coat. They did not mean to murder her, then. They meant to take her away, and even then a spark of hope lit up in the girl's bosom. For even with her illusions crushed she still clung to life with all the passion of her young soul.

The two women stood and looked at her; and then Adéle Rossignol burst out laughing. Vauquier approached the girl, and Celia had a moment's hope that she meant to free her altogether, but she only loosed the cords which fixed her to the pillar and the high stool.

"Mademoiselle will pardon me for laughing," said Adéle Rossignol politely; "but it was mademoiselle who invited me to try my hand.

And really, for so smart a young lady, mademoiselle looks too ridiculous."

She lifted the girl up and carried her back writhing and struggling into the salon. The whole of the pretty room was within view, but in the embrasure of a window something lay dreadfully still and quiet. Celia held her head averted. But it was there, and, though it was there, all the while the women joked and laughed, Adéle Rossignol feverishly, Héléne Vauquier with a real glee most horrible to see.

" I beg mademoiselle not to listen to what Adéle is saying," exclaimed Héléne. And she began to ape in a mincing, extravagant fashion the manner of a saleswoman in a shop. " Mademoiselle has never looked so ravishing. This style is the last word of fashion. It is what there is of most *chic*. Of course, mademoiselle understands that the costume is not intended for playing the piano. Nor, indeed, for the ballroom. It leaps to one's eyes that dancing would be difficult. Nor is it intended for much conversation. It is a costume for a mood of quiet reflection. But I assure mademoiselle that for pretty young ladies who are the favourites of rich old women it is the style most recommended by the criminal classes."

All the woman's bitter rancour against Celia, hidden for months beneath a mask of humility, burst out and ran riot now. She went to Adéle Rossignol's help, and they flung the girl face downwards upon the sofa. Her face struck the cushion

at one end, her feet the cushion at the other. The
breath was struck out of her body. She lay with
her bosom heaving.

Héléne Vauquier watched her for a moment with
a grin, paying herself now for her respectful
speeches and attendance.

" Yes, lie quietly and reflect, little fool!" she said
savagely. "Were you wise to come here and
interfere with Héléne Vauquier? Hadn't you
better have stayed and danced in your rags
at Montmartre? Are the smart frocks and the
pretty hats and the good dinners worth the price?
Ask yourself these questions, my dainty little
friend!"

She drew up a chair to Celia's side, and sat down
upon it comfortably.

" I will tell you what we are going to do with
you, Mlle. Célie. Adéle Rossignol and that kind
gentleman, M. Wethermill, are going to take you
away with them. You will be glad to go, won't
you, dearie? For you love M. Wethermill, don't
you? Oh, they won't keep you long enough
for you to get tired of them. Do not fear! But
you will not come back, Mlle. Célie. No; you
have seen too much to-night. And every one will
think that Mlle. Célie helped to murder and rob
her benefactress. They are certain to suspect
some one, so why not you, pretty one?"

Celia made no movement. She lay trying to
believe that no crime had been committed, that
that lifeless body did not lie against the wall. And

then she heard in the room above a bed wheeled roughly from its place.

The two women heard it too, and looked at one another.

"He should look in the safe," said Vauquier. "Go and see what he is doing."

And Adéle Rossignol ran from the room.

As soon as she was gone Vauquier followed to the door, listened, closed it gently, and came back. She stooped down.

"Mlle. Célie," she said, in a smooth, silky voice, which terrified the girl more than her harsh tones, "there is just one little thing wrong in your appearance, one tiny little piece of bad taste, if mademoiselle will pardon a poor servant the expression. I did not, mention it before Adéle Rossignol; she is so severe in her criticism, is she not? But since we are alone, I will presume to point out to mademoiselle that those diamond eardrops which I see peeping out under the scarf are a little ostentatious in her present predicament. They are a provocation to thieves. Will mademoiselle permit me to remove them?"

She caught her by the neck and lifted her up. She pushed the lace scarf up at the side of Celia's head. Celia began to struggle furiously, convulsively. She kicked and writhed, and a little tearing sound was heard. One of her shoe-buckles had caught in the thin silk covering of the cushion and slit it. Héléne Vauquier let her fall. She felt composedly in her pocket, and drew from it an aluminium flask—the same flask which Lemerre was afterward to snatch up in the bedroom in Geneva. Celia stared at her in dread. She saw the flask flashing in the light. She shrank from it. She wondered what new horror was to grip her. Héléne unscrewed the top and laughed pleasantly.

" Mlle. Célie is under control," she said. " We shall have to teach her that it is not polite in young ladies to kick." She pressed Celia down with a hand upon her back, and her voice changed. " Lie still," she commanded savagely. " Do you hear ? Do you know what this is, Mlle. Célie ?" And she held the flask towards the girl's face. "This is vitriol, my pretty one. Move, and I'll spoil these smooth white shoulders for you. How would you like that ? "

Celia shuddered from head to foot, and, burying her face in the cushion, lay trembling. She would have begged for death upon her knees rather than suffer this horror. She felt Vauquier's fingers lingering with a dreadful caressing touch upon her shoulders and about her throat. She was within an ace of the torture, the disfigurement, and she knew it. She could not pray for mercy. She could only lie quite still, as she was bidden, trying to control the shuddering of her limbs and body.

" It would be a good lesson for Mlle. Célie," Héléne continued slowly. " I think that if Mlle. Célie will forgive the liberty I ought to inflict it. One little tilt of the flask and the satin of these pretty shoulders——"

She broke off suddenly and listened. Some sound
heard outside had given Celia a respite, perhaps
more than a respite. Héléne set the flask down
upon the table. Her avarice had got the better of
her hatred. She roughly plucked the earrings out
of the girl's ears. She hid them quickly in the
bosom of her dress with her eye upon the door.
She did not see a drop of blood gather on the lobe
of Celia's ear and fall into the cushion on which
her face was pressed. She had hardly hidden them
away before the door opened and Adéle Rossignol
burst into the room.

"What is the matter?" asked Vauquier.

"The safe's empty. We have searched the room.
We have found nothing," she cried.

"Everything is in the safe," Héléne insisted.

"No."

The two women ran out of the room and up the
stairs. Celia, lying on the settee, heard all the quiet
of the house change to noise and confusion. It was
as though a tornado raged in the room overhead.
Furniture was tossed about and over the room, feet
stamped and ran, locks were smashed in with heavy
blows. For many minutes the storm raged. Then
it ceased, and she heard the accomplices clattering
down the stairs without a thought of the noise
they made. They burst into the room. Harry
Wethermill was laughing hysterically, like a
man off his head. He had been wearing a long
dark overcoat when he entered the house; now
he carried the coat over his arm. He was in a

dinner-jacket, and his black clothes were dusty
and disordered.

"It's all for nothing!" he screamed rather than
cried. "Nothing but the one necklace and a
handful of rings!"

In a frenzy he actually stooped over the dead
woman and questioned her.

"Tell us—where did you hide them?" he cried.

"The girl will know," said Hélène.

Wethermill rose up and looked wildly at Celia.

"Yes, yes," he said.

He had no scruple, no pity any longer for the
girl. There was no gain from the crime unless she
spoke. He would have placed his head in the
guillotine for nothing. He ran to the writing-table,
tore off half a sheet of paper, and brought it over
with a pencil to the sofa. He gave them to Vauquier
to hold, and drawing out the sofa from the wall
slipped in behind. He lifted up Celia with Rossignol's help, and made her sit in the middle of
the sofa with her feet upon the ground. He un-
bound her wrists and fingers, and Vauquier placed
the writing-pad and the paper on the girl's knees.
Her arms were still pinioned above the elbows; she
could not raise her hands high enough to snatch
the scarf from her lips. But with the pad held up
to her she could write.

"Where did she keep her jewels? Quick! Take
the pencil and write," said Wethermill, holding her
left wrist.

Vauquier thrust the pencil into her right hand,

and awkwardly and slowly her gloved fingers moved across the page.

"I do not know," she wrote; and, with an oath, Wethermill snatched the paper up, tore it into pieces, and threw it down.

"You have got to know," he said, his face purple with passion, and he flung out his arm as though he would dash his fist into her face. But as he stood with his arm poised there came a singular change upon his face.

"Did you hear anything?" he asked in a whisper.

All listened, and all heard in the quiet of the night a faint click, and after an interval they heard it again, and after another but shorter interval yet once more.

"That's the gate," said Wethermill in a whisper of fear, and a pulse of hope stirred within Celia.

He seized her wrists, crushed them together behind her, and swiftly fastened them once more. Adéle Rossignol sat down upon the floor, took the girl's feet upon her lap, and quietly wrenched off her shoes.

"The light," cried Wethermill in an agonised voice, and Héléne Vauquier flew across the room and turned it off.

All three stood holding their breath, straining their ears in the dark room. On the hard gravel of the drive outside footsteps became faintly audible, and grew louder and came near. Adéle whispered to Vauquier:

" Has the girl a lover ? "

And Héléne Vauquier, even at that moment, laughed quietly.

All Celia's heart and youth rose in revolt against her extremity. If she could only free her lips! The footsteps came round the corner of the housé, they sounded on the drive outside the very window of this room. One cry, and she would be saved. She tossed back her head and tried to force the handkerchief out from between her teeth. But Wethermill's hand covered her mouth and held it closed. The footsteps stopped, a light shone for a moment outside. The very handle of the door was tried. Within a few yards help was there—help and life. Just a frail latticed wooden door stood between her and them. She tried to rise to her feet. Adéle Rossignol held her legs firmly. She was powerless. She sat with one desperate hope that, whoever it was who was in the garden, he would break in. Were it even another murderer, he might have more pity than the callous brutes who held her now; he could have no less. But the footsteps moved away, and took with them all her hopes. Celia heard Wethermill behind her draw a long breath of relief. That seemed to Celia almost the cruellest part of the whole tragedy. They waited in the darkness until the faint click of the gate was heard once more. Then the light was turned up again.

"We must go," said Wethermill. All the three of them were shaken. They stood looking at one another, white and trembling. They spoke in whispers. To get out of the room, to have done with the business—that had suddenly become their chief necessity

Adéle picked up the necklace and the rings from the satin-wood table and put them into a pocket-bag which was slung at her waist.

"Hippolyte shall turn these things into money," she said. "He shall set about it to-morrow. We shall have to keep the girl now—until she tells us where the rest is hidden."

"Yes, keep her," said Héléne. "We will come over to Geneva in a few days, as soon as we can. We will persuade her to tell." She glanced darkly at the girl. Celia shivered.

"Yes, that's it," said Wethermill. "But don't harm her. She will tell of her own will. You will see. The delay won't hurt now. We can't come back and search for a little while."

He was speaking in a quick, agitated voice. And Adéle agreed. The desire to be gone had killed even their fury at the loss of their prize. Some time they would come back, but they would not search now—they were too unnerved.

"Héléne," said Wethermill, "get to bed. I'll come up with the chloroform and put you to sleep."

Héléne Vauquier hurried upstairs. It was part of her plan that she should be left alone, chloroformed, in the Villa. Thus only could suspicion be averted from herself. She did not shrink from it now. She went, the strange woman, without a tremor to her ordeal. Wethermill took the length of rope which had fixed Celia to the pillar.

"I'll follow," he said, and as he turned he stumbled over the body of Mme. Dauvray. With a shrill cry he kicked it out of his way and crept up the stairs. Adéle Rossignol quickly set the room in order. She removed the stool from its position in the recess, and carried it to its place in the hall. She put Celia's shoes upon her feet, loosening the cord from her ankles. Then she looked about the floor and picked up here and there a scrap of cord. In the silence the clock upon the mantelshelf chimed the quarter past eleven. She screwed the stopper on the flask of vitriol very carefully, and put the flask away in her pocket. She went into the kitchen and fetched the key of the garage. She put her hat on her head. She even picked up and drew on her gloves, afraid lest she should leave them behind; and then Wethermill came down again. Adéle looked at him inquiringly.

"It is all done," he said, with a nod of the head. "I will bring the car down to the door. Then I'll drive you to Geneva and come back with the car here."

He cautiously opened the latticed door of the window, listened for a moment, and ran silently down the drive. Adéle closed the door again, but she did not bolt it. She came back into the room; she looked at Celia, as she lay back upon the settee,

with a long glance of indecision. And then, to
Celia's surprise—for she had given up all hope—the
indecision in her eyes became pity. She suddenly
ran across the room and knelt down before Celia.
With quick and feverish hands she untied the cord
which fastened the train of her skirt about her
knees.

At first Celia shrank away, fearing some new
cruelty. But Adéle's voice came to her ears, speaking—and speaking with remorse.

"I can't endure it!" she whispered. "You are
so young—too young to be killed."

The tears were rolling down Celia's cheeks. Her
face was pitiful and beseeching.

"Don't look at me like that, for God's sake,
child!" Adéle went on, and she chafed the girl's
ankles for a moment.

"Can you stand?" she asked.

Celia nodded her head gratefully. After all,
then, she was not to die. It seemed to her
hardly possible. But before she could rise a
subdued whir of machinery penetrated into the
room, and the motor-car came slowly to the front
of the villa.

"Keep still!" said Adéle hurriedly, and she
placed herself in front of Celia.

Wethermill opened the wooden door, while Celia's
heart raced in her bosom.

"I will go down and open the gate," he whispered.
"Are you ready?"

"Yes."

Wethermill disappeared; and this time he left the door open. Adéle helped Celia to her feet. For a moment she tottered; then she stood firm.

" Now run !" whispered Adéle. " Run, child, for your life ! "

Celia did not stop to think whither she should run, or how she should escape from Wethermill's search. She could not ask that her lips and her hands might be freed. She had but a few seconds. She had one thought—to hide herself in the darkness of the garden. Celia fled across the room, sprang wildly over the sill, ran, tripped over her skirt, steadied herself, and was swung off the ground by the arms of Harry Wethermill.

" There we are," he said, with his shrill, wavering laugh. " I opened the gate before." And suddenly Celia hung inert in his arms.

The light went out in the salon. Adéle Rossignol, carrying Celia's cloak, stepped out at the side of the window.

"She has fainted," said Wethermill. "Wipe the mould off her shoes and off yours too—carefully. I don't want them to think this car has been out of the garage at all."

Adéle stooped and obeyed. Wethermill opened the door of the car and flung Celia into a seat. Adéle followed and took her seat opposite the girl. Wethermill stepped carefully again on to the grass, and with the toe of his shoe scraped up and ploughed the impressions which he and Adéle Rossignol had made on the ground, leaving those which Celia had made. He came back to the window.

"She has left her footmarks clear enough," he whispered. "There will be no doubt in the morning that she went of her own free will."

Then he took the chauffeur's seat, and the car glided silently down the drive and out by the gate. As soon as it was on the road it stopped. In an instant Adéle Rossignol's head was out of the window.

"What is it?" she exclaimed in fear.

Wethermill pointed to the roof. He had left the light burning in Héléne Vauquier's room.

"We can't go back now," said Adéle in a frantic whisper. "No; it is over. I daren't go back." And Wethermill jammed down the lever. The car sprang forward, and humming steadily over the white road devoured the miles. But they had made their one mistake.

CHAPTER XX

THE GENEVA ROAD

THE car had nearly reached Annecy before Celia woke to consciousness. And even then she was dazed. She was only aware that she was in the motor-car and travelling at a great speed. She lay back, drinking in the fresh air. Then she moved, and with the movement came to her recollection and the sense of pain. Her arms and wrists were still bound behind her, and the cords hurt her like hot wires. Her mouth, however, and her feet were free. She started forward, and Adéle Rossignol spoke sternly from the seat opposite.

"Keep still. I am holding the flask in my hand. If you scream, if you make a movement to escape, I shall fling the vitriol in your face," she said.

Celia shrank back, shivering.

"I won't! I won't!" she whispered piteously. Her spirit was broken by the horrors of the night's adventure. She lay back and cried quietly in the darkness of the carriage. The car dashed through Annecy. It seemed incredible to Celia that less than six hours ago she had been dining with Mme. Dauvray and the woman opposite, who

283

was now her jailer. Mme. Dauvray lay dead in the
little salon, and she herself—she dared not think
what lay in front of her. She was to be persuaded—
that was the word—to tell what she did not know.
Meanwhile her name would be execrated through
Aix as the murderess of the woman who had saved
her. Then suddenly the car stopped. There were
lights outside. Celia heard voices. A man was
speaking to Harry Wethermill. Celia started, and
saw Adéle Tacé's arm flash upwards. She sank
back in terror; and the car rolled on into the
darkness. Adéle Tacé drew a breath of relief.
The one point of danger had been passed. They
had crossed the Pont de la Caille; they were in
Switzerland.

Some long while afterwards the car slackened its
speed. By the side of it Celia heard the sound of
wheels and of the hooves of a horse. A single-horsed
closed landau had been caught up as it jogged
along the road. The motor-car stopped; close by
the side of it the driver of the landau reined in
his horse. Wethermill jumped down from the
chauffeur's seat, opened the door of the landau,
and then put his head in at the window of the car.

"Are you ready? Be quick!"

Adéle turned to Celia.

"Not a word, remember!"

Wethermill flung open the door of the car. Adéle
took the girl's feet and drew them down to the
step of the car. Then she pushed her out. Wethermill caught her in his arms and carried her to the

landau. Celia dared not cry out. Her hands were helpless, her face at the mercy of that grim flask. Just ahead of them the lights of Geneva were visible, and from the lights a silver radiance overspread a patch of sky. Wethermill placed her in the landau; Adéle sprang in behind her and closed the door. The transfer had taken no more than a few seconds. The landau jogged into Geneva; the motor turned and sped back over the fifty miles of empty road to Aix.

As the motor-car rolled away, courage returned for a moment to Celia. The man—the murderer—had gone. She was alone with Adéle Rossignol in a carriage moving no faster than an ordinary trot. Her ankles were free, the gag had been taken from her lips. If only she could free her hands and choose a moment when Adéle was off her guard 'she might open the door and spring out on to the road. She saw Adéle draw down the blinds of the carriage, and very carefully, very secretly, Celia began to work her hands behind her. She was an adept; no movement was visible, but, on the other hand, no success was obtained. The knots had been too cunningly tied. And then Mme. Rossignol touched a button at her side in the leather of the carriage. The touch turned on a tiny lamp in the roof of the carriage, and she raised a warning hand to Celia.

" Now keep very quiet."

Right through the empty streets of Geneva the landau was quietly driven. Adéle had peeped from

time to time under the blind. There were few
people in the streets. Once or twice a *sergent-de-
ville* was seen under the light of a lamp. Celia
dared not cry out. Over against her, persistently
watching her, Adéle Rossignol sat with the open
flask clenched in her hand, and from the vitriol Celia
shrank with an overwhelming terror. The carriage
drove out from the town along the western edge of
the lake.

"Now listen," said Adéle. "As soon as the
landau stops the door of the house opposite to which
it stops will open. I shall open the carriage door
myself and you will get out. You will stand close
by the carriage door until I have got out. I shall
hold this flask ready in my hand. As soon as I
am out you will run across the pavement into the
house. You won't speak or scream."

Adéle Rossignol turned out the lamp and drew
up the carriage blinds.

Ten minutes later the carriage passed down the
little street and attracted Mme. Gobin's notice.
Marthe Gobin had no light in her room. Adéle
Rossignol peered out of the carriage. She saw
the houses in darkness. She could not see the
busybody's face watching the landau from a dark
window. She cut the cords which fastened the
girl's hands. The carriage stopped. She opened
the door. Celia sprang out on to the pavement.
She sprang so quickly that Adèle Rossignol caught
and held the train of her dress. But it was the fear
of the vitriol which had made her spring so nimbly.

It was that, too, which made her run so lightly and
quickly into the house. The old woman who acted
as servant, Jeanne Tacé, received her. Celia offered
no resistance. The fear of vitriol had made her
supple as a glove. Jeanne hurried her down the
stairs into the little parlour at the back of the house,
where supper was laid, and pushed her into a chair.
Celia let her arms fall forward on the table. She
had no hope now. She was friendless and alone in
a den of murderers, who meant first to torture, then
to kill her. She would be held up to execration as
a murderess. No one would know how she had
died or what she had suffered. She was in pain,
and her throat burned. She buried her face in her
arms and sobbed. All her body shook with her
sobbing. Jeanne Rossignol took no notice. She
treated Celia just as the others had done. Celia
was *la petite*, against whom she had no animosity,
by whom she was not to be touched to any tenderness. *La petite* had unconsciously played her useful
part in their crime. But her use was ended now,
and they would deal with her accordingly. She
removed the girl's hat and cloak and tossed them
aside.

"Now stay quiet until we are ready for you," she
said. And Celia, lifting her head, said in a
whisper:

"Water!"

The old woman poured some from a jug and held
the glass to Celia's lips.

"Thank you," whispered Celia gratefully, and

Adèle came into the room. She told the story of the night to Jeanne, and afterwards to Hippolyte when he joined them.

"And nothing gained!" cried the older woman furiously. "And we have hardly a five-franc piece in the house."

"Yes, something," said Adèle. "A necklace—a good one—some good rings, and bracelets. And we shall find out where the rest is hid—from her." And she nodded at Celia.

The three people ate their supper, and, while they ate it, discussed Celia's fate. She was lying with her head bowed upon her arms at the same table, within a foot of them. But they made no more of her presence than if she had been an old shoe. Only once did one of them speak to her.

"Stop your whimpering," said Hippolyte roughly. "We can hardly hear ourselves talk."

He was for finishing with the business altogether to-night.

"It's a mistake," he said. "There's been a bungle, and the sooner we are rid of it the better. There's a boat at the bottom of the garden."

Celia listened and shuddered. He would have no more compunction over drowning her than he would have had over drowning a blind kitten.

"It's cursed luck," he said. "But we have got the necklace—that's something. That's our share, do you see? The young spark can look for the rest."

But Hélène Vauquier's wish prevailed. She was

the leader. They would keep the girl until she came to Geneva.

. They took her upstairs into the big bedroom overlooking the lake. Adéle opened the door of the closet, where a truckle-bed stood, and thrust the girl in.

"This is my room," she said warningly, pointing to the bedroom. "Take care I hear no noise. You might shout yourself hoarse, my pretty one; no one else would hear you. But I should, and afterwards—we should no longer be able to call you 'my pretty one,' eh?"

And with a horrible playfulness she pinched the girl's cheek.

Then with old Jeanne's help she stripped Celia and told her to get into bed.

"I'll give her something to keep her quiet," said Adéle, and she fetched her morphia-needle and injected a dose into Celia's arm.

Then they took her clothes away and left her in the darkness. She heard the key turn in the lock, and a moment after the sound of the bedstead being drawn across the doorway. But she heard no more, for almost immediately she fell asleep.

She was awakened some time the next day by the door opening. Old Jeanne Tacé brought her in a jug of water and a roll of bread, and locked her up again. And a long time afterwards she brought her another supply. Yet another day had gone, but in that dark cupboard Celia had no means of judging time. In the afternoon the newspaper

came out with the announcement that Mme.
Dauvray's jewellery had been discovered under the
boards. Hippolyte brought in the newspaper, and,
cursing their stupidity, they sat down to decide
upon Celia's fate. That, however, was soon
arranged. They would dress her in everything
which she wore when she came, so that no trace
of her might be discovered. They would give her
another dose of morphia, use the vitriol as soon
as she was unconscious to destroy any possibility
of recognition, sew her up in a sack, row her far out
on to the lake, and sink her with a weight attached.
They dragged her out from her cupboard, always
with the threat of that bright aluminium flask
before her eyes. She fell upon her knees, imploring
their pity with the tears running down her cheeks;
but they sewed the strip of sacking over her face
so that she should see nothing of their preparations.
They flung her on the sofa, secured her as Hanaud
had found her, and, leaving her in the old woman's
charge, Adéle went downstairs for her needle and
Hippolyte to get ready the boat. As Hippolyte
opened the door into the garden he saw the launch
of the Chef de la Sûreté glide along the bank.

CHAPTER XXI

HANAUD EXPLAINS

THIS is the story as Mr. Ricardo wrote it out from the statement of Celia herself and the confession of Adèle Rossignol. Obscurities which had puzzled him were made clear. But he was still unaware how Hanaud had worked out the solution.

"You promised me that you would explain," he said, when they were both together at Aix after the trial was over. The two men had just finished luncheon at the Cercle and were sitting over their coffee. Hanaud lighted a cigar.

"There were difficulties, of course," he said; "the crime was so carefully planned. The little details, such as the footprints, the absence of any mud from the girl's shoes in the carriage of the motor-car, the dinner at Annecy, the purchase of the cord, the want of any sign of a struggle in the little salon, were all carefully thought out. Had not one little accident happened, and one little mistake been made in consequence, I doubt if we should have laid our hands upon one of the gang. We might have suspected Wethermill; we should hardly have secured him, and we should very likely never have known of the Tacé family. That mistake was, as you no doubt are fully aware——"

"The failure of Wethermill to discover Mme. Dauvray's jewels," said Ricardo at once.

"No, my friend," answered Hanaud. "That made them keep Mlle. Célie alive. It enabled us to save her when we had discovered the whereabouts of the gang. It did not help us very much to lay our hands upon them. No; the little accident which happened was the entrance of our friend Perrichet into the garden while the murderers were still in the room. Imagine that scene, M. Ricardo. The rage of the murderers at their inability to discover the plunder for which they had risked their necks, the old woman crumpled up on the floor against the wall, the girl writing laboriously with fettered arms 'I do not know' under threats of torture, and then in the stillness of the night the clear, tiny click of the gate and the measured, relentless footsteps. No wonder they were terrified in that dark room. What would be their one thought? Why, to get away—to come back perhaps later, when Mlle. Célie should have told them what, by the way, she did not know, but in any case to get away now. So they made their little mistake, and in their hurry they left the light burning in the room of Héléne Vauquier, and the murder was discovered seven hours too soon for them."

"Seven hours!" said Mr. Ricardo.

"Yes. The household did not rise early. It was not until seven that the charwoman came. It was she who was meant to discover the crime. By that time the motor-car would have been back three hours ago in its garage. Servettaz, the chauffeur, would have returned from Chambéry some time in the morning, he would have cleaned the car, he would have noticed that there was very little petrol in the tank, as there had been when he had left it on the day before. He would not have noticed that some of his many tins which had been full yesterday were empty to-day. We should not have discovered that about four in the morning the car was close to the Villa Rose and that it had travelled, between midnight and five in the morning, a hundred and fifty kilometres."

"But you had already guessed 'Geneva,'" said Ricardo. "At luncheon, before the news came that the car was found, you had guessed it."

"It was a shot," said Hanaud. "The absence of the car helped me to make it. It is a large city and not very far away, a likely place for people with the police at their heels to run to earth in. But if the car had been discovered in the garage I should not have made that shot. Even then I had no particular conviction about Geneva. I really wished to see how Wethermill would take it. He was wonderful."

"He sprang up."

"He betrayed nothing but surprise. You showed no less surprise than he did, my good friend. What

I was looking for was one glance of fear. I did
not get it."

" Yet you suspected him—even then you spoke of
brains and audacity. You told him enough to hinder
him from communicating with the red-haired woman
in Geneva. You isolated him. Yes, you suspected
him."

" Let us take the case from the beginning. When
you first came to me, as I told you, the Commissaire
had already been with me. There was an interesting piece of evidence already in his possession.
Adolphe Ruel—who saw Wethermill and Vauquier
together close by the Casino and overheard that
cry of Wethermill's, ' It is true : I must have
money ! '—had already been with his story 'to the
Commissaire. I knew it when Harry Wethermill
came into the room to ask me to take up the case.
That was a bold stroke, my friend. The chances
were a hundred to one that I should not interrupt
my holiday to take up a case because of your
little dinner-party in London. Indeed, I should not
have interrupted it had I not known Adolphe Ruel's
story. As it was I could not resist. Wethermill's
very audacity charmed me. |Oh yes, I felt that
I must pit myself against him. So few criminals
have spirit, M. Ricardo. It is deplorable how few.
But Wethermill ! See in what a fine position he
would have been if only I had refused. He himself
had been the first to call upon the first detective in
France. And his argument ! He loved Mlle. Célie.
Therefore she must be innocent ! How he stuck to

it! People would have said, 'Love is blind,' and all the more they would have suspected Mlle. Célie. Yes, but they love the blind lover. Therefore all the more would it have been impossible for them to believe Harry Wethermill had 'any share in that grim crime."

Mr. Ricardo drew his chair closer in to the table.

"I will confess to you," he said, "that I thought Mlle. Célie was an accomplice."

"It is not surprising," said Hanaud. "Some one within the house was an accomplice—we start with that fact. The house had not been broken into. There was Mlle. Célie's record as Héléne Vauquier gave it to us, and a record obviously true. There was the fact that she had got rid of Servettaz. There was the maid upstairs very ill from the chloroform. What more likely than that Mlle. Célie had arranged a séance, and then when the lights were out had admitted the murderer through that convenient glass door?"

"There were, besides, the definite imprints of her shoes," said Mr. Ricardo.

"Yes, but that is precisely where I began to feel sure that she was innocent," replied Hanaud dryly. "All the other footmarks had been so carefully scored and ploughed up that nothing could be made of them. Yet those little ones remained so definite, so easily identified, and I began to wonder why these, too, had not been cut up and stamped over. The murderers had taken, you see, an excess of precaution to throw the presumption of guilt upon

Mlle. Célie rather than upon Vauquier. However, there the footsteps were. Mlle. Célie had sprung from the room as I described to Wethermill. But I was puzzled. Then in the room I found the torn-up sheet of notepaper with the words, 'Je ne sais pas,' in mademoiselle's handwriting. The words might have been spirit-writing, they might have meant anything. I put them away in my mind. But in the room the settee puzzled me. And again I was troubled—greatly troubled."

"Yes, I saw that."

"And not you alone," said Hanaud, with a smile. "Do you remember that loud cry Wethermill gave when we returned to the room and once more I stood before the settee? Oh, he turned it off very well. I had said that our criminals in France were not very gentle with their victims, and he pretended that it was in fear of what Mlle. Célie might be suffering which had torn that cry from his heart. But it was not so. He was afraid—deadly afraid —not for Mlle. Célie, but for himself. He was afraid that I had understood what those cushions had to tell me."

"What did they tell you?" asked Ricardo.

"You know now," said Hanaud. "There were two cushions, both indented, and indented in different ways. The one at the head was irregularly indented—something shaped had pressed upon it. It might have been a face—it might not; and there was a little brown stain which was fresh and which was blood. The second cushion had two separate impressions, and between them the cushion was forced up in a thin ridge; and these impressions were more definite. I measured the distance between the two cushions, and I found this: that supposing—and it was a large supposition—the cushions had not been moved since those impressions were made, a girl of Mlle. Célie's height lying stretched out upon the sofa would have her face pressing down upon the one cushion and her feet and insteps upon the other. Now, the impressions upon the second cushion and the thin ridge between them were just the impressions which might have been made by a pair of shoes held close together. But that would not be a natural attitude for any one, and the mark upon the head cushion was very deep. Supposing that my conjectures were true, then a woman would only lie like that because she was helpless, because she had been flung there, because she could not lift herself—because, in a word, her hands were tied behind her back and her feet fastened together. Well, then, follow this train of reasoning, my friend! Suppose my conjectures—and we had nothing but conjectures to build upon—were true, the woman flung upon the sofa could not be Héléne Vauquier, for she would have said so; she could have had no reason for concealment. But it must be Mlle. Célie. There was the slit in the one cushion and the stain on the other which, of course, I had not accounted for. There was still, too, the puzzle of the footsteps outside the glass doors. If Mlle.

Célie had been bound upon the sofa, how came she to run with her limbs free from the house? There was a question—a question not easy to answer."

"Yes," said Mr. Ricardo.

"Yes; but there was also another question. ·Suppose that Mlle. Célie was, after all, the victim, not the accomplice; suppose she had been flung tied upon the sofa; suppose that somehow the imprint of her shoes upon the ground had been made, and that she had afterwards been carried away, so that the maid might be cleared of all complicity—in that case it became intelligible why the other footprints were scored out and hers left. The presumption of guilt would fall upon her. There would be proof that she ran hurriedly from the room and sprang into a motor-car of her own free will. But, again, if that theory were true, then Héléne Vauquier was the accomplice and not Mlle. Célie."

"I follow that."

"Then I found an interesting piece of evidence with regard to the strange woman who came: I picked up a long red hair—a very important piece of evidence about which I thought it best to say nothing at all. It was not Mlle. Célie's hair, which is fair; nor Vauquier's, which is black; nor Mme. Dauvray's, which is dyed brown; nor the char-woman's, which is grey. It was, therefore, the visitor's. Well, we went upstairs to Mlle. Célie's room."

" Yes," said Mr. Ricardo eagerly. " We are coming to the pot of cream."

"In that room we learnt that Héléne Vauquier, at her own request, had already paid it a visit. It is true the Commissaire said that he had kept his eye on her the whole time. But none the less from the window he saw me coming down the road, and that he could not have done, as I made sure, unless he had turned his back upon Vauquier and leaned out of the window. Now at the time I had an open mind about Vauquier. On the whole I was inclined to think she had no share in the affair. But either she or Mlle. Célie had, and perhaps both. But one of them—yes. That was sure. Therefore I asked what drawers she touched after the Commissaire had leaned out of the window. For if she had any motive in wishing to visit the room she would have satisfied it when the Commissaire's back was turned. He pointed to a drawer, and I took out a dress and shook it, thinking that she may have wished to hide something. But nothing fell out. On the other hand, however, I saw some quite fresh grease-marks, made by fingers, and the marks were wet. I began to ask myself how it was that Héléne Vauquier, who had just been helped to dress by the nurse, had grease upon her fingers. Then I looked at a drawer which she had examined first of all. There were no grease-marks on the clothes she had turned over before the Commissaire leaned out of the window. Therefore it followed that during the few seconds when he was watching

me she had touched grease. I looked about the
room, and there on the dressing-table close by the
chest of drawers was a pot of cold cream. That
was the grease Héléne Vauquier had touched. And
why—if not to hide some small thing in it which,
firstly, she dared not keep in her own room ; which,
secondly, she wished to hide in the room of Mlle.
Célie; and which, thirdly, she had not had an
opportunity to hide before ? Now bear those three
conditions in mind, and tell me what the small
thing was."

Mr. Ricardo nodded his head.

" I know now," he said. " You told me. The
earrings of Mlle. Célie. But I should not have
guessed it at the time."

"Nor could I—at the time," said Hanaud. " I
kept my open mind about Héléne Vauquier; but
I locked the door and took the key. Then we went
and heard Vauquier's story. The story was clever,
because so much of it was obviously, indisputably
true. The account of the séances, of Mme. Dauvray's
superstitions, her desire for an interview with Mme.
de Montespan—such details are not invented. It
was interesting, too, to know that there had been
a séance planned for that night ! The method of
the murder began to be clear. So far she spoke
the truth. But then she lied. Yes, she lied, and
it was a bad lie, my friend. She told us that the
strange woman Adéle had black hair. Now I
carried in my pocket-book proof that that woman's
hair was red. Why did she lie, except to make

impossible the identification of that strange visitor?
That was the first false step taken by Héléne
Vauquier.

"Now let us take the second. I thought nothing
of her rancour against Mlle. Célie. To me it was
all very natural. She—the hard peasant woman
no longer young, who had been for years the
confidential servant of Mme. Dauvray, and no doubt
had taken her levy from the impostors who preyed
upon her credulous mistress—certainly she would
hate this young and pretty outcast whom she has
to wait upon, whose hair she has to dress.
Vauquier—she would hate her. But if by any
chance she were in the plot—and the lie seemed
to show she was—then the séances showed me
new possibilities. For Héléne used to help Mlle.
Célie. Suppose that the séance had taken place,
that this sceptical visitor with the red hair professed
herself dissatisfied with Vauquier's method of
testing the medium, had suggested another way,
Mlle. Célie could not object, and there she would
be neatly and securely packed up beyond the power
of offering any resistance, before she could have a
suspicion that things were wrong. It would be an
easy little comedy to play. And if that were true—
why, there were my sofa cushions partly explained."

"Yes, I see!" cried Ricardo, with enthusiasm.
"You are wonderful."

Hanaud was not displeased with his companion's
enthusiasm.

"But wait a moment. We have only conjectures

so far, and one fact that Héléne Vauquier lied about
the colour of the strange woman's hair. Now we
get another fact. Mlle. Célie was wearing buckles
on her ,shoes. And there is my slit in the sofa
cushions. For when she is flung on to the sofa,
what will she do ? She will kick, she will struggle.
Of course it is conjecture. I do not as yet hold
pigheadedly to it. I am not yet sure that Mlle.
Célie is innocent. I am willing at any moment
to admit that the facts contradict my theory. But,
on the contrary, each fact that I discover helps it to
take shape.

"Now I come to Hélène Vauquier's second
mistake. On the evening when you saw Mlle. Célie
in the garden behind the baccarat-rooms you
noticed that she wore no jewellery except a pair
of diamond eardrops. In the photograph of her
which Wethermill showed me, again she was
wearing them. Is it not, therefore, probable that
she usually wore them ? When I examined her
room I found the case for those earrings—the case
was empty. It was natural, then, to infer that she
was wearing them when she came down to the
séance."

" Yes."

" Well, I read a description—a carefully written
description—of the missing girl, made by Hélène
Vauquier after an examination of the girl's ward-
robe. There is no mention of the earrings. So
I asked her —' Was she not wearing them ? '
Hélène Vauquier was taken by surprise. How

should I know anything of Mlle. Célie's earrings?
She hesitated. She did not quite know what
answer to make. Now, why? Since she herself
dressed Mlle. Célie, and remembers so very well
all she wore, why does she hesitate? Well, there
is a reason. She does not know how much I know
about those diamond eardrops. She is not sure
whether we have not dipped into that pot of cold
cream and found them. Yet without knowing she
cannot answer. So now we come back to our pot
of cold cream."

"Yes!" cried Mr. Ricardo. "They were there."

"Wait a bit," said Hanaud. "Let us see how it
works out. Remember the conditions. Vauquier
has some small thing which she must hide, and
which she wishes to hide in Mlle. Célie's room.
For she admitted that it was her suggestion that
she should look through mademoiselle's wardrobe.
For what reason does she choose the girl's room,
except that if the thing were discovered that would
be the natural place for it? It is, then, something
belonging to Mlle. Célie. There was a second
condition we laid down. It was something Vauquier had not been able to hide before. It came,
then, into her possession last night. Why could
she not hide it last night? Because she was not
alone. There were the man and the woman, her
accomplices. It was something, then, which she
was concerned in hiding from them. It is not rash
to guess, then, that it was some piece of the plunder
of which the other two would have claimed their

share—and a piece of plunder belonging to Mlle. Célie. Well, she has nothing but the diamond eardrops. Suppose Vauquier is left alone to guard Mlle. Célie while the other two ransack Mme. Dauvray's room. She sees her chance. The girl cannot stir hand or foot to save herself. Vauquier tears the eardrops in a hurry from her ears—and there I have my drop of blood just where I should expect it to be. But now follow this! Vauquier hides the earrings in her pocket. She goes to bed in order to be chloroformed. She knows that it is very possible that her room will be searched before she regains consciousness, or before she is well enough to move. There is only one place to hide them in, only one place where they will be safe. In bed with her. But in the morning she must get rid of them, and a nurse is with her. Hence the excuse to go to Mlle. Célie's room. If the eardrops are found in the pot of cold cream, it would only be thought that Mlle. Célie had herself hidden them there for safety. Again it is conjecture, and I wish to make sure. So I tell Vauquier she can go away, and I leave her unwatched. I have her driven to the depôt instead of to her friends, and searched. Upon her is found the pot of cream, and in the cream Mlle. Célie's eardrops. She has slipped into Mlle. Célie's room, as, if my theory was correct, she would be sure to do, and put the pot of cream into her pocket. So I am now fairly sure that she is concerned in the murder.

"We then went to Mme. Dauvray's room and

discovered her brilliants and her ornaments. At once the meaning of that agitated piece of handwriting of Mlle. Célie's becomes clear. She is asked where the jewels are hidden. She cannot answer, for her mouth, of course, is stopped. She has to write. Thus my conjectures get more and more support. And, mind this, one of the two women is guilty—Célie or Vauquier. My discoveries all fit in with the theory of Célie's innocence. But there remain the footprints, for which I found no explanation.

"You will remember I made you all promise silence as to the finding of Mme. Dauvray's jewellery. For I thought, if they have taken the girl away so that suspicion may fall on her and not on Vauquier, they mean to dispose of her. But they may keep her so long as they have a chance of finding out from her Mme. Dauvray's hiding-place. It was a small chance, but our only one. The moment the discovery of the jewellery was published the girl's fate was sealed, were my theory true.

"Then came our advertisement and Mme. Gobin's written testimony. There was one small point of interest which I will take first: her statement that Adéle was the Christian name of the woman with the red hair, that the old woman who was the servant in that house in the suburb of Geneva called her Adéle, just simply Adéle. That interested me, for Héléne Vauquier had called her Adéle too when she was describing to us the unknown visitor. 'Adéle' was what Mme. Dauvray called her."

"Yes," said Ricardo. " Héléne Vauquier made
a slip there. She should have given her a false
name."

Hanaud nodded.

" It was the one slip she made in the whole of the
business. Nor did she recover herself very cleverly.
For when the Commissaire pounced upon the name,
she at once modified her words. She only thought
now that the name was Adéle, or something like
it. But when I went on to suggest that the name
in any case would be a false one, at once she went
back upon her modifications. And now she was
sure that Adéle was the name used. I remembered
her hesitation when I read Marthe Gobin's letter.
That helped to confirm me in my theory that she
was in the plot ; and that made me very sure that
it was an Adéle for whom we had to look. So far
well. But other statements in the letter puzzled me.
For instance, ' She ran lightly and quickly across
the pavement into the house, as though she were
afraid to be seen.' Those were the words, and
the woman was obviously honest. What became
of my theory then ? The girl was free to run, free
to stoop and pick up the train of her gown in
her hand, free to shout for help in the open
street if she wanted help. No ; that I could not
explain until that afternoon, when I saw Mlle.
Célie's terror-stricken eyes fixed upon that flask as
Lemerre poured a little out and burnt a hole in the
sack. Then I understood well enough. The fear
of vitriol !" Hanaud gave an uneasy shudder.

"And it is enough to make any one afraid! That I can tell you. No wonder she lay still as a mouse upon the sofa in the bedroom. No wonder she ran quickly into the house. Well, there you have the explanation. I had only my theory to work upon even after Mme. Gobin's evidence. But as it happened it was the right one. Meanwhile, of course, I made my inquiries into Wethermill's circumstances. My good friends in England helped me. They were precarious. He owed money in Aix, money at his hotel. We knew from the motor-car that the man we were searching for had returned to Aix. Things began to look black for Wethermill. Then you gave me a little piece of information."

"I!" exclaimed Ricardo, with a start.

"Yes. You told me that you walked up to the hotel with Harry Wethermill on the night of the murder and separated just before ten. A glance into his rooms which I had—you will remember that when we had discovered the motor-car I suggested that we should go to Harry Wethermill's rooms and talk it over—that glance enabled me to see that he could very easily have got out of his room on to the verandah below and escaped from the hotel by the garden quite unseen. For you will remember than whereas your rooms look out to the front and on to the slope of Mont Revard, Wethermill's look out over the garden and the town of Aix. In a quarter of an hour or twenty minutes he could have reached the Villa Rose. He could

have been in the salon before half-past ten, and
that is just the hour which suited me perfectly.
And, as he got out unnoticed, so he could return.
So he did return! My friend, there are some
interesting marks upon the window-sill of Wethermill's room and upon the pillar just beneath it.
Take a look, M. Ricardo, when you return to your
hotel. But that was not all. We talked of Geneva
in Mr. Wethermill's room, and of the distance between Geneva and Aix. Do you remember that?"

"Yes," replied Ricardo.

"Do you remember too that I asked him for a
road-book?"

"Yes; to make sure of the distance. I do."

"Ah, but it was not to make sure of the distance
that I asked for the road-book, my friend. I asked
in order to find out whether Harry Wethermill had
a road-book at all which gave a plan of the roads
between here and Geneva. And he had. He
handed it to me at once and quite naturally. I
hope that I took it calmly, but I was not at all
calm inside. For it was a new road-book, which,
by the way, he bought a week before, and I was
asking myself all the while—now what was I asking
myself, M. Ricardo?"

"No," said Ricardo, with a smile. "I am growing
wary. I will not tell you what you were asking
yourself, M. Hanaud. For even were I right you
would make out that I was wrong, and leap upon
me with injuries and gibes. No, you shall drink
your coffee and tell me of your own accord."

"Well," said Hanaud, laughing, "I will tell you. I was asking myself: 'Why does a man who owns no motor-car, who hires no motor-car, go out into Aix and buy an automobilist's road-map? With what object?' And I found it an interesting question. M. Harry Wethermill was not the man to go upon a walking tour, eh? Oh, I was obtaining evidence. But then came an overwhelming thing— the murder of Marthe Gobin. We know now how he did it. He walked beside the cab, put his head in at the window, asked, 'Have you come in answer to the advertisement?' and stabbed her straight to the heart through her dress. The dress and the weapon which he used would save him from being stained with her blood. He was in your room that morning when we were at the station; as I told you, he left his glove behind. He was searching for a telegram in answer to your advertisement. Or he came to sound you. He had already received his telegram from Hippolyte. He was like a fox in a cage, snapping at every one, twisting vainly this way and that way, risking everything and every one to save his precious neck. Marthe Gobin was in the way. She is killed. Mlle. Célie is a danger. So Mlle. Célie must be suppressed. And off goes a telegram to the Geneva paper, handed in by a waiter from the café at the station of Chambéry before five o'clock. Wethermill went to Chambéry that afternoon when we went to Geneva. Once we could get him on the run, once we could so harry and bustle him that he must take risks—why, we had him. And that afternoon he had to take them."

"So that even before Marthe Gobin was killed you were sure that Wethermill was the murderer?"

Hanaud's face clouded over.

"You put your finger on a sore place, M. Ricardo. I was sure, but I still wanted evidence to convict. I left him free, hoping for that evidence I left him free, hoping that he would commit himself. He did, but—— well, let us talk of some one else. What of Mlle. Célie?"

Ricardo drew a letter from his pocket.

"I have a sister in London, a widow," he said. "She is kind. I, too, have been thinking of what will become of Mlle. Célie. I wrote to my sister, and here is her reply. Mlle. Célie will be very welcome."

Hanaud stretched out his hand and shook Ricardo's warmly.

"She will not, I think, be for very long a burden. She is young. She will recover from this shock She is very pretty, very gentle. If—if no one comes forward whom she loves and who loves her—I—yes, I myself, who was her papa for one night, will be her husband for ever."

He laughed inordinately at his own joke; it was a habit of M. Hanaud's. Then he said gravely:

"But I am glad, M. Ricardo, for Mlle. Célie's sake that I came to your amusing dinner-party in London."

Mr. Ricardo was silent for a moment. Then he asked :

" And what will happen to the condemned ? "

" To the women imprisonment for life."

" And to the men ? "

Hanaud shrugged his shoulders.

" Perhaps the guillotine ; perhaps New Caledonia How can I say ? I am not the President of the Republic."

THE END

Printed by Hazell, Watson & Viney, Ld., London and Aylesbury.

Lightning Source UK Ltd.
Milton Keynes UK
UKHW012052230219
337878UK00014B/1277/P

9 781440 097270